Protect and Serve

Holly Capella

To my good friend, John D. Kempker!
Live, Laugh, Love

ACKNOWLEDGMENTS

Copella Books: First Paperback Edition 2023
SelfPubBookCovers.com/ Shardel
Model by Grafvision
Model: Attila Hajnal
Printed by KDP, an Amazon.com Company

PUBLISHER'S NOTE

Chapter One

The white, two-and-a-half-story plantation-style mansion was situated on a five-acre estate with landscaping, gardens, and large weeping willow trees. The home itself had a "Gone with the Wind" appeal. Several large pillars were in the front, with floor-to-ceiling windows and a massive wraparound porch. Set back far enough on the property, the home appeared almost secluded from the rest of the world. Isolated and peaceful. It was already late afternoon. Within the house, the front sitting room was light and bright, with many large windows, white walls, and a tall ceiling. The furniture was dainty, possibly antique, with large floral print of pink and cream. An attractive woman in her early forties sat in the front sitting room sipping her tea from her favorite mug rather than a china teacup.

Natalie Raymour was a taller woman, possibly five foot seven, with dark shoulder-length hair. Considered the 'lady of the house', she wasn't exactly an aristocrat, being more down to earth than one would expect from a wealthy woman. Most often, she dressed fashionably casual, wearing house slippers rather than uncomfortable shoes. The live-in maid, Betty, bustled about the sitting room, straightening what she could. Although there wasn't much that needed straightening or cleaning, Natalie enjoyed the company. Betty was a nice-looking young woman in her mid-twenties with light brown hair worn up in a messy ponytail. She didn't wear a conventional maid's uniform. Instead, she wore black pants and a light-colored top, keeping with the casual theme. Natalie's house wasn't exceptionally formal.

"Will Mr. Raymour be home for dinner tonight?" Betty asked while straightening a stack of magazines on the coffee table. "Abby could keep something warm for him if he's going to be late."

Natalie frowned while staring across the room at nothing in particular. "No, he won't be home for dinner tonight," she responded in something resembling a scoff. "He's off on another one of his three-day *business* trips."

Betty straightened and attempted to hide her surprise. Her reaction indicated she knew exactly what Natalie wasn't saying.

"I'll be sure to let Abby know the change in dinner plans," Betty replied somewhat sympathetically.

Natalie glanced at the young maid and tensed slightly. "When Kasey gets home, I'd prefer if she didn't know what's going on between her Uncle Vincent and me and not a word about the private investigator."

Betty forced a tiny, sympathetic smile. "She won't hear anything from me," she replied. "I have a very short memory."

"Thank you, Betty," Natalie replied gently.

"Mom?" a male voice called out from the hallway just moments before a handsome man in his mid-twenties appeared in the sitting room doorway.

"Dillon," Natalie announced cheerfully while springing up from the sofa. "I didn't hear you come in."

Natalie's stepson, Dillon Raymour, was tall, handsome, and built somewhere between athletic and muscular. His light brown hair was a little longer, but he kept it slicked back with not a hair out of place. He had a short, thin beard that was a shade lighter than his hair, almost ginger in color. His expensive, stylish clothes, handsome features, and daddy's money made him practically irresistible. Despite being Vincent's son from his first marriage, Natalie essentially raised the young man, who was only twelve when she got together with his father. Of course, he accepted her as his mother years ago, readily calling her 'mom'. Dillon approached Natalie and kissed her on the cheek while maintaining his grin.

"I slipped in through the kitchen," he announced, then flashed a half-eaten cookie. "Don't tell Abby I pinched one of her cookies."

"She'll yell for sure," Natalie announced with a tiny laugh. "She baked those for Kasey."

"That's why I stopped by," Dillon announced, then shook his head while looking around. "Where is the college co-ed? I wanted to be the first to wish her happy birthday."

After Kasey's mother died seven years ago, Natalie took in her sister's twelve-year-old daughter. Dillon and his cousin Kasey lived in the same house together for two years before Dillon went off to college. Now, Kasey was in college and would graduate next year.

Natalie offered a tiny, humored smile. "You realize her twentieth birthday isn't until this weekend, right?"

"Yeah, I know."

"Well, she won't be home until late tonight," Natalie informed him. "Not until one or two in the morning, I'm afraid. It's a long drive from the airport."

"That late?" Dillon asked, then frowned. "If it were earlier, I'd offer to pick her up myself, but I'm meeting some friends for a yacht party."

"She's going to be home all summer," Natalie replied, excited at the thought. "I'm sure you'll see plenty of her. Go to your party. It sounds like a lot of fun."

Dillon took another bite from his cookie. "Yeah, wish me luck," he announced. "Maybe I'll finally meet a nice girl."

"In that case, good luck," Natalie announced while grinning. "Did you want to stay for dinner?"

"No, I need to run back to my apartment to shower and change," he replied. "I'll get something to eat on the ride home."

"Not junk food," Natalie called after him as he left the sitting room.

Dillon gave an acknowledging wave, meaning he heard her but didn't intend to do as she requested. While frowning, Natalie looked around the quiet sitting room, then returned to her seat. She picked up her tea mug just as the butler, Embry, entered the room. Embry was a good-looking man in his early fifties with short dark hair peppered with gray and a clean-cut face. He was shorter than average, being about five foot eight. Unlike the almost casually dressed maid, Embry liked to dress to impress. He almost always wore an expensive black suit, although he only wore a tie on special occasions. Embry was a polite and proper gentleman who took excellent care of the house, the employees, and some finances during his seven years of employment. His attention to detail was second to none.

"Mrs. Raymour," Embry announced politely. "I just got off the phone with Miss Warrick."

"Kasey?" Natalie asked as a smile returned to her face. Her smile immediately vanished. "She's still coming home, isn't she?"

"Yes, of course," Embry replied while maintaining his own smile. "She was able to get an earlier flight. It lands around ten-thirty."

"Oh, that's wonderful," Natalie announced with increasing enthusiasm. "I can't wait to see her. I know I saw her over spring break, but it feels like a lifetime ago."

"I feel the same," Embry remarked. "If you wouldn't mind, I'd like permission to take one of the cars and pick her up."

"Are you sure?" Natalie asked, a little surprised by the request. "You probably won't get back here until midnight."

"I'm aware, Mrs. Raymour," Embry replied while equally enthusiastic. "It'd be my honor to greet her at the airport."

"That's a wonderful idea," Natalie announced.

"You're more than welcome to ride along," Embry informed her.

Natalie considered it and then frowned. "I doubt I'd be very good company tonight." She smiled while waving him off. "You two catch up. I'll see her when she gets home."

"Very well, Mrs. Raymour," Embry announced, then left the room.

Chapter Two

Night. Natalie's impressive master bedroom suite had a balcony, a massive fireplace, and a private bath. The king-sized bed contained a frilly comforter as well as many decorative pillows. Natalie sat in bed dressed in white satin pajamas while reading a book. It was getting close to midnight, and her niece was expected home within the hour, provided the flight was on time. Natalie was trying to get into her book but was too excited about Kasey returning home for the summer. She heard a faint clunk coming from the first floor. It might have been the front door, but she hadn't heard the car pulling up as usual. Natalie lowered her book and listened for a moment. When she heard nothing, she decided to get up and investigate.

Natalie slipped into a matching satin robe and left her room. After a short walk down the hallway in her bare feet, she reached the grand staircase. She could see the stairs and the front door through the dim lighting. Usually, some lights were left on within most of the mansion, but it was darker than usual tonight.

"Kasey?" she called down the stairs. "Are you home?"

When there was no response, Natalie headed down the massive, carpeted staircase. She reached the bottom of the stairs, shrouded in shadows, and slipped on something wet. She caught her balance and immediately pulled back with some surprise, feeling the lukewarm liquid on her bare foot. It hadn't been raining, so it seemed odd that anything would be wet on the floor. Natalie looked down at the dark puddle near her feet but couldn't tell what it was. She headed across the hall, past the stairs, and toward the wall light switch. When she saw the outline of a young woman lying motionless on the floor, panic filled her. Even without the lights, she could now see it was blood pooling at the base of the stairs.

"Kasey," she gasped in horror.

Natalie was about to lunge for the light switch when she saw a man dressed in black step into the open doorway from the sitting room. He wore a dark mask over his face and held a blood-covered knife in his gloved hand. Natalie screamed, darting away from him, and ran back for the stairs. The intruder slashed at her with the large hunting knife but missed the nimble woman. As she bolted up the stairs, he charged after her. Natalie ran into the master bedroom and slammed the door behind her, locking it. Only steps behind her, the man struck the door with a loud thud, but it didn't budge. Natalie pushed her body against it, ensuring it stayed closed while collecting her wits. There was a loud, startling bang, and the knife blade pierced the door not far from her face.

Natalie screamed and ran to the nightstand. She grabbed the phone and dialed 9-1-1 as the door vibrated from the man repeatedly throwing his body against it. When she heard nothing through the phone, she hesitated and tried again. There was no dial tone! The door again vibrated, causing her to jump at the sound.

§

The expensive black town car pulled up to the mansion near the back terrace and kitchen entrance. Embry got out of the car and immediately approached the trunk, removing a large suitcase on rolling wheels. A young, attractive woman no older than twenty exited the vehicle and waited for Embry by the terrace steps. Kasey Warrick was of average height and build for a young college woman. She wore her dark hair up in a ponytail for travel purposes and was casually dressed for the same reason. Travel days were exhausting, particularly sitting on a plane and in an airport for hours. Embry pulled Kasey's suitcase behind him and toted it up the three steps to the terrace.

"I appreciate you picking me up, Embry," Kasey announced while hiding her weary smile. "Though, you didn't have to. I know how early you get up in the morning. You must be exhausted. I could have taken a cab."

"It's my pleasure," Embry insisted while grinning. "Besides, some of those cabs are filthy. You don't want to know what's on those seats."

"Still, it's not your job," she reminded him as they approached the kitchen door.

Embry stopped before the door and unlocked it. "I know it's not my job," he replied, then smiled warmly. "But I missed you."

Kasey couldn't help but smile and gently pat his lower arm. "I missed you too."

Kasey entered the dimly lit kitchen with Embry and her rolling suitcase only a few steps behind. The kitchen was large and airy, with a beautiful whitish-gray marble floor. There was an island counter with four tall chairs for counter seating and a kitchen table that comfortably sat six. The kitchen had state-of-the-art appliances and heavy-duty cutlery on the wall behind the main counter. A nearly concealed back staircase led to the second floor, and a doorway beyond the island counter led to the staff quarters. Embry shut the back door behind him and reached for the alarm. He hesitated and stared at the 'disarm' button that was already lit.

"Huh, I could have sworn I set that before I left," he remarked more to himself.

"Everything okay?" Kasey asked.

Embry managed a smile while turning to face her. "Yes, I guess I'm just forgetting myself," he remarked, rolling her bag to the back stairs. "Why don't you get settled into your room, and I'll bring you some nice hot tea?"

Kasey tried hard to hide her smile. Embry was such a cute, dear man. "I'm not a little girl anymore, Embry," she reminded him.

"A dirty martini, then?" he asked while grinning.

"You're sweet, but I'm just going to take a bath and go to bed," she informed him. "We'll do our morning tea ritual tomorrow."

"I'm looking forward to it," Embry replied. "Did you want me to take your bag upstairs?"

"I can manage," she insisted, then kissed him on the cheek. "Goodnight, Embry."

"Goodnight, Kasey."

As Kasey grabbed her bag and headed up the back stairs, Embry stood at the bottom and watched her with a contended smile. Once she was gone, he returned to the door, locking it and setting the alarm. He turned, about to walk away, when he hesitated and looked back at the alarm. The disarm light remained lit. Embry returned to the alarm and pressed the engage button again. Nothing happened. He frowned and slammed his palm against the unit.

"Piece of shit alarm."

Embry turned the deadbolt and headed across the dimly lit kitchen toward the servants' quarters.

11

Despite the dim lighting, a bloody handprint on the door leading to the staff wing was unmistakable. Embry immediately tensed at the sight and approached slower. He looked at the floor and saw blood droplets followed by a streak of blood just past the counter. Embry lurched for the wall switch, turning on the lights. An older, heavyset woman in her mid-fifties was lying on a bloody heap behind the island counter. Embry withheld his horrified gasp and crouched alongside the dead cook.

"Abby?"

Embry gently turned her over. The entire front of her shirt was covered in blood from a pronounced slit across her throat, and her dead eyes seemed to stare at him. Embry stared back at the dead woman, momentarily horrified, then slowly straightened. The slightest creak from the staff wing doorway alerted him to someone's presence. Embry spun and saw a masked man dressed in black standing directly behind him with a bloodied hunting knife clutched in his gloved hand. Embry gasped with surprise as the blade was thrust at him.

Chapter Three

Kasey's bedroom was almost as big as Natalie's master bedroom. She, too, had a fireplace, balcony, and a private bathroom. Her room was very grownup for a college student, refurbished after graduating high school. She had a queen-sized bed with less frilly pillows and comforter than her aunt's room, but it was still rather feminine. Kasey held her cell phone to her ear as she walked across her bedroom in her bra and underwear while the bathtub was heard filling.

"I told you I'd call you when I got home," she announced, then laughed. "I literally just walked in the door."

"Literally just walked in the door, huh?" the man announced from the other end, then chuckled. "Then why do I hear bath water running."

"How can you possibly hear that?" she demanded, hiding her smile.

"Finely tuned ears," he replied, then chuckled. "By the sounds of it, you're parading around in your underwear."

Kasey immediately stopped and looked at her windows. The curtains were securely closed.

"That's just creepy the way you do that, Colton," she informed him, then laughed it off. "Are you sure I didn't wake you?"

"It's not even midnight yet," her friend, Colton, insisted from the other end. "You know I can't sleep until I've bitten a few virgins on the neck. It would be unheard of."

"I did wake you."

"Not your fault," Colton replied. "I'm watching a dull movie. If it were the least bit interesting, I never would have fallen asleep in the first place."

"I should go; my bath is calling," Kasey informed him. "You got your obligatory 'I made it home alive' phone call. Go to bed."

"Why don't we go out for dinner tomorrow and then check out the clubs?" Colton suggested before she could hang up.

"You're on," she announced. "I'll call Jamie."

"Hmm, a threesome," he replied, then chuckled. "I'd like that."

"Funny," she scoffed while again hiding her smile. "I think my bath is ready. I don't want it to overflow. I'll talk to you tomorrow."

"Serious question, though," he announced, then fell silent. "What are you wearing?"

Kasey groaned and chuckled softly. "You're a terrible flirt, Colton."

"I'm an excellent flirt," he corrected from the other end. "You're just not dirty enough to appreciate it."

"Goodnight, Colton."

"Goodnight, Kasey," he replied. "I'll be over to bite your neck a little later."

Kasey laughed and disconnected the call before tossing her cell phone onto her bed. "I don't know how I ever became friends with such a pervert."

Kasey was about to head into the bathroom when she heard movement in the hallway. She hesitated, then slipped into an oversized shirt and buttoned it while approaching her bedroom door. She opened it and looked into the hallway. There was no one there. She considered it only a moment, then headed into the bathroom and shut off the water. Kasey crossed her room, entered the hallway, and approached the master bedroom. She lightly knocked, but there was no response. Kasey hesitated when she saw the inch-long slit in the middle of the door. She ran her finger along the small gap, considered it only a moment, and opened the door. It made a terrible creaking sound. The room was dimly lit by the part in the curtains, revealing her aunt beneath the covers on the bed. Kasey stood in the doorway for a moment.

"Aunt Nat?" she asked, feeling unusually tense now. "Are you awake? I just got home."

There was no response. Kasey felt slightly chilled by the lack of response. Something felt off. She entered the room and approached the bed with some apprehension.

"Aunt Nat?"

Kasey gently touched her aunt's exposed shoulder, but she didn't move. Kasey lunged for the bedside light, and the room brightened. Blood could be seen soaking through the sheet covering her motionless aunt. Kasey withheld her gasp and nervously pulled back the covers. Her Aunt Natalie was surrounded in blood from multiple stab wounds to her abdomen. Her white satin pajamas and the bed surrounding her were soaked in blood. By her defensive wounds to her hands and arms, she'd put up a fight. Kasey stared in horror, too frightened to move. The light suddenly went out. Kasey cried out, spun toward the nightstand, and saw the outline of a man only a foot or two from her. There was no mistaking the outline of the knife in his hand.

Kasey screamed and attempted to move as the man lunged for her. As he tackled Kasey to the bed, she grabbed his wrist, holding back the knife, and wedged her foot between them. Kasey hit the mattress, falling against her aunt's butchered body. With her foot wedged between her and her attacker, she managed to flip him off her and across the bed. Kasey screamed while leaping off the bed. She could feel her aunt's blood soaking through the back of her nightshirt and against her skin. She saw her aunt's blood on her hands and felt panic sweep through her. For a moment, she was paralyzed with fear, but the voice in her head screamed for her to run. Kasey came back to life and ran from the room, slamming the door behind her.

Chapter Four

Kasey thundered along the second floor hallway and raced down the grand staircase. Her feet were moving so fast, she was amazed she didn't fall down the stairs. As she reached the bottom, she slipped on a large pool of blood and fell to the floor, landing hard on her backside. Kasey was slightly dazed, uncertain how she even got on the floor and pulled herself to her feet using the banister. When she saw the dead maid, Kasey stifled her horrified gasp.

"Betty," she whispered, then backed up a step before running down the hallway for the kitchen, leaving partial bloody footprints on the floor.

Kasey needed to reach Embry in the staff wing to warn him and for additional security. She ran into the well-lit kitchen and grabbed the phone on the wall near the island counter.

"Embry!" she cried out while punching 9-1-1 on the phone.

Though Embry didn't respond, she was preoccupied with her phone call, placing the receiver to her ear. She realized there was no dial tone when she heard nothing through the phone. It was then that she saw a bloodied body between the counter and the island counter. Kasey dropped the phone and took a step closer to the island counter, uncertain what she'd find. She stared at the dead cook in horror, then looked around the well-lit kitchen. More blood was rapidly pooling just beneath the servant's wing doorway. For a brief moment, she feared Embry was dead as well. If he had gone back to his bedroom, he would have seen the cook's body, and she was almost positive someone was lying dead in the servant's wing corridor.

Self-preservation again kicked in. Kasey lunged for the knife rack and removed the boning knife. It wasn't the biggest knife, but it was the sharpest. She scanned the kitchen for a moment, partially frozen in terror, not knowing what to do next. Her mind was racing, and she felt almost paralyzed with fear.

"Embry!" she screamed, panic-stricken and almost down to tears.

There was still no response confirming what she had already suspected. If Embry were capable, he'd answer her, which meant something had happened to him. And now that she screamed, she'd given her position away to the killer. Kasey knew she needed to stop playing the role of a victim and start thinking like a survivor. Rational thinking took control. Embry undoubtedly had the sedan keys on him, so she had no car. Running out the door wasn't an option. The estate was secluded, which meant help was too far away. The phones weren't working, but her cell phone was upstairs in her bedroom. She needed to reach her cell phone, call the police, and lock herself in her room until help arrived.

The interior kitchen door suddenly burst open to reveal the masked man in black with his bloodied hunting knife clutched in his hand. Kasey cried out and ran for the back stairs, her blood-covered feet slipping on the marble floor. She nearly fell and caught the railing on the back stairs. The intruder was now almost on top of her. Kasey darted out of his path just as he plunged the knife downward. His knife struck the doorframe and became embedded in the wood. She screamed and swiped randomly with the boning knife, slicing his arm. He cried out in pain while yanking his knife free simultaneously. Kasey screamed again and ran up the back stairs with the killer on her heels. She ran along the second floor hallway and darted into her bedroom, slamming and locking the door behind her. She jumped back as the door vibrated, briefly recalling the slice in her aunt's bedroom door.

Was this the same horror her aunt went through right before she was killed? Kasey realized the door wouldn't hold. He'd gotten to her aunt, and he'd get to her. She needed to move fast. Kasey ran to the bed and grabbed her cell phone with trembling hands. With her sticky, bloodied fingers, she pressed 9-1-1. The emergency operator answered, giving her a moment of hope just before the door cracked and flew open. Kasey screamed as the killer charged across the room for her with his knife, ready to strike. She cast her cell phone aside and caught his wrist with her free hand. Then, without even thinking, she immediately followed through with an upward thrust with the boning knife. The killer moved just far enough to prevent a fatal blow, but the blade grazed his side. His painful grunt indicated she'd at least done some damage.

The killer responded by knocking the knife from her hand and backhanded her across the face with his free hand. Kasey fell back and struck the thick bedpost, slightly dazed from the hard slap and her head striking the heavy bedpost. Enraged that she'd cut him, he grabbed her by the throat and threw her onto the bed while just about jumping on top of her. He placed the knife to her neck and then seemed to hesitate. Kasey was breathing almost as heavily as the intruder. She felt the sharp blade against her throat, positive he was going to kill her, but he again hesitated. Despite the mask, she could see his attention fall upon her partially exposed bra and cleavage.

Kasey easily read his thoughts in that brief moment and felt the ensuing panic. While keeping the knife to her throat, he ripped her shirt open with his free hand. Kasey gasped in horror, frantically plotting her next move with reckless abandon. Any move she made would undoubtedly end with her dying, but she had already decided to fight him with everything she had. When he moved the knife from her throat to cut her underwear, it was her last chance, and she had to take it. Kasey cried out in a mixture of fear and anger while thrusting the palm of her hand into his exposed nose. As her palm connected, his nose made a distinctive crunching sound. He jumped back while crying out and clutched his bleeding nose.

Kasey shot up into a sitting position and attempted to take the knife from him. He suddenly grabbed her throat with his left hand and slammed her back against the mattress. Kasey gasped for air and attempted to loosen his grip while clutching his wrist, keeping the knife back with her other hand. Her legs wildly thrashed, attempting to kick him to no avail. He kneeled over her, holding pressure on her throat, possibly trying to suffocate her into unconsciousness. Unable to breathe, Kasey felt unusually lightheaded. She knew she'd be unconscious and vulnerable in mere seconds. With the parting of air, a black blur struck the masked man in the face. He was thrown off her and struck the floor at the foot end of the bed. Kasey gasped for air while frantically sitting up on the bed.

There was a haze of darkness and a buzzing sound in her ears from lack of oxygen and sitting up too fast. Despite being on the brink of passing out, Kasey could finally see straight. She saw Embry standing alongside her bed, staring at the masked intruder with the coldest look she'd ever seen from the primarily docile man. Embry had blood streaking down his temple and along the corner of his mouth, possibly having suffered a beating. The intruder slowly moved to his feet, fixated on Embry, while reclaiming his knife. Instead of running or backing away, Embry took two quick steps toward the menacing, masked man. When the killer thrust the knife at Embry's side, Kasey was almost certain Embry was a dead man. Embry used his leg to block the blow in what looked like a karate move, causing the knife to become embedded in his thigh.

The meek butler cried out with a mixture of pain and anger but somehow maintained his forward momentum, refusing to stop on his path to the killer. Embry grabbed the larger man by the throat, forcing him to release the knife, which remained partially embedded in Embry's thigh. Embry plowed forward while pushing the man backward across the room with speed and force until they reached the window. The back of the man's head struck the window, cracking the thick glass. With what little strength the killer had left, he clutched Embry's wrist, attempting to free himself. To Kasey's surprise and horror, Embry pulled the knife from his thigh, painfully grunting and sneering. He then swiftly flipped the knife in his free hand and, without hesitation, plunged it into the man's jugular.

The killer appeared momentarily horrified before gasping and spitting up blood, realizing his fate. Embry released the man and, without emotion, watched him drop to the floor. He stared momentarily at the intruder bleeding out on the floor, then looked at Kasey as his emotionless, cold expression immediately softened.

"Are you okay?" Embry gasped.

Kasey jumped off the bed, ran to Embry, and clung to him, releasing a tiny sob and a relieved sigh. He held her against him for a moment while panting softly.

"Kasey," he announced while releasing a tiny gasp. "Call an ambulance."

The words barely left his mouth as he sank against her on his way to the floor. Kasey cried out while attempting to keep him from falling.

Chapter Five

One year later. It was a little after seven o'clock in the morning. Embry leaned against the island counter in the kitchen while reading a book and sipping his pre-breakfast morning tea. Kasey appeared on the back stairs and approached the island counter while smiling pleasantly at the butler. She'd just graduated college and was officially home. An entire summer of morning tea with her favorite man. Naturally, that title should have gone to her uncle, but Embry held a special place in her heart from the moment her aunt hired him eight or nine years ago, and those feelings were reinforced last year when he saved her life. He not only killed the man in her bedroom, but he also killed another intruder in the staff wing corridor, suffering injuries on both accounts. Despite that he refused to take any credit for what he'd done; he was a hero in her book.

"Morning, Embry."

Embry saw her and straightened while smiling. "Good morning, Kasey," he announced cheerfully. "Are you having tea with me?"

Kasey jumped onto one of the counter chairs with noted enthusiasm. "Of course I am," she announced while in a particularly good mood this morning. She then turned curious. "We're not having tea on the back patio this morning?"

Embry poured tea into her favorite mug and placed it before her. "I wish we could, but your uncle is up early this morning," he announced, then eyed her. "As much as I hate gossip--"

Kasey grinned and snickered while leaning across the counter. "Sure you do."

Embry couldn't hide his smile at the comment and also leaned on the counter closer to her. "I believe that Hunter character is in some sort of trouble," he remarked.

"Already?" she asked, genuinely humored, then straightened and sipped her tea. "How hard is it to stand there and look intimidating? He's got that look down pretty good if you ask me."

"Well, he's had a good run," Embry remarked with an overly dramatic sigh. "He's lasted longer than the other bodyguards your uncle hired to protect you this past year."

"Yeah, I kind of miss Jughead," Kasey replied with a soft sigh.

"Juggernaut," Embry corrected.

"I'm kind of wishing I hadn't gotten him fired," she remarked and had to giggle. "He was so dense; he was almost funny. A hell of a lot easier to lose then this one." She then frowned. "Colton can't stand Hunter, and I think the feeling is mutual."

"That's because Colton is wound too tight, and Hunter is so low-key he's almost comatose," Embry remarked while snickering.

"He has Jamie's vote, though. She thinks he's cute," Kasey informed him, then sighed dramatically. "Of course, that's not saying much, considering she 'got it on' with Jughead."

Embry looked at her with surprise. "Jamie slept with Juggernaut?"

"Trust me, there was no sleeping involved," Kasey remarked dryly. "They did it in the back of the limo when we went out to one of the dance clubs."

"Jamie is almost as wild as your boy toy, Colton," Embry remarked, then returned to his book. "I don't even want to know about your behavior when you're around those two."

"You don't need to worry," Kasey informed him, then grinned. "You raised me to choose wisely and play hard to get."

Embry glanced at her and smiled proudly. "That's the nicest thing you've ever said to me."

"Don't get me wrong," Kasey announced. "I love my Uncle Vincent and my Aunt Nat, but you were the one who was there for me the last nine years after my mother died."

"Actually, eight years," he corrected, then turned sympathetic. "I'm sorry I never had a chance to meet your mother. I'm sure I would have adored her as much as I do you."

"My mother was much like my Aunt Nat," she informed him. "I guess those two were a handful growing up."

"I find it interesting that I'd heard all about your stepfather," Embry remarked, then appeared curious. "But you never mentioned your real father."

"Not much to mention," Kasey replied. "He died before I was born. My mother said he was a war hero and died in combat."

"I didn't know that," Embry remarked, considering it. "I guess I just assumed he was in finance."

"You mean because of all this?" she replied while indicating the house, then shrugged. "The estate belonged to my grandparents and was left to my mother and Aunt Nat."

"So does that mean your uncle inherited the estate as your aunt's surviving spouse?" Embry asked, now curious.

"I suppose so," Kasey replied. "When my mother died, provisions were made for my education, a home here until I'm twenty-five, and a trust fund that I receive when I turn twenty-one."

"That's right," Embry announced while grinning. "Someone has a milestone birthday coming up next week."

"Oh, my God, you're right," Kasey replied, playing along. "I'll finally be the legal drinking age. No more drinking soda at the nightclubs and raiding my uncle's liquor cabinet."

"Your uncle will need to hire another bodyguard," Embry remarked somewhat dryly. "Someone needs to keep Colton from getting you drunk and humping you."

Kasey glared at Embry and raised a brow. "Colton isn't like that, Embry," she informed him. "We're just friends."

"He's a pervert."

"Yes, but that's all for show," she insisted. "He'd never actually do anything."

Embry rolled his eyes, silently disagreeing with her. The kitchen door opened, revealing a very well-dressed, noble-looking man in his mid-forties, Vincent Raymour. Kasey's Uncle Vincent was tall and lean with a certain regal charm about him, but he wasn't exactly handsome, even if his string of young girlfriends over the last few months would disagree. He had a full head of light brown hair with some gray at the temples. He was always meticulously clean-shaven and dressed as a wealthy businessman would.

Although widowed only a year, he had been dating women half his age publicly for the last six months. Behind closed doors, Kasey was sure he saw one or two women less than a month after her Aunt Natalie was killed.

A rather ruggedly handsome, thirty-year-old man followed Vincent. Hunter Kane was Kasey's latest bodyguard. One of several over the past year since her aunt and the staff were murdered. Her Uncle Vincent insisted she had protection since that tragic night, and humoring him was easier than fighting him over it. Hunter was at least six foot two with an athletic to muscular build and wore his signature, lightweight, black leather jacket. He was an impressive sight to behold from a purely physical standpoint. There was no denying he was easy on the eyes. He had short dark hair and a neatly trimmed beard that was already showing signs of gray in the chin. His dark eyes were moderately ruthless, and the permanent scowl on his face was particularly intimidating.

But intimidating was what her uncle was paying for, and Hunter didn't disappoint. He intimidated everyone, from her cousin Dillon to the guys approaching her in nightclubs. That made him public enemy number one in Kasey's book. Regarding Hunter's intelligence, the jury was still out on that one. Hunter wasn't big on small talk, but he always seemed one step ahead of Kasey, particularly when she attempted to ditch him a few times. He was definitely smarter than Jughead. Embry turned away from the island counter and pretended to be busy for Vincent's benefit. Hunter didn't say a word as he walked behind the island counter to the main counter and poured coffee into his favorite mug. He already had a favorite mug, which meant he wasn't planning on quitting anytime soon. Vincent smiled pleasantly and kissed Kasey on the cheek.

"Good morning, dear," Vincent announced.

"Morning, Uncle Vincent," she announced cheerfully, then disinterestedly eyed Hunter. *"And associate."*

Hunter lacked emotion as he eyed Kasey and sipped his black coffee without comment. Vincent sat at the island counter next to Kasey.

"I wanted to talk to you about your graduation slash birthday cruise next week," her uncle announced as Embry placed a coffee mug on the counter before him.

The comment caught Kasey off guard. "Oh, come on," she groaned, immediately turning defensive. "I thought we'd settled that. I've made the cruise reservations already, and it's paid in full. I'm going. No take backs."

"I wouldn't dream of telling you that you can't go, Kasey," Vincent informed her while adding sugar to his coffee and stirring it. "I know how important it is for you to get away with your friends for your twenty-first birthday. I'm not arguing the point with you. You're old enough to make your own decisions."

"Really?" she asked, surprised by the reversal, and fidgeted, unsure how to handle the remark. "Well, thank you."

"However--"

She immediately rolled her eyes. "Not the *however* speech."

"*However*," he announced a little louder, then sipped his coffee while avoiding eye contact. "I'm sending Hunter with you."

Kasey stared at her uncle with a somewhat stunned look. "You've got to be kidding," she scoffed while nodding across the kitchen at Hunter. "He's a killjoy. I mean, he's not even properly housebroken yet. How can I take him on a cruise ship with normal people?"

"After what happened here last year--"

"I know what happened here," she announced with a low groan. "You don't have to keep reminding me about it. I still have nightmares, but those men are dead. Embry killed both of them." She shifted on her chair and then straightened proudly. "You made an exception regarding Hunter following me around while I was on campus at college. I would think security should be even tighter on some exclusive luxury cruise ship. I'll be fine."

"College campus was different," Vincent insisted. "Hunter was there the moment you set foot off campus after classes. I want you to be safe, Kasey. I can't lose you too."

Her uncle certainly knew how to guilt her into doing what he wanted, but she was prepared with a rebuttal to his guilt trip.

"Fine, you want me to have protection, then I'll take Embry with me," Kasey announced and casually shrugged. "He's well-mannered and all the protection I need."

"Fine," Vincent replied.

Kasey was surprised that her uncle readily agreed with her. Embry nearly dropped his teacup into the sink and partially looked back, equally surprised by Vincent's acceptance.

"Really?" Kasey asked.

"Yes, take Embry," Vincent announced, then cocked his head. "But Hunter's going too."

Kasey frowned and eyed Hunter by the main counter. Hunter casually sipped his coffee while watching them but offered no comment. Even though he didn't react, Kasey could almost see the twinkle in his eyes, mocking her.

Kasey groaned, feeling defeated. "Fine," she scoffed.

Embry hid his smile and returned to the sink. Apparently, his day just vastly improved with an impromptu vacation on the high seas.

"But I have a few conditions of my own," Kasey boldly announced.

Vincent shifted uncomfortably on his chair and groaned, defeated. "Of course," her uncle replied. "You always do."

"Hunter has to maintain a distance of ten feet from my friends and me," Kasey insisted. "I don't want anyone thinking Mr. Personality is with us. And if he intimidates any cute guys who approach me, he swims home."

"Done," Vincent replied while grinning, then took another sip of coffee. He eyed her and appeared curious. "What are your plans for today?"

"Well, I need to work on my tan so I don't burn to a crisp on the cruise," Kasey informed him, then considered the rest of her day. "And then clothes shopping with Jamie and Colton for some cruise outfits."

"Make sure you're home in time for dinner," Vincent announced. "Dillon and I are taking you out for graduation. We have reservations."

"I'll be back in plenty of time for dinner," she replied.

Vincent looked across the kitchen at Hunter, who leaned against the main counter, watching them while drinking his coffee.

"Make sure she's back no later than five," Vincent announced.

Kasey looked from Hunter back to her uncle. "I'm not taking Hunter shopping with me," she informed her uncle.

"Oh, but you are," Vincent replied with little emotion. "That's why I hired him."

"You realize that's all going to end when I start working and get my own place, right?" Kasey remarked. "He sure as hell isn't living with me."

Her uncle sipped his coffee and seemed almost disinterested. "We have four years to worry about that," Vincent replied.

Kasey stared at her uncle with some surprise at the comment. "Who said anything about four years?" she asked.

Vincent finally looked at her. "This is your home until you turn twenty-five," he informed her. "Your mother made those arrangements."

"It's my option to live here until I'm twenty-five," she corrected. "*Option* being key. I can move out before that."

Her uncle glanced at his watch, then smiled back at her. "We'll discuss that later," Vincent announced while indicating his watch. "I have a meeting this morning."

Vincent stood, quickly kissed her on the cheek, and left the kitchen without allowing her to protest. Kasey glanced at Embry, who offered a sympathetic look while raising his brows. Obviously, it was a battle for another day. She rolled her eyes, admitting defeat, and left the kitchen, leaving Embry alone with Hunter.

Chapter Six

After breakfast, Kasey retreated to her bedroom for nearly thirty minutes, patiently biding her time. Rather than change into her swimsuit, she remained dressed and silently crept down the back stairs with her small clutch purse containing her cell phone, car keys, and wallet. She paused near the bottom of the stairs just out of view of the kitchen and listened a moment. When she heard nothing, she crept down the last few steps and looked around. Embry sat at the island counter, reading his book while sipping his second cup of tea. He almost immediately saw her and appeared curious.

"I thought--?"

Kasey held her finger to her lips and approached him while scanning the area. "Where's Hunter?" she asked softly.

"If I had to guess, I'd say he's in the bathroom," Embry replied using the same soft tone. He then appeared curious and cocked his head. "Why are we whispering?"

"I'm rebelling," she informed him. "I think I can go clothes shopping without the hired muscle."

"Are you sure you want to do that?" Embry asked. "When 'the good humor man' has to hunt you down, it only makes him cranky."

"He's already cranky," Kasey muttered while folding her arms across her chest. "And I'm getting tired of him giving Colton death glares."

"Colton likes to run his mouth," Embry reminded her. "At times, he even gets on my nerves."

"Not the point," Kasey remarked. "I don't need Hunter standing around and gawking while I'm bikini shopping."

Embry appeared curious and raised his brow. "He gawks?"

"Well, no, but he's always watching me," she replied.

Embry snorted a laugh. "That's kind of his job," he informed her.

"You're not helping," Kasey insisted, waving him off. "I'll be back by five."

Kasey hurried out the side kitchen door, headed down the patio steps, and approached her dark blue Dodge Charger. She hopped into the driver's seat, fastened her seatbelt, and started the car. The passenger side door opened, and Hunter gracefully sank into the cockpit-style seat. He didn't even look at her as he shut the door and fastened his seatbelt. Kasey stared at his profile and his emotionless expression.

"Did Embry rat me out?" she demanded, although she didn't see how he had time.

"Nope," Hunter replied without looking at her as he slipped into his dark sunglasses.

She continued to stare at him in astonishment, then shook her head. "How in the world could you possibly--?"

"Not the first time you've tried to ditch me," he informed her, then turned his head and stared at her through his dark sunglasses. "I'm twelve and zero, in case you were keeping score."

Kasey stared at him, attempting to see his eyes through his dark sunglasses, but it was impossible.

He was lucky he was cute. She sneered at him, threw her car into reverse, and stepped on the gas as he eyed her side mirror.

"Dillon just pulled up behind you," Hunter casually announced.

Kasey slammed on the brakes and looked in her rearview mirror. Dillon got out of his car and threw his arms in the air with an annoyed look. Kasey looked at Hunter in the passenger seat and sneered at him.

"I hate you."

"I know," he replied without emotion.

As Dillon approached Kasey's door, she put the car into park and lowered her window in time to meet his gaze.

"That would have been a pricy fender bender," Dillon remarked. "What do you have against my BMW?"

"Nothing," Kasey announced dryly, then indicated Hunter. "I was driving *distracted*."

Dillon eyed Hunter in the passenger seat and then nodded. "I get it," he replied. "Where are you going so early? I thought we'd spend some time together this morning."

"I'm meeting Jamie and Colton at the mall," she informed him. "Clothes shopping for the cruise."

"Of course, the cruise," Dillon replied with a tiny, sly smile. "The one I wasn't invited to go along on."

"It's nothing personal, Dillon," she informed him, feeling uncomfortable for excluding him.

"I'm just messing with you," Dillon replied while grinning, then nodded back at his car. "Come on; I'll give you a ride to the mall."

Kasey considered it only a moment, then turned her car off as Dillon opened her door. She jumped out and walked with him to his small, powder blue, two-seat sports car. Hunter followed them and cut them off before the passenger side door.

"It's my job to accompany Kasey," Hunter informed Dillon.

Dillon smirked, relaying his dislike for Kasey's bodyguard. "It's okay, big guy," he announced. "She'll be fine. She's with me." He slapped Hunter on the arm. "Take the day off."

Hunter didn't move away from the car door and maintained his glare. "Your father might feel differently."

Dillon chuckled while stepping closer to Hunter, who had at least two inches on him, and stared into his sunglasses.

"Are you going to run and tell my daddy?" Dillon asked, mocking him.

"Dillon," Kasey softly scolded her cousin, knowing mocking Hunter wasn't a very good idea. "Don't provoke him."

"What's he going to do?" Dillon demanded without taking his eyes off Hunter while maintaining his arrogant grin. "Hit me? He'll be fired before he lands a punch."

Hunter removed his sunglasses, placed them in his jacket pocket, and glared at Dillon with a chilling look that almost certainly intimidated Kasey's cousin, even if he would never admit it. Dillon remained arrogant, doubling down on his threat.

"Step away from my car," Dillon snarled without taking his eyes off Hunter.

Kasey watched the two men as they stared into each other's eyes without blinking. Kasey felt her anxiety increasing at the stand-off. She couldn't understand why Dillon would intentionally provoke Hunter. There was no version where Dillon won in a fair fight against someone like Hunter. When neither man was willing to back down, Kasey couldn't take the tension any longer and stepped between the two men, turning her back to Hunter.

"It's okay, Dillon," she announced, attempting to defuse the situation. "An entire afternoon of shopping at the mall is punishment enough for Hunter. Jamie and I will make him hold our purses while we shop for lingerie."

Dillon frowned and finally backed away, although maintaining his sneer. Kasey then turned to Hunter and handed him her car keys.

"You can drive," she informed him. "Mall parking sucks."

Hunter accepted the car keys and followed her back to her sports car. He politely opened the passenger side door for her, then shut the door once she was inside. Hunter glared at Dillon as he rounded the car to the driver's side. Dillon sneered back at him.

Chapter Seven

One week later. The small, luxury cruise ship sailed along the calm, peaceful ocean without any other signs of life on the water. It was a gorgeous, sunny afternoon with a light salty breeze blowing. The ship was geared toward the rich and famous, often carrying at least one or two known Hollywood celebrities. The ship consisted of four decks with a large pool, three restaurants, four bars, and two nightclubs. There were only one hundred passengers and twice as many crew to pamper the cruise liner's wealthy guests. Given the size of the ship and the limited number of passengers, the pool and deck seemed relatively empty, although the hot tub was almost always at maximum capacity. The many deck lounge chairs were broad and comfortable, with attentive wait staff buzzing about, quick to refill drinks.

It was the first day of their ten-day, all-inclusive cruise and a perfect day to enjoy the sun on deck around the pool. Embry wore a pair of sunglasses while sitting on one of the deck chairs reading a book. Although he didn't loosen up enough to wear shorts, he did wear a pair of light tan slacks, a short-sleeved button shirt, and a pair of loafers without socks. The meek, hardworking butler appeared to be enjoying his spontaneous vacation, compliments of Kasey's overbearing uncle. Seeing Embry chilling out by the pool was a rare treat for Kasey, although she was disappointed he didn't wear shorts. She was curious to see how white his legs were. Kasey occupied the deck chair alongside Embry and tanned while wearing a conservative black bikini. She already had a good base tan from swimming in the pool at home, wanting to ensure she didn't burn on her trip.

Kasey's other travel companions were also on deck with them. Being her best friend since high school, Jamie Holt was a beautiful blonde bombshell with shoulder-length hair and generous curves. Jamie was that friend who always had the popular guys chasing after her throughout high school. It didn't hurt that she was also intelligent and fun-loving, rounding out the entire package. Jamie dated enough for both of them. Her friend hadn't found love yet, but she enjoyed browsing. Jamie wore a sexy, hot pink bikini that had already attracted plenty of attention from the single male population onboard. Kasey envied Jamie. Her friend knew how to have a good time, and the guys loved her. Kasey wished she could be half as outgoing as her friend.

Then there was her more recent best friend, Colton Stark. He'd been friends with Kasey and Jamie for almost a year and a half now. Colton was a lanky but dashing man in his mid-twenties. Although he wasn't hunky leading man handsome, he was cute enough to get his foot in the door. His personality was his ace in the hole. Colton had short dark hair that he kept spikey on top, blue eyes, and a dazzling smile. He was the life of any party and always kept Kasey and Jamie entertained. If his personality wasn't big enough to satisfy, he was also an incredible dance club partner. Although he was a tremendous flirt, both women turned a blind eye to his slightly dirty nature. Colton wore colorful swim trunks that went half-way down his thighs and a white button shirt. With his designer sunglasses, he looked ready to surf the waves at Bondi Beach. Colton sipped his fruity drink while casually scanning the deck for hot women.

"I can't believe your uncle made you bring Hunter," Colton muttered as he finished his first fruity drink of their vacation. "God, ten days of that rent-a-killer. He's always giving me dirty looks. I'm afraid he's going to kill me in my sleep."

"You aren't the one sharing a room with him," Embry muttered under his breath.

All four glanced across the deck twenty feet from them, where Hunter casually leaned against the railing while facing them. With his dark sunglasses, it was impossible to tell if he was watching them or not. Although dressed casually, he still didn't fit in with the other sunbathers on deck. He wore black jeans, military-style boots, a white button shirt, and his black leather jacket that he had never been without. It was unclear whether he would jump on a Harley, raid a military bunker, or shoot a mob boss. Jamie lowered her sunglasses while taking in a sweeping eyeful of the tall, ruggedly handsome bodyguard.

"Hmm, ten days to corrupt his morals," Jamie remarked, then replaced her sunglasses. "I'm actually looking forward to that."

"*You're* going to corrupt *his* morals?" Embry remarked, then chuckled, clearly amused. "That's a good one."

"What is it about my uncle's bodyguards that turns you into such a sex maniac?" Kasey asked while shaking her head.

"Mostly that quiet, dangerous vibe they give off," Jamie replied, then grinned almost playfully. "They're also animals in bed."

"Okay, I wish I hadn't eaten so much at the buffet," Kasey muttered, then felt compelled to take in another eyeful of Hunter.

Jamie wasn't entirely wrong. There was something sexually appealing about Hunter, and Kasey could see why Jamie might be attracted to the moderately frightening man. The first time she looked at him, she thought the same thing.

"He's going to scare all of the cuties away," Colton muttered, returning Kasey to reality. He then glanced at his friend. "Not to mention any shot you'll have with the guys. Remember last month when the guy at the club wanted to dance with you? He scared him off with one look."

"He has to stay ten feet away," Kasey reminded her friend. "It's one of the conditions."

"He looks like Secret Service," Jamie announced. "That's *so* hot."

"Look out," Colton remarked and chuckled. "Jamie's on the prowl."

"Though I still haven't figured out how to make him speak yet," Jamie remarked, then glanced at her friend. "Is there a particular cue word you use like 'speak, boy speak'?"

"Usually, I only get one-line sarcastic responses from him," Kasey informed her friend. "Most times, I get the icy glare or his ever-so-famous, shit-eating grin."

Colton chuckled softly, then focused his attention on Jamie and lowered his sunglasses, eyeing her. "You could always try the old-fashioned approach," he announced.

"What's the old-fashioned approach?" Jamie asked, now interested.

"Grab his trouser snake and lick his ear," Colton replied, then put his sunglasses back in place. "That's a pretty good icebreaker."

Kasey groaned softly. She was pretty sure that wasn't a legitimate icebreaker. At least, she hoped it wasn't.

"We'll call that Plan B," Jamie remarked, flashing a humored smile.

The waitress brought Embry another fruity drink with an umbrella in it. All three eyed Embry and his third colorful drink in under two hours.

"He's going to be drunk the whole trip, isn't he?" Colton asked just loud enough for Kasey and Jamie to hear.

"Hey, at least he's enjoying himself," Kasey informed him. "I mean, what does my uncle think is going to happen here?"

"I don't know, there's the very real threat of you getting groped in the nightclub," Colton remarked, then grinned almost slyly. "I know because I wrote it on my itinerary. *Grope Kasey.*"

"You're always hitting on Kasey," Jamie remarked while folding her arms across her chest, almost pouting. "You never hit on me."

"Probably because you hit back," Colton remarked and again eyed her.

Jamie couldn't hide her smile and giggled. "Just the one time," she replied, then offered a tiny grimace. "Maybe twice. Sorry about that."

"Too bad," Colton announced while turning his head away from her. "You fooled me twice. There won't be a third time."

"On that note, I'm going to flirt with the muscle," Jamie announced.

"And what are you going to say?" Kasey felt compelled to ask, wishing she could listen in on the whole flirting process.

Jamie stood, slipped into her strapless high heels, and smiled. "I don't know, but I'm cute," she announced with a shrug. "Words don't matter. It's all in the body language."

Jamie walked seductively along the deck, catching the attention of several men, who noticed and watched the blonde beauty in the pink bikini. Colton again lowered his sunglasses and watched her from behind. He groaned softly.

"And her body speaks many languages," Colton remarked.

Embry lowered his book and seemed compelled to watch Jamie as well, but not for the same reason. He leaned closer to Kasey.

"Is she going to flirt with--?"

Kasey smiled and raised her brows in silent response. All three felt compelled to watch, suddenly interested in Hunter's mating rituals. Jamie approached Hunter by the railing, momentarily catching his attention, but the sunglasses made his reaction hard to gauge. He maintained little to no expression as she paused before him. Jamie wore her best come-hither smile while talking to him. As she spoke, she allowed her hand to travel up his shirt to where it was unbuttoned near the top. Although he didn't appear to react, Hunter said something in response. Jamie immediately pulled her hand back, frowned, and returned to her chair without further interaction or comment.

Colton and Embry attempted to hide their smiles while Kasey cringed, sympathetic for her friend's feelings.

"I'm guessing that didn't go so well," Kasey remarked.

"What did he say?" Colton eagerly asked while leaning closer to her.

"None of your business," Jamie scoffed while folding her arms across her chest and lightly pouted after her interaction with Hunter.

"Oh, come on," Kasey just about begged, dying to know.

"I told him I was hot for him," Jamie remarked, then frowned before continuing. "He offered to throw me overboard."

Colton grinned and chuckled softly. Embry raised his book to hide his humored smile.

Chapter Eight

Kasey's luxury stateroom was a two-thousand-square-foot, two-bedroom suite with two bathrooms and a private balcony. There was a huge living area with plush furniture, a large television, a small dining area, and a wet bar. She was sharing the massive suite with Jamie and Colton. Colton had a bedroom to himself while she and Jamie shared the master bedroom. Hunter and Embry also shared a suite, although theirs wasn't nearly as spacious as Kasey's, only having one bedroom with two full beds and one bathroom. Kasey's master bedroom was slightly larger than Colton's bedroom, but each room had its own television, private bathroom, and access to the balcony.

Colton was showering in his bathroom while Jamie was finishing up in her shared bedroom with Kasey. Having showered first, Kasey sat in her official cruise line bathrobe on the plush chaise portion of the sectional sofa. Now that she was alone for the first time, she was lost in her thoughts. Despite the ten-day birthday and graduation celebration, Kasey had a lot on her mind. Jamie appeared from the bedroom, shower-fresh in her matching white cruise line robe while brushing her wet hair. She glanced at Kasey and immediately noticed her distant look.

"Hey," Jamie asked while joining her on the sectional sofa. "Everything okay? You aren't sea sick, I hope."

"No, I'm fine," Kasey replied, then groaned softly and shifted uncomfortably. "No, I'm not okay." She ran her fingers through her damp hair and looked at her friend. "I'm just a little, well--"

"It's okay to be nervous," Jamie informed her with a reassuring smile, then gently rubbed her shoulder. "No one's forcing you to do this, you know."

"I know," Kasey replied while remaining tense. "It's just, well, I'm going to be twenty-one tonight at midnight." She again shifted uncomfortably. "I just think I've been, well, *you know*, for too long."

"If you're this nervous, maybe you should wait until you're not, well, *conflicted*," Jamie informed her. "It's not as if you'll turn into a pumpkin if you're still a virgin two seconds after you turn twenty-one."

"I know," Kasey replied somewhat softly. She then cringed and looked at Jamie. "Would it be weird if I asked Colton?"

Jamie appeared just about horrified. "To be your first?" she gasped, then vigorously shook her head. "No, Kasey. I strongly suggest against that. If it gets awkward, you'll lose a good friend."

"Why would it get awkward?"

Jamie groaned. "Okay, you're nowhere near ready for this," she announced. "Find a nice guy. Date him for a week or so, and let that guy be your first. Then, if you break up with him, it won't matter. You don't have to do this tonight. There's no rush."

"No rush for what?" Colton asked as he appeared from his bedroom wearing his matching cruise line bathrobe while drying his hair. He eyed them and grinned. "Hey, we're all wearing matching bathrobes.

Now would be a great time for Hunter to pop in. He'd think we were filming a porno."

Both women stared at Colton and groaned. He tossed his towel aside and sat on the foot end of Kasey's chaise lounge.

"So what are we talking about?" he asked, leaning on Kasey's bent knees. "I thought I heard my name mentioned."

"You were mistaken," Jamie informed him somewhat firmly. "Go get dressed. It takes you forever to primp."

"Hey," Colton announced while straightening, then indicated his body. "This doesn't just happen. It requires work." He again cocked his head, not letting go of what he'd heard. "What were you two talking about?"

"Nothing," Jamie snarled. "Now, go away. This is girl talk."

"Oh, I see," Colton announced with little emotion, turning serious. "Kasey's looking to deflower tonight, huh?"

Jamie groaned, placed her hand over her eyes, and had to look away. Kasey grimaced slightly with embarrassment.

"Relax," Colton announced to Jamie. "Kasey told me about the whole 'like a virgin' thing she has going on." He appeared almost offended. "Kasey and I girl talk too, you know."

Jamie looked at Kasey with some surprise while indicating Colton. "You actually talked to *him* about this?" she asked. "The mutt in heat?"

"I resent that," Colton scoffed, then looked at Kasey with sympathy. "Don't do anything you're not ready to do. I don't want to sound like a condom commercial, but you'll know when the time is right. Besides, over the next ten days, there's plenty of time for a little shipboard romance."

Jamie stared at Colton with some surprise. "Wow, that's the first time you didn't sound like a total perv," she remarked.

"Don't sound so surprised," Colton scoffed, then looked back at Kasey while remaining serious. "And if that doesn't happen, I'd like you to remember I'm at your service."

Jamie rolled her eyes and groaned. "And he's back."

Colton was again offended. "I think it's very nice of me to offer," he informed Jamie. "I'm not just amazing on the dance floor, you know. But, as her friend, I'd be doing her a favor."

"This is getting awkward," Kasey remarked under her breath.

"Getting?" Jamie gasped.

"So what is the plan if one of us meets someone tonight?" Colton then asked. "I mean, I have my own room, but what if Kasey does meet some guy for a little love on the high seas? The two of you are sharing a room."

"The answer is obvious," Jamie informed Colton while raising her brows. "You give up your room and sleep on the sofa."

"Why do I sleep on the sofa?" Colton practically pouted.

"Because you're a gentleman," Jamie reminded him.

"Well, that's debatable," Colton muttered, then gave her a curious look while cocking his head. "What if I meet someone too?"

"Odd man out gets the sofa," Kasey informed them. "And if that happens to be me, Hunter gets kicked out of his room, he gets the sofa, and I'll bunk with Embry. They have two beds in their suite."

"Solid plan," Colton announced and placed his fist out.

Jamie stared at Colton's fist. "I'm not fist-bumping you," she informed him.

"You're no fun," Colton huffed, then looked at Kasey.

Kasey groaned and fist-bumped him.

"Dorks," Jamie grumbled.

Chapter Nine

Kasey, Jamie, and Colton wore their club attire to dinner that evening so they wouldn't have to change for the dance club later. Both women wore sexy, short, form-fitting dresses and high heels. Both dresses offered more than a generous view of each woman's cleavage, which Colton openly admired and provided plenty of commentary. Kasey liked black dresses, while Jamie liked colors that popped. The one she wore tonight was the same color as her bikini, hot pink. Colton wore fashion slacks, a white button shirt, and a flashy jacket that was mostly black with some purple marbleized throughout. He was always the best-dressed man on the dance floor, and the ladies noticed him. Although Hunter enjoyed getting under his skin and often told him that he looked like a pimp.

The ship's main dining room, located on the top level, seated about fifty guests with mostly small, intimate tables that sat either two or four guests. Being it was the main dining room, there was live entertainment and even a small dance floor for those who weren't into the club scene. Most of the passengers were under forty, but some were older than that. The top-level dining room was also the fanciest of the three. It had crystal chandeliers, a large bar, and tuxedo-dressed servers. Kasey, Colton, and Jamie sat at their table and sipped drinks while actively interested in the table not too far from them.

Embry, dressed in proper dinner attire that looked suspiciously like his butler uniform, sat at a table with Hunter for their evening meal. Embry was quite possibly drunk and chattered away with enthusiasm. On the other hand, Hunter, who hadn't bothered changing, sat partially slumped in his chair with his hands in his pockets and stared at the burning candle on the table.

"I feel bad for Embry," Colton remarked while frowning. "He's such a cheerful little, drunken chipmunk, and that python across from him is just waiting to strike."

"All that talking," Kasey remarked while shaking her head, then turned curious. "What do you think Embry is saying?"

"We should get Embry laid," Jamie announced, seemingly out of the blue.

Kasey and Colton looked at Jamie with some surprise at the comment. Particularly since it had nothing to do with the current conversation. Jamie eyed them and turned surprised.

"I didn't mean me; I just meant we should find a nice, easy woman and introduce him," Jamie insisted, then turned almost casual. "Why should he have to put up with Hunter the entire cruise?"

"That's probably why he's drunk," Colton muttered.

"I have to know what he's saying," Kasey announced, her curiosity getting the best of her. "It's killing me. I've never seen him chatter so much before."

Kasey stood and approached Embry's table several feet away. Hunter straightened in his chair while Embry partially stood, offering a drunken smile.

"Hey, darling," Embry announced and indicated the vacant chair. "Care to join us?"

"Just for a few minutes," Kasey replied, sitting with them.

Embry placed his chin on his fist, leaned closer to her, and smiled. "You're so pretty."

Hunter shot a surprised look at Embry, then just as quickly looked away.

Embry suddenly yelped, "Ouch!" He looked at Hunter with surprise. "Did you kick me?"

Hunter didn't respond.

Embry looked back at Kasey and pointed at Hunter. "He kicked me."

"Yes, he has bad manners."

Embry seemed to dismiss what had just happened, or he'd already forgotten and resumed smiling at Kasey.

"This is fun," Embry announced, conveying his level of drunkenness. "Thanks for bringing me."

"I'm glad you're enjoying yourself," Kasey replied cheerfully, then turned somewhat serious. "Would you do me a favor, Embry?"

"Sure, anything."

"Well, I was hoping you'd come with us for a little while tonight, being it's my birthday, and dance with Jamie and me," Kasey informed him, "but you might be a little too intoxicated."

"Oh, I'll switch to tea," Embry insisted while remaining enthusiastic. "I'd love to dance with you, especially on your birthday." He again looked at her with loving eyes. "You're so pretty."

Hunter suddenly yelped.

Without looking away from Kasey, Embry smiled slyly. "I kicked him that time."

"Good for you," Kasey announced, then looked at Hunter. "Will you watch how much he drinks? I don't want him falling overboard."

"Oh, I can swim," Embry insisted, interrupting her conversation with Hunter. "I'm an excellent swimmer."

"He's fine," Hunter muttered, possibly disinterested in babysitting the hired help.

Kasey studied Hunter for a moment with disapproval. "You know, if you'd prefer to be alone, he can join us for dinner," she informed him. "I can't imagine you being anyone's idea of good company."

Hunter maintained his emotionless expression and didn't comment.

Kasey groaned softly and stood, having had enough. "I'd like to talk to you, Hunter," she announced, then turned stern. "*Alone.*"

Kasey walked away from the table and left the dining room.

As Hunter stood, Embry smiled deviously and chuckled. "Someone's getting spanked."

§

Kasey stood by the deck railing and stared into the dark ocean, lost in her thoughts. Hunter appeared on deck only a moment later, approached her, and casually leaned on the railing while facing her. Kasey turned toward him and glared her disapproval at his behavior.

"I realize I can't fire you, and you have no intention to listen to anything I say--"

"Allow me to stop you right there," Hunter announced sternly while straightening, now towering over her.

Kasey was surprised by his commanding tone and presence. Even though he technically worked for her, she felt a little threatened.

"You may not have the power to fire me, but you've gotten four men fired before me," Hunter informed her. "We both know watching over you is a baby sitting job, but what you did to your other bodyguards was cold and unfeeling." His eyes narrowed while he stared into her eyes. "So go ahead, throw your tantrum, and stomp your feet. You're not the first spoiled little rich girl I've baby sat."

Kasey stared at him with some surprise, not expecting that sort of speech from him. Despite her reddened cheeks, her hostility quickly returned.

"Sounds like you're the one throwing a tantrum," she scoffed while folding her arms across her chest.

"We both know you're looking for a way to get me fired," Hunter remarked, then gestured. "Like sending your friend over to seduce me by the pool. That's how you got the last guy fired, right?"

Kasey stared at him a moment longer, rethinking what she wanted to say now that he had caught her off guard. He didn't look away or back down. Why did she feel as if she were standing in front of her high school principal? She finally blurted out the first thing that came to mind, whether good or bad.

"Hey, you want to fuck around, be my guest," Kasey scoffed, projecting her anger to cover her insecurities. "And I *had* an opportunity to get you fired last week but didn't take it."

Hunter appeared curious about the comment. "What's that supposed to mean?"

"The incident with Dillon," Kasey announced, then scaled back her hostility and became uncomfortable while avoiding eye contact. "Dillon wanted you fired over the incident by his car." She again shifted and met his gaze. "My uncle asked if I wanted you replaced." Kasey hesitated, frowned, and rubbed her chilled bare shoulders. "I said no."

There was a long moment of silence as Hunter seemed to process the new information. Kasey then came back to life, feeling the need to vindicate herself. She didn't want to come across as soft or having any sympathy for Hunter.

"I don't really give a shit what you and Jamie do," Kasey informed him. "I only care about that poor, sweet drunken man in there who thinks he's having a good time talking to a cold, unfeeling bastard." Her emotions were again spiking, and she couldn't seem to control her hostility. "Would it kill you to say two words to him?" She threw her hands in the air. "You're miserable; I get it. Go be miserable somewhere else. I won't let you treat that dear, sweet man the way you treat everyone else."

Kasey turned toward the railing and fought her tears. She hated being so emotional, particularly anywhere near such an emotionless man like Hunter. Kasey nearly lost Embry the night her aunt was murdered, and she had become overly protective of him as a result. An uncomfortable moment passed, and she wasn't sure if Hunter was looking at her or not. She saw him move out of the corner of her eye, but she didn't want to let him know she was watching him.

Hunter leaned his back against the railing and groaned softly. "If that's really all you're worried about, I'll take him to the casino after dinner," he informed her. "He wants to try his hand at craps. I'll sober him up at the craps table, and we'll meet you in the club around ten."

Kasey hesitated, then turned toward him with some surprise. "You'd do that?" she asked in a softer tone.

Hunter eyed her and offered a disinterested shrug. "Won't kill me," he replied. "Consider it my birthday present to you."

"Thank you, Hunter," she replied and finally smiled. "And you have my word; I had nothing to do with Jamie coming on to you." Kasey considered the comment and then snorted a tiny laugh while indicating the ship. "And you have my word that I won't use anything that happens on this cruise as ammunition to get you fired."

"Really?" he asked, now curious.

"What happens on the high seas stays on the high seas," she replied, then cocked her head. "Of course, I expect a little quid pro quo. You don't report my every move back to my uncle either."

Hunter studied her a long moment, then offered what appeared to be a sincere smile and nodded. "Okay, you've got yourself a deal."

Chapter Ten

Eight o'clock that evening. Even though the ship wasn't as big as most cruise liners, the casino was surprisingly huge. It had many slot machines as well as dozens of table games. Typical of most casinos, there was tacky, bolt print carpeting, crystal chandeliers, and plenty of flashing lights. Embry and Hunter stood around the craps table with several other players, placing large bets everywhere. The table minimum was twenty-five dollars, but most were playing black, one-hundred-dollar chips. The table was highly enthusiastic each time the dice rolled, followed by cheers at another win and more chips tossed in every direction. Embry joined in on the enthusiasm in his drunken condition, seeming livelier than ever as well as a little richer.

Hunter attempted to curb Embry's overly zealous gambling, but the butler appeared disinterested and continued pressing his winnings. His pile of chips on the play area was more than two thousand dollars, and letting it ride with each roll was risky. Against Hunter's gentle insistence that he pull some chips back, Embry rolled the dice again while Hunter covered his eyes and cringed. The entire table screamed at the big win for everyone, particularly for Embry. A lavishly dressed woman standing alongside Embry, who hadn't even been playing, excitedly hugged him. Once she released him, Embry eyed Hunter and offered a devious smile, indicating the *friendly* woman. Hunter just rolled his eyes. Embry had to know the woman was a high-priced call girl. And maybe he didn't.

Hunter again insisted Embry pull back some of his winnings, making a motion for his stack of chips on the table. Embry slapped his hand and wagged his finger at him, scolding him.

§

The fast, thumping, never-ending club music blared throughout the large crowded room of mostly twenty-somethings, all dressed to impress. The dance club was dimly lit except for the strobe lights on the dance floor. A large bar along the back wall offered no seating, but there were intimate tables of four and larger tables of six for the passengers. Scantily clad dressed waitresses brought drinks to thirsty patrons. The dance floor was packed with men and women dancing to the heart-stopping music, and nearly all the tables were filled throughout the room, making it standing-room only. Kasey, Jamie, and Colton impressed on the dance floor with sexy and stylish moves, astonishing other men and women in the club with their dirty dancing threesome.

Colton appeared in his glory, with the two gorgeous women paying so much attention to him, which drew other women closer. Where most single men had 'wing men', Colton liked to refer to Jamie and Kasey as his 'wing women'. Something about a man hanging out with attractive women seemed to entice other women. Perhaps the 'good ones are always taken' motto drew in the women. Whatever the reason, Colton always had more than his fair share of attractive women approaching him. After their latest round of dirty dancing, Kasey, Jamie, and Colton finally returned to their table, deciding it was time for a break and more drinks. It was around ten o'clock, prompting Kasey to glance around. She saw Hunter standing at the bar across the room, casually watching them. Kasey realized Embry wasn't with him and frowned in disapproval.

"Great," Kasey scoffed loudly above the music and gestured at the bar, alerting her friends. "The bastard ditched Embry."

Jamie and Colton glanced across the crowded club as well. Kasey left the table in a huff and approached Hunter at the bar. Unfortunately, she had to stand close to him, and he had to lean down, so they could hear each other over the loud music.

"What happened to Embry?" she asked while attempting to keep her temper in check despite wanting to lash out.

Kasey found his closeness slightly uncomfortable, but it was the only way they could hear each other. Kasey rarely spoke to him when they went to the clubs back home, so it was never an issue.

"I put him to bed," he announced close to her ear above the music.

"I thought you were bringing him here," Kasey remarked as her hostility increased.

"He was completely wasted," Hunter informed her. "He won a couple of grand at craps and had every high-priced call girl on the ship trying to part him from his winnings."

Kasey appeared slightly surprised by the admission, then met his gaze, his face being unusually close to her.

"Oh?" she asked, then had to smile. "Well, it sounds like he at least had fun."

"Yeah, a little too much."

While at the bar, Kasey saw two relatively handsome men in their late twenties approach Jamie at the table and talk to her. It obviously irritated Colton when they unexpectedly took the two vacant seats. Kasey knew what Jamie was up to, and she wasn't sure she was entirely comfortable, despite what she may have said about her birthday plans during the weeks leading up to the cruise. Kasey returned her attention to Hunter, placed her hand on his shoulder, and stood on her tip toes to speak closer to his ear. He again leaned down to hear her, although placing his hand on her lower back this time.

"Why don't you loosen up and enjoy yourself?" she suggested, practically shouting in his ear while very aware of his hand on her lower back. "Mingle a little. Have some fun. I'm sure you'll notice if someone tries to kill me."

"I'm too old for this crowd," he responded near her ear. "Just a bunch of kids."

Kasey cast a slightly offended look at him. "They're my age or older," she reminded him.

"Yeah, like I said, a bunch of kids," Hunter replied, then straightened and grinned at her expense while removing his hand from her back.

Kasey glared at him, not humored by the comment. She beckoned him to lean back down, which he obliged and immediately returned his hand to her lower back. Kasey subconsciously placed her hand on his shoulder in response, putting them closer together.

"You're not funny, Hunter."

Hunter lowered his mouth to her ear and chuckled warmly, sending a tiny shiver through her body from his warm breath.

"I'm not paid for my personality," he reminded her as his beard lightly brushed against her face near her ear.

"No kidding," she scoffed.

At that moment, Kasey realized she was pressed against Hunter as he basically held her. He met her gaze with his face close to hers while mocking her. She stared at him for a moment, almost mesmerized by his smile. His smile was oddly warm and genuine, which was odd. Kasey smirked, gave him a slight shove, and pulled away from him. She quickly retreated back to her table to avoid Hunter. Kasey discovered that one of Jamie's two new admirers now occupied her seat. Both men were tall and athletically built, keeping their dark hair neat and short. Kasey eyed the man in her seat and indicated her chair with a cleverly raised brow. It was easier than trying to talk to him above the music, and she didn't want to get that close to some stranger. Instead of moving, he grinned and patted his lap.

Kasey just glared at him, not humored. She snatched her drink from the table, approached Colton, and sat on his lap instead.

"Hmm," Colton announced while grinning proudly and placing his arms around her waist from behind. "My luck is changing already."

"Yeah, you just behave," Kasey announced.

Jamie looked at Kasey on Colton's lap, appeared slightly humored, and then indicated the two men. "This is Brad and Thomas," she announced loudly above the music.

Kasey managed a smile but remained irritated about being offered Thomas's lap. With the next song, Jamie and Brad stood and headed for the dance floor together. Kasey moved off Colton's lap, disappointing him, and sat on Jamie's chair. Thomas moved onto the vacant chair closer to Kasey and leaned in to speak to her above the music.

"Want to take a walk on deck?" Thomas asked.

Kasey eyed the man and managed a smile while shaking her head.

"Oh, come on," Thomas moaned while playfully grinning, then moved in closer than necessary so she could hear him. "You still mad about trying to get you on my lap? I was just joking around."

Colton leaned closer to Kasey and glared at Thomas. "She's with me," he snarled loudly across the table. "Take a hike."

Thomas frowned and left the table, joining Brad and Jamie on the dance floor. Colton read Kasey's moods well and knew she wasn't interested in the new fella. Although it was possible he had overheard her earlier conversation with Jamie and was trying to impress her, so she'd ask him to be her first, but that really wasn't Colton's style. Jamie returned to the table two songs later and flopped onto her chair with a huff.

"What a jerk," Jamie scoffed.

"Which one?" Kasey asked.

"Brad," Jamie replied, folding her arms across her ample cleavage. "One dance, and he's already trying to get me alone on deck."

"And this is a bad thing?" Colton asked, seeming confused.

"It's code for 'next stop my cabin'," Jamie informed him.

Colton was somewhat surprised by the response. "I'd better remember that so I don't accidentally offend someone," he remarked, then appeared curious. "I thought you were looking for a little shipboard romance."

"Romance, yes," Jamie announced. "Not a quickie on deck. I want to find a guy I can be with during the entire trip. You know, a week-long fling." She then frowned. "And since Hunter is obviously out--"

Colton groaned, apparently giving in. "Fine, I'll have a fling with you," he announced. "But only because you're my friend, and I care about your happiness."

Jamie and Kasey both looked at Colton and raised their brows. He attempted to hide his smile but couldn't. Jamie rolled her eyes but had to smile as well.

Chapter Eleven

Midnight. Jamie, Kasey, and Colton danced on the crowded dance floor with dozens of other young men and women. The sober passengers were becoming fewer, but excessive alcohol brought the self-conscious patrons out of their comfort zones and onto the dance floor. Kasey and Colton danced fast and close to the pulsating music while Jamie appeared to have found a new conquest. Kasey and Colton finally returned to the table for their drinks, leaving Jamie on the dance floor with her new man. Kasey was now feeling the full effects of the strong mixed drinks, making her giddy and possibly a little too affectionate, but she was having a good time. She laughed at her slightly unsteady gait while clinging to Colton, who remained mostly sober.

Colton rarely drank much when they went out, possibly because he often drove himself. When Jamie was old enough to drink six months ago, Kasey became the designated driver. Now, it was Kasey's turn to drink too much and make bad decisions. Since it was her twenty-first birthday, the ship's bartender allowed Kasey to drink a few hours before she officially turned twenty-one. When Colton noticed their nearly empty glasses, he indicated the bar and leaned over Kasey's shoulder to speak close to her ear so he didn't have to shout.

"I'm going to get another round," Colton announced. "I'll be right back."

Colton approached the bar near Hunter and said something to him. Whatever he'd said, Hunter glared at him, clearly not amused, but didn't respond. Perhaps it was just the alcohol, but Kasey was suddenly intrigued by Colton and Hunter's interaction at the bar. As Jamie approached the table with her new man, Kasey headed to the bar, now feeling the full effects of the alcohol. She'd gotten a buzz a few times, but this was definitely different. She liked the euphoric feeling, compliments of vodka in cranberry juice. It had been a rough year. Kasey squeezed between Hunter and Colton, placing her hands on both men's shoulders, hanging on them, and instantly getting attention from each. She leaned closer to Colton so he could hear her over the loud music.

"Tell the bartender to go easy on the vodka," Kasey remarked.

"You've got it," Colton replied.

"You're so cute," she informed her friend.

Colton grinned in response, enjoying his friend's drunken, slightly flirtatious behavior. Kasey turned to face Hunter, smiled drunkenly while leaning on his shoulder, and used her free hand to straighten his jacket. Since she was feeling a little too good, she didn't even care that she was hanging on Hunter. Kasey was actually questioning why she had so many issues with her handsome bodyguard. Obviously, she had misjudged him. Hunter certainly wasn't as bad as she made him out to be. He couldn't be. He was so cute!

"I'm a little drunk," she announced and giggled while hanging on him.

Hunter smiled, obviously humored, while gently supporting her against him with his hand on her lower back.

"Yes, you are," he replied, seeming unusually cheerful about something, although she wasn't sure what.

"Come and join us," Kasey announced, unaware of her flirting while pressed against him and gazing into his eyes. "I promise to play nice."

Colton shot a look at Kasey's profile, having heard the comment. Hunter, on the other hand, appeared humored and grinned, enjoying her flirty drunkenness. As Kasey gazed into Hunter's eyes, possibly for the first time, she now saw something undeniably sexy about him. She suddenly couldn't remember why she had a problem with the handsome man. And why hadn't she noticed that incredible smile of his? Without waiting for a response, Kasey affectionately took Hunter's hand and led him back to their table. Colton stared after his friend with some surprise at her behavior, then grabbed their drinks and hurried after them.

Jamie and her new friend, Brock, were sitting close to each other at the table, looking rather intimate, while attempting to converse over the loud music. Brock was Jamie's usual type; tall, handsome, and moderately muscular. This particular beefcake had a shaved head, making him look like one of many action adventure movie stars. The man probably didn't have a personality, but meeting men in nightclubs wasn't about conversation anyway. Kasey led Hunter to one of the vacant seats, with Colton only a step or two behind them. Colton set the drinks down and quickly took his seat, attempting to coax Kasey back onto his lap. Instead, Kasey sat on Hunter's lap, surprising Colton *and* Hunter.

Jamie was too busy getting to know her new friend to notice the building drama happening at the table.

While comfortably seated on Hunter's lap, Kasey casually sipped her drink and caught a glimpse of Colton, who appeared unusually annoyed while watching her.

"Do you know whose lap you're on?" Colton finally asked.

Hunter grinned at Colton, mocking him. "Relax, Huggy Bear, she's fine," he remarked while reaching past Kasey with his free arm and setting his drink on the table.

"I'm *not* dressed like a pimp," Colton scoffed, further humoring Hunter.

Kasey caught Hunter's hand, noted the time on his watch, and smiled gleefully as she allowed his hand to fall on her leg. Hunter didn't bother removing his hand from her leg, but Colton noticed and didn't appear pleased.

"It's after midnight," Kasey announced, giddy with excitement. "It's officially my birthday!"

Jamie and Colton cheered while holding up their drinks to her. "Happy birthday, Kasey!"

Kasey giggled and clinked glasses with her friends across the table, then took a large swallow of the strong drink. Despite being drunk, she tasted the alcohol and made a face.

"How about a birthday kiss?" Colton suggested while leaning closer, eager to steal a kiss from the birthday girl.

Kasey considered the idea only a moment, then set her glass on the table and looked back at Hunter, unable to hide her devious smile. She affectionately touched his face and then warmly kissed him on the lips. Despite his surprise, Hunter immediately returned the kiss while his arm tightened around her waist and his free hand firmly caressed her leg. Jamie cheered them on when she saw what was happening while Colton silently fumed. Kasey broke off the kiss and met Hunter's gaze with her mouth close to his.

There was no doubt in her mind, no matter how drunk she may have been, whom she had just kissed--and she didn't care.

"What happens on the high seas--" she cooed, reaffirming her earlier stance on shipboard behavior as she affectionately clung to him.

Hunter returned the smile, placed his hand on her face, and eagerly kissed her. Jamie cried out and clapped excitedly.

§

One o'clock in the morning. Kasey and Jamie, now fully intoxicated, danced with Colton and Brock on the dance floor among other rowdy passengers. Colton mostly danced with Kasey now that Jamie found a suitable replacement and possibly overnight company in Brock. Since Colton didn't even appear to be trying to get close to other women, it looked as if he'd be the one sleeping on the sofa in their suite tonight. Kasey wasn't even thinking about any of that in her drunken mind. She was just having a good time with her two best friends. When it was finally time for a break from dancing, Kasey and Jamie stumbled to the bathroom for one of many quick pit stops before returning to their table.

Had Kasey been sober, finding Hunter waiting outside the ladies' room would have irritated her, but she was too drunk to notice or care. In her increasingly vulnerable position, Hunter wasn't taking any chances with the young, horny drunken men roaming around the club. Kasey giggled when she saw Hunter leaning against the wall outside the restrooms and immediately sauntered up to him. She placed her arms around his waist and rested her head on his chest while grinning at Jamie, who wasn't even fazed by the action. Ironically, it all suddenly seemed perfectly natural. Hunter placed his arms securely around her, returning the embrace.

"Isn't he adorable?" Kasey asked.

Jamie grinned almost slyly, then suggestively raised her brows. "Very interesting choice," she announced. "You get first dibs on the master suite. Colton can have the couch."

Kasey and Jamie laughed at the comment, although Hunter was a bit puzzled by it, not privy to Kasey's birthday plans.

"My drink and that handsome stud are calling," Jamie informed them, then headed back into the noisy club.

A slow song played, and Kasey pulled away from Hunter while taking his hands in hers.

"Dance with me," she announced, leaving no room for protest as she pulled him back into the crowded club.

Once on the dance floor, Hunter held Kasey in his arms and slow danced with her. She happily clung to him while they swayed to the music, barely moving. It seemed as if the slow song was over too soon, and the fast song overlapped, cutting the slow dance short. Kasey clung to Hunter, partly for balance, as they returned to the table while others headed onto the dance floor for the next round of fast songs. Hunter no sooner sat down when Kasey popped onto his lap and immediately hung on him. He didn't seem to mind, keeping his arm securely around her waist. Both sipped their drinks while the loud music blared throughout the large room.

Colton once again eyed Kasey on Hunter's lap and didn't appear pleased. After having a few minutes to rest, Jamie pulled Brock and Colton back onto the dance floor, leaving Kasey alone on Hunter's lap. Kasey now clung to Hunter while lightly caressing his beard with her free hand. She was unusually fascinated by his beard and couldn't keep her hands off it. He warmly caressed her thigh in response while watching her closely with a strange sort of smile but didn't comment. She wasn't even aware he was watching her while she was lost in her own world. Kasey finally met his gaze and smiled lustfully before leaning closer to his ear to speak.

"Want to hear my birthday wish?" she cooed, brushing her lips past his beard.

"Sure."

"I want to lose my virginity," she whispered in his ear.

Hunter's entire body seemed to tense at her words, and his hand lightly gripped her leg in reflex. Kasey kept her lips close to his ear while gently nuzzling her face against his.

"I'd like it to be with you," she whispered while adding a soft sigh that seemed to make him shiver. "Will you stay with me tonight?"

Kasey finally pulled back just far enough to meet his gaze and gauge his reaction. Hunter couldn't hide his overly pleased grin and even chuckled softly.

"Are you sure you've got the right guy?" he asked as his smile increased into something almost sinister. "What's my name?"

"I'm not drunk," she insisted boldly while searching his eyes.

"You're not?" Hunter asked with some humor, knowing damned well she was.

"I know what I'm doing," she informed him matter-of-factly, attempting to convince him that she wasn't drunk. "You're a very sexy man, Hunter." Kasey bit her lower lip while grinning, then looked down, gauging what she felt while on his lap before again meeting his gaze. "Can I take *that* as an enthusiastic 'yes'?"

Hunter didn't take his eyes off hers while grinning like a schoolboy. "If it makes you feel safer having me around," he announced. "Of course, I'll stay in your room with you." He repositioned her on his lap and smiled more naturally, losing some of his arrogance. "And I promise I'll make sure you don't do anything you'll regret in the morning."

Kasey giggled, somehow misinterpreting his response as acceptance. "Okay, then," she replied and kissed him.

Hunter cupped her face and eagerly returned the kiss, pulling her tightly against him. While they kissed, he took a selfie with his cell phone of them together, then broke off the kiss and pulled back just far enough to meet her gaze as his sly grin returned.

"Well, maybe one *small* regret," he remarked, then slipped his cell phone into his pocket and resumed kissing her.

Chapter Twelve

After last call at two in the morning, the club had less than a dozen patrons remaining. When the last slow song played before the bar closed, Colton stole Kasey away from Hunter, securing the last dance with his best girl. Despite Kasey spending the better portion of the evening on Hunter's lap, Colton held Kasey close while they danced. He periodically glanced back at the table to gauge Hunter's reaction, but the bodyguard appeared unreactive.

"Maybe you'd better stick close to me on the way back to the cabin," Colton remarked to his friend while they slow danced.

Kasey drunkenly met his gaze and managed a tiny humored laugh. "I'm fine, Colton," she insisted. "I'm only a tiny bit drunk. Besides, it's Hunter's job to keep me safe. He needs to earn his keep."

Colton frowned while studying her, despite her head returning to his shoulder. "Are you sure you want to go that route?" he finally asked.

Kasey lifted her head and met his gaze. "That route?"

"With Hunter," he replied, then tensed. "You've been stoking that fire all evening. He might take your flirting seriously and expect an invite."

Kasey smiled warmly and gently touched Colton's face. "You're a good friend, Colton, and I love you dearly," she announced, then smoothed his jacket while they continued to slow dance. "I already talked to Hunter. It's all good."

"Meaning--?"

She giggled softly and again rested her head on his shoulder. "It means it's all good," she insisted without elaborating.

Finally, the slow song ended, and the music ceased, leaving the club eerily quiet. The deafening silence was code for 'go home'. As they headed back to the table, Colton kept an arm securely around Kasey's waist, keeping her steady. Jamie sat on Brock's lap, and they kissed like two teenagers at prom while Hunter sat not far from them and casually glanced at his watch. When Colton and Kasey paused by the table, Hunter stood.

"I'm exhausted," Kasey announced with a weary sigh. "I'm ready to go."

"Yeah," Colton replied with a soft chuckle while securing his arm around her. "I think they're about to lock the doors on us."

When Hunter approached them, Kasey pulled away from Colton, slipped her arms around Hunter's mid-section, and rested her head against his chest. As Hunter placed his arms around her, holding her against him, she shut her eyes. Colton eyed Kasey clinging to Hunter, and frowned.

"Figures," Colton muttered.

All three looked at Jamie and Brock, who continued making out, unaware of everything else happening around them. Colton cleared his throat, but the happy couple was oblivious to his presence. Colton approached Jamie on Brock's lap and shoved their chair slightly. As the chair jolted and creaked, they both jumped while breaking off the kiss and looked at Colton with drunken disorientation.

"Time to go," Colton announced.

Jamie attempted to move off Brock's lap and nearly fell to the floor. She drunkenly laughed while catching her balance. Brock also stood while laughing and helped stabilize her, which she also found amusing. Although Kasey felt drunk, tired, and mostly disorientated, she felt unusually contented while nestled against Hunter. It had been an enjoyable night and the beginning of her birthday celebration. Although Kasey was tired, she was sure plenty of excitement was yet to come as she secretly caressed Hunter's body. While Jamie clung to Brock, all five finally headed across the club toward the main exit behind a few other patrons.

Colton casually walked alongside Jamie and Brock. "Your call, Jamie," he announced while glancing at his drunken friend, sending her some secret message with a single look. "Do you want us to walk you to your room?"

It seemed like a weird thing to say, being the three of them were staying in the same suite, but the hidden message was enough to rouse Jamie. She stopped in her tracks and looked at Brock, with whom she clung. She slipped back into reality, released him, and looked at Colton.

"Yes, you should probably take me to my room," Jamie replied, then looked back at Brock while offering a tiny, sympathetic smile. "Sorry, I'm too drunk tonight. I'd really like to get together tomorrow, though."

Brock was obviously disappointed that his plans for overnight company were squashed, but he managed a smile and a nod before quickly departing ahead of them.

Jamie gave Colton a tiny, weary smile. "Thanks, Colton."

Colton sighed and placed his arm around her shoulder. She immediately clung to him much the same way Kasey clung to Hunter.

"That's what friends are for," Colton replied, hugging her and affectionately kissing the top of her head.

When they finally reached the door, Colton pushed on it, but it appeared to be stuck. He hesitated and looked back at Hunter, somewhat puzzled. Hunter released Kasey, quickly approached the door, and pushed on it as well.

Colton looked across the nightclub at the bartender. "Hey, the door is locked or something," he called to the man.

The bartender walked out from behind the bar and approached. "It shouldn't be," he remarked, then pushed on the door as well. When it didn't budge, he nodded toward the far end of the club. "Use the back exit."

They turned and headed across the mostly empty club toward the back exit. Colton, Kasey, and Jamie had a difficult time keeping up with Hunter's long, fast strides. He suddenly appeared to be in a hurry. Besides the two waitresses and the bartender, only one other couple and three men were still inside the club. Brad and Thomas were among those three men remaining. Hunter approached the back exit and eyed a drunken man in his late twenties leaning against the wall not far from the door while attempting to light his cigarette. His lighter didn't appear to work, and he looked at Hunter.

"Hey, buddy," the man announced. "You have a light?"

Hunter eyed the drunken man, who now straightened while reaching inside his jacket. Hunter slammed the man against the wall without warning and grabbed his wrist. Kasey gasped with surprise at the action and was about to scold Hunter when she saw the gun in the man's hand. Jamie and Kasey screamed as Hunter wrestled the man for control of the weapon. Colton panicked and pulled the two women low to the floor with lightning-fast reflexes while looking across the room.

"Call security!" Colton yelled to one of the waitresses.

The waitress immediately reacted and hurried across the club. Brad suddenly removed a gun affixed with a silencer and shot the waitress. The bullet struck her in the head, projecting a large blood spatter across the nightclub, and she immediately dropped to the floor. The second waitress screamed while the remaining couple dove to the floor. Thomas now pulled a weapon as well and shot the man not far from him. By the rear exit door, Hunter continued to fight the man for his weapon. Hunter finally snapped the man's arm, snatched his gun, and fired back at Brad and Thomas. With the silencers, little sound was heard as bullets struck floors and walls. Despite the lack of sound from the weapons, those caught in the crossfire screamed. Unfortunately, their screams would go unheard in the heavily soundproofed dance club. Hunter fired multiple shots, striking Brad twice in the chest and winging Thomas.

"Go!" Hunter cried out while motioning toward the door.

Colton kept Kasey and Jamie low as he hurried them through the door. Hunter fired at the remaining gunman, giving the second waitress time to usher the remaining patrons to safety behind the bar with the bartender.

Chapter Thirteen

Colton hurried his frightened friends along the eerie, empty back corridor. Hunter stormed from the club and ran after them only a few seconds later, having mysteriously secured another magazine for his borrowed weapon. As they approached the door leading onto deck, Brock appeared in the corridor, saw them, and smiled.

"Hey, Jamie," Brock announced with a drunken laugh. "I forgot my cell phone."

Jamie was about to shout a warning to Brock about the shooting in the nightclub when she was interrupted.

"Wrong door," Hunter remarked aloud but seemingly to himself.

Colton suddenly gasped and shoved Jamie and Kasey against the wall while shielding them with his body. When Hunter aimed his gun past them at Brock, Jamie let out a horrified scream, possibly frightened Hunter would shoot her would-be boyfriend. Brock gasped with alarm and held his hands up.

"Whoa, what's going on?" Brock cried out. "Money! I got money!" He then reached inside his inner jacket pocket.

"Hands where I can see them!" Hunter shouted loud enough to raise the rafters. There was no doubt that he'd pull the trigger without compliance to his orders.

"Yeah! Okay!" Brock cried out and again raised his hands.

When the rear nightclub door flew open behind them, Hunter glanced back briefly, and Brock again reached inside his jacket. Hunter saw the movement and immediately fired, winging Brock in the shoulder and dropping him to the floor. Jamie screamed, terrified that Brock had been shot.

"You shot him!" Jamie cried out.

"Go!" Hunter yelled as he fired back at the injured gunman in the nightclub doorway.

Colton grabbed Kasey and Jamie, hurrying them along the corridor. The injured man fired several shots and then dived back into the club. Jamie screamed as she was pushed past Brock, who was now clutching his bleeding shoulder while still attempting to reach inside his jacket.

"He shot him!" Jamie screamed again as she looked back at the bleeding man, writhing in agony.

"He left the club through the main entrance right before it was locked," Colton shouted at Jamie with panic in his voice. "And then he shows up at the rear entrance just as we're fleeing for our lives? Think about it!"

Hunter swiftly removed the gun from Brock's concealed shoulder holster, indicating their theory had been correct, and hurried after Colton and the girls to the deck door. Once outside, the promenade deck was virtually abandoned, as it would be during the late hour. Colton hurried Kasey and Jamie along the silent and moderately creepy deck. While Jamie sobbed softly, Kasey kept an arm around her and remained alert. Despite being drunk only a few minutes earlier,

Kasey suddenly felt instantly sober, although a little dizzy.

Hunter followed them along the deck with both guns, keeping watch behind them. Colton stopped by the corner and cautiously looked beyond it. A man dressed in a white crewman's uniform suddenly grabbed Colton and held a knife to his throat. Before he could slice Colton's throat, Hunter took a step closer and shot the man in the head, painting the wall with his blood. The crewman was dead before he hit the deck. While Jamie sobbed, Kasey could only stare at the emotionless expression on Hunter's face. She'd spent the last two months berating and mocking this man to his face, and now she didn't even recognize him. She was genuinely frightened by how easily he pulled the trigger, ending lives without care. They hurried past the dead man and the blood that was swiftly pooling across the deck.

"We need to get off this ship," Colton cried out while unsuccessfully trying to remain calm despite being jacked.

"Are you insane?" Jamie gasped between sobs. "And go where? We need to find ship's security!"

"That was security," Hunter scoffed, then glared at Kasey, raising his brows. "Your uncle has some explaining to do."

Colton hurried toward the ship's bow and rifled through a bench seat containing life jackets. As Kasey joined him, she saw Jamie dart to the railing and immediately vomit over the side. Kasey had to look away, now feeling slightly sickened herself. Colton started tossing out life jackets.

"Put those on," Colton commanded.

Kasey was practically in a fog, unable to grasp what was happening around her. People reacted differently under extreme pressure, which is what Kasey witnessed at that moment. Jamie was falling apart while Colton was completely lucid and following his heightened flight instinct. Hunter was thinking rationally and kept his head, reacting much like a soldier in battle. As Jamie slowly stumbled back to them, she had one hand on her abdomen and the other against her mouth, fighting the urge to throw up some more. She looked even worse now that she'd thrown up. Kasey handed Jamie one of the life preservers while trembling with her own fears and a surge of adrenaline.

Kasey quickly slipped into one of the life jackets while Jamie seemed to have trouble, fumbling with hers. Colton put one on as well before extending one to Hunter. Hunter just glared at Colton. Colton frowned, tossed it aside, and continued to look through the bench.

"What the hell is going on?" Kasey demanded, starting to lose her emotions to fear as her body began to tremble. "Why are they doing this?"

"Do you want to stop and ask?" Hunter snarled in response.

Kasey twitched and stepped back from him, genuinely afraid of the man she was now seeing. She knew she needed to give him some space. Kasey couldn't fall apart and potentially distract Hunter. Jamie was doing enough of that for all of them.

"A raft," Colton cried out and straightened. "I found a raft."

"We can use that," Hunter announced.

"You're insane," Jamie launched while just about down to tears once again while clutching her stomach, still feeling sick.

"Maybe," Hunter replied. "But I'm not the one trying to kill you."

Colton removed a small bag, unzipped it, and eyed the contents before tossing it to Hunter.

"Is that something useful?" Colton asked.

Hunter peered into the bag. "It's a satellite phone," he remarked with some surprise at the find. "I believe we found their escape plan. Well, it's ours now." He then looked at Colton while giving a firm nod to the ocean. "Get them into the water."

Colton opened the gate in the back railing without question and held his hand out to Jamie. She stared at him in disbelief, with large mascara stains now under her eyes.

"How can you have that much faith in him?" Jamie gasped while shivering uncontrollably.

"Because he's the only one not trying to kill us," Colton replied and again indicated the water just a few feet below. "Get your ass in the water, or I'm throwing you in!"

Colton was seriously losing it, and there was no doubt he'd follow through with his threat. Kasey approached Jamie and hugged her, clinging to her.

"It's going to be okay," Kasey whispered.

Without releasing her friend, Kasey took a deep breath and jumped into the water, taking Jamie with her. Colton tossed the raft overboard while pulling the cord, then jumped into the water after the raft and his friends. Hunter secured one gun down the back of his pants and one down the front before jumping in after them. All four surfaced above the water while gasping. Despite the warm night, the water was surprisingly cold. The ocean seemed so dark, with the only light coming from the moon and the ship's bow. Kasey's head was spinning as she attempted to get her bearings after the shock of the cold water. The shootout in the club may have sobered her, but she wasn't feeling sober now. She was feeling confused and disorientated.

Jamie cried hysterically while floundering despite her life vest keeping her afloat. Kasey finally collected her wits and forced her friend to swim toward the large raft, heaving her up over the side and into it. As Kasey began climbing into the raft, Colton appeared behind her and gave her buttocks a solid boost, tossing her into the raft. He then climbed in after her. Hunter easily heaved himself into the raft, joining them. Despite his effortless entry, Kasey grabbed onto his jacket, helping secure him in the raft. Jamie immediately leaned over the side of the raft and again hurled. Kasey held her own sour stomach and fought the temptation to puke. As the ship sailed away from them, several men appeared on deck and fired at them.

The bullets struck the water several feet from the raft, but they were already too far away. Hunter removed the pack containing the satellite phone and pulled it out. He also found a compass, removed it, and handed it to Colton. Colton glanced at the compass, attempting to read it, then finally looked back at Hunter.

"Who do you think they were?" Colton asked, still unable to relax after his adrenaline rush.

"If we're to believe Kasey's uncle, they are the same group of people who killed his wife," Hunter replied. "Although, they're a little more skilled than he led me to believe. I thought he meant disgruntled employees or something. These guys could be Mafia, drug lords, or even terrorists."

"How would my uncle know those kinds of people?" Kasey demanded. "He's in real estate."

"Doubtful," Hunter muttered.

Kasey was surprised by the comment. "You're saying my uncle might be into something criminal?" she asked.

"Yeah, *might* would be a stretch," Hunter replied while fiddling with the satellite phone. "Your uncle is dirty up to his elbows."

"Who do you intend to call with that thing?" Colton asked, holding it together better than the women. "Can we trust the Coast Guard?"

"I trust about five people in this world," Hunter informed him. "And one of them is resourceful and not too far from here." He pressed several numbers and then held the phone to his ear. There was a moment of silence. "Admiral, it's Kane. This is an emergency. I need to call in a favor."

Chapter Fourteen

Four o'clock in the morning. The four had been floating in the raft for almost an hour since they fled the cruise ship. Jamie and Colton clung to each other to keep warm in the raft while Hunter held Kasey against his damp body. After their impromptu dip in the cold water, they were left soaked and chilled from their wet clothes. After her spike in adrenaline wore off, Kasey's head was left spinning from too much alcohol and exhaustion. As she clung to Hunter, she knew she wasn't thinking straight. She was frightened and suspicious of Hunter and even her friends, yet she couldn't pry herself away from this man she no longer trusted. It was almost as if she tossed rational thinking out the window and chose to embrace what frightened her most.

Kasey felt as if she'd jump out of her skin at any moment, reliving the horror of the night from one year ago that left three people dead and Embry in the emergency room. Despite her best effort, she couldn't even remember the last hour or how she ended up in Hunter's arms. Everything after the nightclub attack was a blur. Thankfully, Jamie stopped crying. It was possible she was too busy shivering as she clung to Colton for warmth. At least compassionate, lovable Colton returned and comforted her. That lucid version of Colton on deck was a bit scary, but he had their backs when they needed him most. A lesser man may have run the moment the bullets started flying.

Kasey was conscious of Hunter's hand repetitively rubbing her bare arm while holding her securely against him, keeping her warm. The side of his face was pressed against her head, allowing her to feel the warmth of his breath against her skin. Although Hunter's body against hers was comforting, she could feel the hard metal of the gun down the front of his pants pressing against her. It was a chilling reminder of the horrors in the nightclub and the ease with which Hunter shot and killed several men. Over the gentle lapping of the water against the raft, they heard a low thumping sound coming from somewhere. Hunter and Colton immediately looked at the sky. There was a light. It was a helicopter approaching in the darkness!

Hunter released Kasey, swiftly moved across the raft, and turned on a flashing beacon. As the helicopter came into view, its search light scanned the water. The beacon revealed their position, and the spotlight finally settled upon them. As the helicopter hovered over them, Hunter waved from the raft. Once a rope with a clamp was dropped from the helicopter, Hunter attached the clamp to the raft. After it was secured, he motioned they were clear. Hunter returned to Kasey and held her close to him as the helicopter swiftly pulled them along the water.

They zipped along the water for quite some time, bouncing across the tiny ripples. The speed at which they were traveling made both women slightly ill. Kasey clung to Hunter; her eyes closed, fighting the urge to vomit. After gliding along the water for miles, they finally saw land. They were approaching fast, which was a little frightening to both women. The helicopter hovered just over the beach as the raft slid gracefully and fully onto the sand. Hunter removed the clamp, signaled, and the helicopter immediately flew off. Hunter jumped out of the raft onto the beach and helped Kasey and Jamie out. Both women were unusually unsteady, possibly due to all the alcohol still in their systems. Kasey and Jamie had earlier removed their shoes in the raft and now held them in their hands. Walking through the sand in high heels would be almost impossible anyway.

Maybe it was too much alcohol, but despite everything that had just happened to them, Kasey couldn't help but admire the beauty of the moonlit beach. How was it possible to feel as if the world had fallen apart yet find beauty in nature? Colton didn't appear to share her appreciation while looking around the isolated, dimly lit beach.

"Please tell me that's not all there is to the plan," Colton grumbled. "We're on an island in the middle of nowhere."

Hunter removed the compass and looked around before pointing down the beach. "The admiral has an island retreat about a mile down the beach that way," he announced. "He'll give us cover until we can figure out who was trying to kill us."

"You mean trying to kill Kasey," Colton reminded him, then indicated himself and Jamie. "Jamie and I have nothing to do with this."

"You saw their faces, and they saw yours," Hunter informed him. "You're in this just as deep as Kasey. We need to find out who has a grudge against her uncle and how far of a reach they have before we contact anyone."

"You're paranoid; you know that?" Colton remarked.

"And that's the only reason you're still alive," Hunter informed him, now turning stern. "You want to stay that way; you do what I say."

Hunter motioned them along the beach, once again taking control of the situation. Colton frowned and nodded for Kasey and Jamie to follow him. He placed his arms around both of their shoulders for security and comfort. Jamie clung to his hand on her shoulder and shivered from the damp dress clinging to her body.

"I don't trust him," Jamie whispered while watching Hunter a few feet ahead of them. "He scares me."

"I don't trust him either," Colton muttered, "but I don't see what choice we have."

Kasey was lost in her own thoughts and just stared at Hunter ahead of them on the beach as they walked. Her rational thought seemed to return. She released Colton and hurried to catch up to Hunter, walking alongside him.

"What about Embry?" Kasey asked, worried about her friend.

"What about him?" Hunter replied without looking at her.

"Is he in any danger because of me?"

"Best guess--no," Hunter replied. "He didn't see anything, and he doesn't know anything." His lack of emotion about the subject was troubling. "He'll contact your uncle when he doesn't find you in the morning. They'll discover the massacre in the club, conduct a search, and conclude we were killed and thrown overboard."

"Embry will think I'm dead?" Kasey gasped in horror.

"It's best he thinks that for now," Hunter assured her. "If your uncle starts poking around too much, he's liable to get himself and more innocent people killed." He finally looked at her, and his expression seemed to soften. "I know you're upset, Kasey, but you're going to have to trust me. I have this under control. I can protect you."

"It's not safe for Colton and Jamie to be anywhere near me, is it?"

"We don't have much choice in the matter," Hunter reminded her.

"Your friend, the admiral, he can take them someplace far from here--far from me," she insisted. "I don't want anything happening to them because of me."

"It's not because of you, Kasey," Hunter informed her, attempting to ease her mind. "This has nothing to do with you. This is your uncle's mess. You're just collateral damage."

"Is that supposed to make me feel better?" she demanded.

"Did it?"

"No."

"I'm afraid that's all I've got to offer."

"Would he be willing to take them someplace safe away from me?" Kasey then asked.

"They're safer here than anywhere else," Hunter insisted. "Hell, I'm not even sure where we are exactly. That has to be a good sign."

Kasey was less than convinced but knew there was no point arguing about it. Her fears had gotten the better of her, and nothing was going to ease her anxiety at this point. She insecurely clung to Hunter's arm, possibly surprising him. Her actions were a bit of a surprise to her as well, but she needed that comfort. The calm he projected gave her a sense of security, even if it was a false one. Hunter glanced at her as they walked along the beach.

"It's going to be okay, Kasey," he reassured her in possibly the softest and most sincere tone she'd heard from him. "I promise."

"I want to believe you," she whispered while nuzzling her head against his damp leather jacket sleeve.

Hunter removed his arm from hers and placed it over her shoulder, pulling her against his side. She immediately clung to his waist with both arms as they continued to walk. Fear made people do strange things, and cozying up to Hunter was definitely high on that list.

Chapter Fifteen

The admiral's elegant, old mansion sat fifty yards inland from the beach. Most of the three-story house was surrounded by palm trees, leaving only a small portion of the structure visible. The home had a large porch on the first floor and stylish balconies on the second and third floors. Possibly because it was close to the beach, nearly a dozen steps led up to the front porch, elevating the home on its concrete base and adding to its grandeur. Although no outside lights were lit, there was a faint glow inside, barely visible to those on the beach. As they got closer, the mansion had an almost eeriness about it. Although Hunter showed little concern regarding the home, Kasey and her friends were apprehensive about the creepy mansion on a seemingly deserted island.

Kasey clung to Hunter's hand as he just about pulled her closer to the mansion. She looked around, but the admiral's helicopter was nowhere to be found. It seemed odd that he had rescued them less than an hour ago, yet now his helicopter was conspicuously missing, and he wasn't even on the beach to greet them. Kasey had difficulty tackling the many steps, realizing how drunk she had actually been and possibly still was. She glanced back to see how Jamie was fairing. Colton clung to Jamie and just about pulled her up each step. Jamie was even more frightened by the home than Kasey had been. When they reached the porch, Hunter finally released Kasey's hand and checked the door, which was unlocked. There seemed little reason why it would need to be locked.

As Hunter entered the mansion, Kasey reclaimed his hand and followed him, lacking trust and enthusiasm. Colton guided Jamie across the threshold into the foyer while keeping his arm securely around her shoulder. She clung to him like a security blanket. All four looked around the massive entrance way. The large area looked more like a hotel lobby than a home, being extensive and open. The grand staircase wrapped around and overtop the main entrance, with a cathedral ceiling up to the second floor. The white marble hallway went straight back to the opposite end of the house while crystal chandeliers lined the ceiling.

There were massive doorways to many rooms on either side of the hall, most of which remained open. Antique chairs and end tables lined the hallway while expensive artwork hung on the walls. Not surprisingly, the grand staircase was massive with elegant stained wood and decorative wrought iron railing, taking the class level up another notch. Although there was a third floor, the stairs to the third floor were not visible from the entranceway.

"This friend of yours must be loaded," Colton remarked while scanning the hallway and staircase, possibly looking for signs of Hunter's mysterious friend.

"Well, I wouldn't exactly call him a friend, but he's someone we can trust," Hunter replied.

Jamie shivered, clinging to Colton's left arm while looking around nervously. "It's cold in here," she muttered.

Kasey couldn't deny she was even colder now than she had been on the beach. Her damp dress clung to her body, keeping her cold and uncomfortable. It was almost unbearable enough that she considered taking the dress off and traipsing around in just her underwear.

"I'm sure we can find some dry clothes to change into in one of the bedrooms," Hunter announced, then turned to Colton and indicated the staircase. "Why don't you take Kasey and Jamie upstairs and see what you can find? I'm going to find the admiral." He consulted his watch. "Let's meet in the kitchen in half an hour."

Colton remained tense while nodding, then uncertainly led Kasey and Jamie by their hands toward the grand staircase. None appeared overly enthusiastic about the entire situation, remaining nervous and mildly suspicious.

§

Colton, Kasey, and Jamie entered the massive kitchen from the back stairs. All three wore dry clothing, although they were men's clothes. Kasey and Jamie wore men's dress shirts with boxer shorts as bottoms, while Colton found pants and a shirt to fit him. The kitchen, although large, didn't have as much workspace as the one at Kasey's house. There was a massive double stove with six burners above two ovens. A tan Formica counter and sink took up one wall, while a large island counter with pub seating was in the middle. The remaining bulk of the kitchen was the glass doors to the patio and a large, informal table that easily sat eight. The entire kitchen floor was refinished hardwood, giving the room a classic, classy appeal.

The three approached Hunter, who stood by the island counter while still dressed in his damp clothes. He set three bottles of water on the counter for them while drinking from his own bottle. They sat at the counter, appearing equally exhausted.

"Well, I spoke with the admiral on the satellite phone," Hunter announced, adding a defeated sigh. "Unfortunately, he's on his way to the mainland for a meeting and won't return for several days. He said to make ourselves at home and help ourselves to anything we needed."

"Well, this just keeps getting creepier," Jamie muttered while sipping her water.

"We're safe," Hunter reminded her. "Nothing's going to happen here. You're just going to have to trust me."

Somehow, his words didn't put Kasey at ease, and she doubted Jamie and Colton felt any safer. Kasey was still feeling some of the effects of the alcohol, which seemed to intensify her anxiety. Of course, the fact that someone wanted to kill her may have been causing her uneasiness. Kasey stared at Hunter, wondering if she actually trusted him. She wasn't feeling particularly trusting right now, but at least she was no longer suspicious of Colton and Jamie. Kasey was grateful that whatever caused those earlier feelings had dissipated.

"I realize everyone is exhausted and probably a little edgy," Hunter continued. "So I suggest we find some guestrooms and get some sleep."

"Are you kidding?" Jamie gasped while staring at Hunter with wide, horror-filled eyes. "You actually think I'm going to stay in a room by myself in this creepy place?"

"I'll stay with you," Kasey replied without missing a beat.

Although it sounded like a suggestion, it actually wasn't. She was not leaving Jamie alone, by herself, anywhere in this house.

"It's not a bad idea to stick together," Colton added. "We'll find a room. You two can have the bed, and I'll sleep in a chair. It's not as if I intend to get much quality sleep anyway."

"What about Hunter?" Kasey asked, then glanced at him, catching his attention. "We shouldn't expect him to stay alone."

"We're safe here," Hunter insisted again. "I'll be fine on my own, but if it makes you feel better, I'll take the room next to yours." He offered a tiny, sincere smile. "Just relax and get some sleep."

Chapter Sixteen

Kasey and Jamie slept in the tall, king-sized bed within the massive, old bedroom while Colton slept on a chaise lounge in the sitting area near the window with a throw blanket covering him. The large bedroom had off-white carpeting throughout, white walls, a white ceiling, and white crown molding, making the room bright and less frightening. Upon entering the bedroom, there was a small sitting area with plush white furniture and access to the balcony. The massive bedroom had limited furniture but plenty of windows. The room was already partially lit from the sunlight, now peeking in through a part in the thick, white curtains. Kasey woke while slightly disoriented and looked around the room. She frowned and groaned softly, disappointed that it hadn't been a bad dream.

Kasey heard a creaking sound in the hall not far from their room. She stared across the room into the sitting area at the closed door for a moment, then quickly slipped off the bed and hurried toward the door, quietly passing Colton asleep on the sofa. She paused before the door and strained to listen for what she'd heard. She could hear soft, muffled voices further down the hall. Kasey was slightly bewildered. She quietly unlocked the door with the old-fashioned key and gently pulled it open. It made a god-awful creaking sound. She cringed, cursed softly, and opened the door the rest of the way, no longer concerned by how much noise it made. Kasey stepped into the doorway in her bare feet and looked up and down the quiet, creepy corridor. Despite that there was no one there, she remained certain she heard someone.

Kasey entered the hallway, gently closing the door behind her, and quietly pattered down the corridor. She approached the bedroom next door, hesitated a moment, and listened. When she didn't hear anything, she lightly knocked on the door.

"Yeah?" Hunter muttered. "It's open."

Kasey pushed open the door, slowly stepped into the doorway, and looked toward the tall king-sized bed. Hunter was partially beneath the covers on his side, bare-chested, clutching his pillow beneath his head, and still attempting to sleep, despite having answered her knock. Hunter's guestroom was smaller than the one Kasey and her friends occupied, although it was also primarily white. There was a balcony and a private bathroom, but he didn't have an additional sitting area, just a couple of plush chairs. Hunter opened his eyes only briefly, groaned, and closed them.

"Shouldn't you be sleeping?" he muttered into his pillow.

Kasey nervously stepped into the room and shut the door behind her. "I heard someone in the hallway."

"You're hearing things," he replied without opening his eyes. "Probably a mouse. You're just tired."

Hunter appeared to doze off despite her presence in the room. Kasey hurried across the cold bedroom floor, hoisted herself onto the tall bed, and sat on the edge facing him.

"I know what I heard," she insisted while remaining tense.

Hunter groaned softly and rolled onto his back, placing his arm over his eyes.

"Two more hours, Kasey," he announced. "Just give me two more hours, and I'll search every nook and cranny of this place. I'll even personally shoot every mouse and spider for you."

Kasey studied him for a moment while he was now on his back. She couldn't help but admire his toned chest with a light coating of hair. Although Hunter's build was similar to her cousin Dillon, she had never given her cousin's bare chest a second glance while they were in the pool during the summer months. So Kasey didn't understand her sudden fascination with Hunter's upper torso and broad shoulders. He had a couple of interesting scars along his shoulders and sides. Possibly battle scars from whatever trouble he'd gotten himself into before becoming a bodyguard. Perhaps they were even due to his current profession. After admiring Hunter's body longer than acceptable, Kasey moved onto her knees on the bed and faced him, resuming her concern with their current situation.

"I know you trust this admiral guy, but I don't," Kasey informed him. "This place is uber-creepy. It doesn't look like anyone's even lived here in years, and now I'm hearing voices in the hallway. How do you know someone else didn't find this place before we arrived?"

"Is there any way you're going to let me sleep?" he asked.

"Give me a gun," she insisted, "and I'll check it out myself."

Hunter removed his arm from his eyes and looked at her with some surprise. "That's not happening," he replied somewhat sternly.

Kasey moved closer to him while still on her knees, sat back on her feet, and pleaded with her eyes.

"Then get up and have a look around," she announced.

Hunter again groaned. "Here's the deal, Kasey," he remarked, partially opening his eyes and meeting her gaze. "Either you let me sleep for another two hours or get under the covers and give me a real good reason to stay awake."

Kasey stared at him a moment in silence, stunned by his response. Her heart skipped a beat, and for a brief moment, she entertained the thought. Her birthday wish had been to get together with a cute guy and lose her virginity. Last night, while she was drunk, Hunter seemed like the perfect choice, but now that she was sober, she felt Hunter was a little too much man for her.

"Enjoy your sleep," Kasey announced.

Hunter shut his eyes while snickering and turned back onto his side, facing her, once again nestling into the pillow. Kasey slowly moved away from him, gently sliding her hand beneath the first pillow. She slowly pulled the gun out and attempted to move off the bed with it. Hunter suddenly grabbed the gun barrel and glared at her disapprovingly. Kasey gasped at his fast reflexes.

"Don't play with my toys," he lightly snarled.

Hunter removed the gun from her hand, propped himself up on his elbow, and casually played with the gun.

"Now I'm awake, *and* I'm pissed," he scoffed and met her gaze.

"Okay, I'm leaving," she announced and sprang off the bed.

Kasey hurried across the room and left, shutting the bedroom door behind her. She stood just outside the door, drew a deep, tense breath, and turned. Kasey nearly collided with Colton, and both cried out in surprise.

"Jesus, Kasey," Colton cried out while clutching his chest. "Don't do that!" He then hesitated and eyed the closed bedroom door. "What the hell where you doing in Hunter's room?"

"Apparently, being emotionally and sexually intimidated," she muttered.

"Excuse me?"

"Nothing," she replied with a soft groan. "I heard someone in the hallway, and when I tried to alert Hunter, he just blew me off."

"You heard someone?" he asked with surprise.

Kasey fidgeted while staring into Colton's eyes. "I don't think we're alone in this house," she informed him.

Colton groaned and shut his eyes a moment before looking back at her. "Please don't say anything to Jamie," he insisted. "She's already on edge." He seemed to consider their options. "Let's let Jamie sleep another hour, then you and she can get something to eat in the kitchen while I search the house with Hunter. He has two guns from last night. I'll ask him to give me one." He offered a warm smile. "Will that make you feel better?"

"Yes," she replied with relief. "Thank you."

Colton smiled and pulled Kasey into his arms, holding her against him. She returned the warm embrace and rested her head on his shoulder. It was surprising how safe she suddenly felt, considering she had been suspicious of him and Jamie just a few hours ago. That was undoubtedly the adrenaline and booze intensifying her distrust.

"I won't allow anyone to hurt you and Jamie," Colton insisted. "You have my word."

Kasey loved Colton dearly, but it was an empty promise at best. Colton wasn't a fighter; he was a lover. If the situation arose, she didn't doubt he'd put forth his best effort to protect them and die very quickly.

Chapter Seventeen

Having slept the entire morning, Kasey and Jamie got up that afternoon and found more than enough food in the refrigerator and pantry to last them a month, if necessary. The two women made breakfast, consisting of bacon and eggs, even though it was technically lunch time. As added security, an old sword sat on the island counter while the guys searched the mansion for a potential intruder. Jamie placed the crispy bacon on a plate while Kasey emptied the scrambled eggs into a large serving bowl. As Colton and Hunter entered the kitchen from the back stairs, Colton grinned and hurried toward the counter.

"I told you I smelled bacon!" Colton announced to Hunter.

Colton seated himself at the island counter and immediately grabbed a plate. While Colton devoured a strip of bacon, Hunter approached the main counter and helped himself to some coffee. Hunter joined Colton at the island counter, set his coffee down, and picked up the sword.

"Where did you find this?" Hunter asked.

"On the wall in the study," Kasey replied, then took it from him and smirked. "Don't play with my toys."

"That blade is dull," Hunter informed her matter-of-factly. "It's not much of a weapon. More like a large letter opener."

"It'll be sharp when I'm finished with it," Kasey informed him.

Kasey set the sword on the main counter behind her and picked at some bacon. Jamie sat alongside Colton at the island counter and fixed herself a plate of bacon and eggs.

"I'm assuming you didn't find anyone or anything," Kasey remarked while eyeing both men.

"Hmm, not entirely true," Colton announced while eating another strip of bacon. "We found a bedroom with women's clothing in the drawers and closet. Maybe the two of you can find something more your size to wear." He then indicated Hunter. "We'll look around down here after Hunter has his morning coffee. He's a bit crabby without it."

"As opposed to his normal crabbiness?" Jamie asked.

"Yeah, let's not irritate him more than necessary," Colton muttered.

"Then you may not want to be present for this," Kasey announced before turning to face Hunter. "I think we should use that satellite phone and call someone who can actually help us."

"We're already being helped," Hunter casually reminded her.

"We're in hiding," Kasey responded.

"And do I need to remind you why?" Hunter then asked while cocking his head.

"Some bullshit about my uncle being involved with seedy people," Kasey announced, then glared at him. "If you know something, we have a right to hear it since it's our asses on the line here. If you only know as much as you told us last night, we need to call in some real help."

"I agree," Jamie replied, joining Kasey. "I don't want to be here either. We're completely cut off."

"Right now, that's what we want," Hunter informed both women. "Those men who attacked us last night were professionals. I counted at least ten of them, and they had guns with silencers. Some were also dressed in crew uniforms."

"Yes, we were there," Kasey remarked.

"Then I don't have to remind you that they killed two people within the club just for being in the wrong place at the wrong time," Hunter continued. "At least three of them were the same men who attempted to cozy up to the two of you last night." He glared at both women. "They knew exactly what they were doing and exactly how they wanted to do it."

"Brock," Jamie muttered, then shuttered slightly and pushed her untouched breakfast plate away.

"Now, you put that together with the attack on the mansion last year, where three people were brutally murdered, and another two narrowly survived," Hunter remarked. "And that gives you a very determined group of people who *really* want their way." He cast looks from Kasey to Jamie. "People like that almost always have police protection in the event of an emergency. In short, you're screwed. If they want you, dead or alive, they will find a way to get you."

Colton fidgeted and pushed his half-eaten breakfast plate away as well. "So much for not alarming them," he muttered to Hunter.

"They need to hear the truth," Hunter snapped back at him and again eyed both women. "Hiding out is your *only* option. So you can trust me to keep you alive, or you can do it your way and possibly end up dead."

Hunter's words made everyone shiver. Kasey understood what he was saying, but it didn't make her feel any better. Either way, she felt she was risking her friends' lives. Kasey studied Hunter briefly, then finally looked at Jamie and Colton.

"Well?" she timidly asked.

"I just want to leave," Jamie replied, insecurely rubbing her chilled arms.

"I'm not that thrilled about being here either, but I'm willing to listen to other options," Colton informed Kasey. "Last night was wicked scary. I think we're lucky we survived."

Hunter casually looked back at Kasey with little expression. Kasey eyed him, frowned, and had to look away.

"You win," Kasey announced with a defeated sigh. "We'll hole up here a little while longer."

Jamie groaned softly and nervously rubbed her forehead.

Colton placed his arm around Jamie's shoulder and held her to his side. "We're going to be fine, Jamie," he reassured her.

Kasey returned to the main counter, feeling mostly defeated, before Hunter approached and hovered over her.

"I don't *win*, Kasey," Hunter gently informed her. "This isn't winning and losing. This is living and dying."

"You just don't understand," she muttered, refusing to look at him.

"I don't, huh?" Hunter remarked. "You feel trapped and isolated. You'd rather be someplace where there are police and sirens because that would make you feel safe."

Kasey glanced at him with some surprise. She was actually thinking something very close to what he'd said. Hunter stared down at her with a somewhat sympathetic look.

"The people who are after you own the police," Hunter informed her. "They were powerful enough to put their people onboard that cruise ship. A cruise ship that caters to rich and famous people with very expensive security." He cocked his head. "If you felt safer there, you're deluding yourself."

Kasey stared at him for a long moment, knowing he was right.

"We were damned lucky last night," he continued. "Now that I know what we're up against, I'm telling you we're safer here." He continued to study her. "I just need you to trust me."

Kasey drew a deep breath and turned to face him, meeting his gaze. "If it were just my life on the line, I'd have an easier time believing you can protect me. As it is, I don't want you protecting me if that means my friends are expendable."

"I never said your friends were expendable," Hunter informed her.

"No, but you were hired to protect me," she reminded him. "My uncle is paying you to protect me. You can understand why I'm concerned."

Hunter groaned softly and raked his fingers through his hair. "The admiral will be back in a few days," he informed her. "Let's just wait for him, and then we can discuss all our options. Are you okay with that?"

Kasey considered his words and then nodded. "Okay," she replied. "We'll wait for the admiral."

Chapter Eighteen

Kasey entered the study with her freshly sharpened sword in hand. Sharpening the mostly ornamental sword with a cutlery sharpener that she found in the kitchen took some time. Although the tip was sharp, the blade wasn't, but she was sure it would still do a fair amount of damage. Jamie followed Kasey into the study while remaining tense. The study was old-school elegant, containing a lot of dark, rich woodwork. A large throw rug covered the hardwood floor beneath the desk and chair, being the only carpet. Besides the large antique desk, there were decorative shelves along the walls. Some contained books, while the others had valuable trinkets on display. The last one had a small bar with a few bottles of top-shelf liquor.

Kasey shut the door behind them and approached the desk. She set the sword on top of the desk and collapsed into the chair behind it while Jamie flopped into the chair before it.

"I can't believe I'm the only one who doesn't trust Hunter," Jamie remarked while resting her temple on her knuckles.

"Trusting Hunter has nothing to do with the decision to stay," Kasey informed her. "I'd rather err on the side of caution. Last night shook me up pretty good."

While Kasey rummaged through the desk drawers, opening each one, she discovered they were all empty except for the bottom drawer, which contained old nautical charts, maps, and a bottle of prescription pills. The name on the pill bottle was worn off, but they were sleeping pills. Kasey recognized the obscure generic brand name, being they were the same pills her uncle used to take to help him sleep.

"I guess because you've been through something like this before, you're a little better equipped to deal with what happened last night than I am," Jamie remarked.

Kasey looked at Jamie with surprise at the comment. "Are you kidding?" she gasped and returned the bottle to the drawer. "I was just as terrified last night as I was the night my aunt died. That's not the sort of thing you get used to."

Jamie stared at Kasey, trying to understand what she'd just said. "Well, you're certainly holding it together better than I am," she insisted. "I was practically hysterical last night, and not in a funny way."

For a moment, Kasey wondered if Jamie was distrustful of her, mirroring how she had felt last night. Being they were childhood friends, they knew they could trust each other.

"Yeah, well, it only appears as if I'm holding it together better," Kasey informed her and removed the nautical charts from the drawer. "You have to remember; we were both drunk last night. That may have added to your perceived hysteria."

"There was nothing perceived," Jamie remarked. "I was a hot mess."

"Which is why you didn't notice how frightened I was," Kasey informed her while sorting through the papers.

"You seemed pretty calm," Jamie insisted, then considered something and cocked her head. "Colton was kind of impressive, though, wasn't he?"

"A little spastic," Kasey remarked, then nodded. "But, yeah, he was thinking rationally. He also did a great job of comforting you." She tossed the nautical charts back into the drawer and then frowned. "Meanwhile, I was glued to Hunter, practically crawling inside him." Kasey shook her head and groaned. "That was so embarrassing."

"Well, to be fair," Jamie announced. "You *were* flirting with him all evening."

Kasey stared at Jamie with surprise and possible horror. "I was not," she scoffed. "Why would you say that?"

"Because you were," Jamie replied matter-of-factly. "You were on the guy's lap half the night, made out with him, and I'm pretty sure you groped him moments before we were almost killed."

Kasey felt her cheeks become hot at the accusation. "You're exaggerating," she insisted. "I'm sure I would have remembered--" She hesitated and mentally reviewed what she remembered from last night before the shooting started. Her expression suddenly dropped. "Oh--"

Jamie grinned almost slyly. "Oh, so you remember now?" she giggled.

Kasey shut her eyes and groaned almost painfully. "Yeah, I remember," she muttered, her eyes flicking open. "I remember inviting him back to my cabin for a sleepover."

Jamie stared at her with some surprise. "Really?" she gasped, then leaned on the desk, now interested. "What did he say?"

"I'm pretty sure he agreed to it," Kasey groaned, dropping her head to the desk. "God knows what else I told him." She lifted her head and rubbed her weary eyes. "How embarrassing."

"Considering our current situation, I'd say you don't need to worry about it," Jamie remarked. "You were drunk at the time, and we nearly died. Case closed."

Kasey straightened with renewed conviction. "Yes, we do have more important things to worry about," she announced, then looked back at her friend. "I'm convinced something here isn't quite right, and I get this nagging feeling that Hunter knows something he isn't telling us about this mansion and his friend, the admiral."

"I agree," Jamie replied. "This place gives me the creeps." She then appeared curious. "So what do we do?"

"I would say we get Hunter to talk, but that's easier said than done," Kasey remarked. "He's not exactly the sort of guy you can make talk."

"He's not easily seduced either," Jamie muttered, then eyed Kasey while raising a clever brow. "Well, not by me, that is."

Kasey glared at her friend. "I don't know if that was meant as a joke or a suggestion, but it's not funny."

"Mostly joking," Jamie replied while adding a tiny smile. "But maybe he turned me down because he has, well, a specific preference in his women. Namely you."

"That is definitely not funny," Kasey scoffed.

"That wasn't meant to be," Jamie replied, leaning on the desk. "I noticed he was a little more 'hands-on' after you made out with him later in the evening."

"Can you stop saying that?" Kasey squawked.

"It's a compliment, Kasey."

"I disagree."

Jamie sat back in her chair and folded her arms across her chest. "Be honest," she announced. "Even drunk, you *chose* to make out with Hunter. Not Hunter *and* Colton. Just Hunter." Jamie raised her brows almost demandingly. "There was some rational thought behind it."

Kasey considered the comment a long moment, then groaned and shook her head. "I don't know," she replied.

"Not an answer," Jamie insisted, not giving up on knowing.

Kasey drew a deep breath and then met Jamie's gaze. "It's just--" she announced, then hesitated. "I guess the alcohol took away my inhibitions, and I got a little cozy with him." She drifted out a moment. "And he, well, smiled at me." Kasey quickly snapped out of her thoughts and eyed her friend. "A real smile. For a moment, I realized what a handsome man he was, and then it just escalated from there."

Jamie offered a tiny smile that quickly turned to a frown. "But now you're not so sure we can trust him?" she asked.

"Maybe it was just seeing him in a different light after the attack," Kasey remarked, then shuttered slightly and rubbed her chilled arms. "Since we've arrived, he seems almost different now, and it has me a little on edge."

"He seems the same to me," Jamie announced, then made a face. "Except I'm a little less attracted to him now, but that's probably because I watched you make out with him half the night in the club." She raised her brows. "He was really into it."

Kasey groaned. "Will you stop bringing that up?" she squawked.

"I could pretend it didn't happen if it'd make you feel better," Jamie informed her with a casual shrug. "But Hunter's not likely to forget."

"What happens on the high seas; stays on the high seas," Kasey muttered.

"What?"

"Nothing."

Chapter Nineteen

Kasey and Jamie ventured into the woman's bedroom that Colton and Hunter had found earlier. The more feminine-looking bedroom contained a lot of pink elements, teetering on the brink of too much. There was pink carpeting, light pink walls, and frilly colorful bedding on the queen-sized bed. There was also a small dressing area with a makeup table and a full-length mirror. A large, walk-in closet was filled with a lot of women's clothing ranging from blouses and slacks to skirts and dresses. Both women tried on several outfits, which most seemed to fit them. While Kasey searched the dresser drawers, Jamie stood before the full-length mirror and checked out the light pink sundress she wore. Kasey opened and closed each drawer with increasing disgust.

"So, who is this woman with a closet full of clothes but not a single photo of anyone anywhere?" Kasey asked without looking at her friend.

"Not even one compact or any lipstick," Jamie remarked while adjusting her bra strap beneath the sundress straps. "Not even lip balm. Seems weird, huh? I mean, what woman living on a tropical island doesn't have lip balm?"

"Yes, it's very strange. Did you notice the toiletries in the bathroom when you showered?" Kasey felt compelled to ask.

"I can't say I was actually paying attention," Jamie replied while admiring herself in the mirror. "I was just happy to take a hot shower after our impromptu swim in the ocean last night. I hate salt water in my hair."

"Everything unused; brand new," Kasey informed her. "It's a ruse. I see women's clothing, but I don't think a woman ever lived here. Honestly, I don't even think a man lives here." Kasey then sank into thought.

Jamie eyed her through the mirror and seemed curious. "So what are you thinking?" she asked. "And is it going to kill us?"

"I don't know," Kasey remarked, then raised a curious brow. "Safe house, perhaps?"

"So maybe Hunter is on the up and up?" Jamie asked.

"It's just weird," Kasey announced with a sigh, then collapsed on the frilly bed and looked around the room. "Nothing personal anywhere. All of these things--" She finally eyed Jamie and turned stern at what she saw. "No, no dresses."

"What?" Jamie asked and gave her a surprised look. "Why not?"

"In case something happens and we have to run again," Kasey insisted. "We need to be prepared this time. Fleeing the nightclub in a dress and high heels nearly cost us our lives. We couldn't run worth a shit."

"Fine, no dresses," Jamie replied.

"Then, later this evening, you and I are taking a little stroll on the beach," Kasey informed her friend matter-of-factly.

"We are?" Jamie asked, somewhat horrified while again eyeing her through the mirror. "I think I had enough of that last night."

"I just want to make sure we can leave the house if we want to."

Jamie turned toward Kasey with a strange look on her face. "Are you suggesting we're being held prisoner?"

Kasey eyed her and raised a cocky brow. "Can you leave the island?"

"Well, no."

"Then we're being held prisoner--for our own good," Kasey replied, then jumped off the bed and went back to searching the drawers. "I just want to test the boundaries a little. If Hunter allows us to take a walk along the beach without his supervision, I'll feel a little better about our situation. Well, at least where he's concerned."

"How about after dinner?"

"Perfect."

Jamie picked up the hairbrush from the dresser and suspiciously looked it over. "Jesus, now you have me doing it."

"Doing what?" Kasey asked.

"Being all suspicious and Sherlock Holmes-like," Jamie replied, then held up the brush. "No hair in the hairbrush."

"Told you so," Kasey scoffed.

Jamie brushed her hair while looking in the mirror, then seemed to drift off a moment. "We should get Hunter drunk."

Kasey eyed her friend with surprise. "Are you serious?"

"Guys have a habit of babbling on and on when they're loaded," Jamie informed her. "You saw how Embry was at dinner. You can't tell me Hunter is the exception."

"Unfortunately, we'd also have to drink," Kasey reminded her. "And that would be counterproductive."

"Not if we get Colton to drink with him," Jamie suggested. "You know, a guy thing. Colton's always bragging about how he can hold his liquor. He can drink Hunter under the table without half trying. I remember seeing some booze in the game room behind the bar."

"And what if Hunter is a nasty drunk?" Kasey asked.

"Then we coal cop him and lock him in a closet," Jamie casually replied.

Kasey smiled and laughed, enjoying the image of Hunter locked in a closet.

§

Around six o'clock that evening, Kasey and Jamie entered the kitchen while discussing the dinner menu and what they would make. Earlier, they had left some frozen ground hamburger on the counter to thaw for dinner. Both women paused when they saw Hunter making hamburger patties from the thawed meat while Colton sliced potatoes to fry. They had limited fresh vegetable side dish options and would have to make do. Jamie and Kasey exchanged looks with tiny, humorous smiles. It was nice to know they didn't have to play mother to the two men while they were stranded together for the next few days.

"That is so cute," Jamie remarked softly to Kasey so the guys wouldn't be aware of their presence. "I didn't even think Colton knew how to cook. I just assumed he lived off of cheesy puffs and take-out food."

"He does," Kasey replied. "Unfortunately for him, the take-out options are limited here."

They remained by the door in silence a moment longer while watching the men prepare dinner. Hunter no longer wore his leather jacket and had his sleeves rolled up while pressing hamburger patties. The first thing Kasey noticed was the leather shoulder holster he wore. He wasn't wearing a shoulder holster on the cruise ship, being weapons weren't allowed. He must have found the admiral's weapon stash but didn't bother telling anyone. Now, Hunter had three weapons. Knowing he was armed should have put Kasey at ease, but it didn't. They finally approached the island counter, alerting the men to their presence. Both sat at the island counter and offered pleasant smiles.

"Who would have guessed you two were domesticated?" Jamie remarked, lightly teasing the guys.

"Hunter discovered the gas grill on the patio," Colton informed them. "And I found some frozen hamburger rolls. Plenty of condiments, too. Sadly, no cheese."

"I guess Hunter found the admiral's weapon arsenal," Kasey remarked, briefly catching Hunter's attention.

"Arsenal, no," Hunter replied as he carried the plate of raw hamburgers to the island counter and met Kasey's gaze. "Although, I'm sure he has one somewhere. I found the shoulder holster and gun in his bedroom closet earlier this afternoon. It completed my ensemble."

Kasey eyed Hunter's mocking grin, which was followed by a wink. She knew he was messing with her.

"Now that you have three guns, maybe you could give up one of them," she announced.

Hunter lightly cocked his head while eyeing her. "Do you know how to handle a firearm safely?" he asked.

"I'm sure I can manage," she insisted.

He snorted a laugh. "Famous last words from every idiot who's ever shot himself with his own weapon," Hunter replied, then smiled more naturally. "If you really want a weapon, I'll give you a gun safety lesson tomorrow and take you target shooting. If you pass, I'll give you a gun."

Kasey considered the proposal, then smiled and nodded. "Okay, you're on," she replied.

Hunter picked up the plate of raw hamburger patties and crossed the kitchen, heading to the patio door.

"I'd like to take that gun safety lesson tomorrow, too," Colton called after Hunter.

Hunter looked back at Colton while pushing open the door. "There's no way in hell I'm ever giving you a gun," he remarked. "You'd definitely shoot yourself in the foot or worse--" He sneered at Colton. "Probably shoot me in the ass."

As Hunter left the kitchen, Colton frowned in disapproval.

"What a dick," Colton scoffed and returned to the stove to fry the potatoes.

§

Sunset. Kasey, Jamie, and Colton walked along the beach in front of the mansion and enjoyed the warm salt air, the gentle breeze, and the magnificent sunset. The colorful sky was pink, orange, and blue with light cloud coverage. It was the perfect sunset. The ocean seemed to extend forever, making them feel as if they were the only people. How could anyone have a problem in the world on such a perfect evening?

"Gorgeous sunset aside, I don't understand why you wanted to take a walk on the beach," Colton remarked, letting the water rush past his feet and watching as it rolled back out again. "Didn't we get enough of this last night?"

Jamie laughed softly, being it was almost exactly what she had said.

"Just testing our boundaries," Kasey remarked with little emotion.

"What boundaries?" Colton asked while looking back at her.

"Of our prison."

"Is that supposed to mean something?" Colton asked, now bewildered.

"I still have this nagging feeling something isn't right," Kasey informed him.

"Probably the part where people were trying to kill us," Colton replied a little too casually and resumed watching the water rushing past his feet.

"I actually meant here in our prison paradise," Kasey informed him, catching his attention. She then cocked her head. "Would you care to do an experiment with us tonight?"

"Something deceitful?" Colton asked, almost concerned.

"A little," Kasey replied.

Colton suddenly grinned. "Well, then, count me in," he enthusiastically announced. "What do you want me to do?"

"Get Hunter drunk."

"Yeah, I'm out," Colton replied, quickly shaking his head. "He's kind of mean and scary when he's sober. Imagine him drunk."

"We need information," Kasey insisted.

"Are you sure you want to go that route?" Colton asked while cringing.

"I think he's hiding something," Kasey informed him. "Jamie's not getting any pillow talk out of him any time soon, and he's certainly not my BFF, so that just leaves the boy's night out."

"I'm sorry I volunteered, but I'll see what I can do," Colton replied with a sigh. "He'd spent his free time that first afternoon of the cruise in the casino. If we can find a deck of cards, I might be able to push some drinks on him, but you two will have to play cards and pretend to drink along."

"I'll pretend, but I'm off alcohol *forever*," Jamie replied almost dramatically. "I don't care if I never see a club again, either."

Colton quickly stepped toward Jamie, twirled her into his arms, and gracefully dipped her while grinning. "But when will we ever dance again?" he asked.

Jamie had to smile and even giggled. "Yes, I would miss that."

Chapter Twenty

The large game room contained a mixture of stone walls, rich hardwood flooring, and tall windows. In addition to the massive bar that seated six, there was a pool table alongside a pub table, old-fashioned slot machines, and a living area with a large, circular sofa across from a huge television. Kasey and Jamie were impressed by the coziness and comfort of the room. It was large yet somehow intimate. The two women sat at the bar and glanced at the back corner where Colton talked to Hunter, who played pool by himself. Whatever was said didn't seem promising. Colton frowned, returned to Kasey and Jamie, and sat on one of the stools near them.

"That would be 'no' to cards of any kind," Colton replied, somehow taking it personally. "Well, he did agree to strip poker. And, although I was all for it, I declined on your behalves." He then hesitated and raised a curious brow. "You wouldn't be interested in playing strip poker, right?"

Kasey and Jamie glared at him, not dignifying the question with a response.

"Yeah, I didn't think so," Colton replied and managed a tiny laugh. "On a positive note, I'm sure he'll agree to play a game of pool with a friendly wager on the side. Do either of you know how to make mixed drinks with maximum alcohol and minimum alcohol taste?"

Kasey shook her head, having little experience with alcohol except what she pinched from her uncle's liquor cabinet.

"Long island iced tea," Jamie suggested.

"Perfect," Colton announced cheerfully. "Fire up some drinks and offer them to us. That's the best I can do."

Jamie grinned slyly and headed around the bar. "I'll make a Long Island Iced Tea that'll knock your socks off." As Colton walked away, Jamie glanced at Kasey while preparing the potent drinks. "What about you, birthday girl? Still have a few more hours left of your big day."

Kasey snorted a laugh. "I can say, with complete honesty, this has been the second worst birthday of my life," she informed her friend.

"Started out with a bang," Jamie remarked, offering a devious grin.

"And then two people were killed, and we nearly died," Kasey reminded her. "Which was followed by diving off the back of a moving cruise ship and being stranded in this lovely place."

"It is actually a lovely place," Jamie countered with a tiny grin.

"Not the point," Kasey replied with a dreary sigh, then cast a quick glance at Hunter, who was racking the balls for a game with Colton.

Jamie leaned across the bar from the inside, resting her chin on her hand while grinning. "Is he a good kisser?"

Kasey glanced back at her friend and saw the dreamy-eyed look on her face.

"We could always abort operation 'boy's night out' if you want to play bedsheet bingo with Hunter instead," Jamie announced, then straightened, giddy at the thought. "I mean, it's still technically your birthday."

Kasey snorted a soft, humored laugh and shook her head. "You know I'm having serious trust issues about him right now, but you think it's a good idea to sleep with the guy."

Jamie casually shrugged. "All I'm saying is, why not?" she remarked. "We almost died last night. If we're going to die, you don't want to die a virgin, do you?"

Kasey considered the question a moment and again glanced back at Hunter. He looked up from chalking his cue stick at that exact moment and caught her gaze. Hunter grinned and winked at her before returning his attention to the table. Kasey's heart skipped a beat at the small action, and her mind reeled. She looked back at Jamie and groaned in frustration.

"As tempting as it is, that would be the biggest mistake ever," Kasey informed her. "Overlooking that whole Jeckle and Hyde thing he has going; if it turns out he is on the up and up, I would have had sex with my bodyguard. And after what happened on the cruise ship, I'm literally stuck with him forever. There's no way my uncle will ever leave me without a bodyguard again."

"Worst case scenario--?" Jamie asked, then shrugged. "Your relationship goes back to 'rude sarcastic'. On the other hand, if he's not a total dick, he'd make a wonderful boy toy."

Kasey considered the comment a moment, lingering over it longer than she should have, which seemed to intrigue Jamie. Kasey blushed and quickly waved Jamie off.

"No," she announced firmly. "Just no."

"You're missing out, Kasey," Jamie informed her as she resumed making a small pitcher of mixed drinks. "That's all I'm saying."

§

Colton and Hunter played pool while nearly finishing their second glasses of Long Island Iced Tea, which resided on the pub table behind them where Kasey and Jamie sat. The two women played five-card stud for clay chips since neither had any actual money on them. Both attempted to eavesdrop on the conversation at the nearby pool table, but most of the talk came from Colton, who seemed excessively chatty tonight. After drinking almost two entire glasses of iced tea each, Hunter appeared completely sober, while Colton already seemed drunk. While Hunter racked the balls for their next game, Colton approached the table and hung on Jamie's shoulder, grinning drunkenly.

"Hey, babe."

Both eyed him.

"Are you drunk?" Kasey asked, now suspicious.

"What happened to pretending to get drunk?" Jamie demanded.

"That tea is out of this world," Colton announced with a little too much enthusiasm.

"So why are you giddy as a school girl and he's not?" Jamie asked with little emotion.

"Ah, he's drunk," Colton insisted while giving a general wave toward Hunter at the pool table. "He's just hiding it better." He maintained his grin. "I'm a happy drunk, and he's, well, he's--" Colton pointed and gestured.

"Master of his domain?" Jamie muttered while folding her arms across her chest.

"Keep it up, and you won't get any tonight," Colton scoffed, straightening almost proudly.

Kasey and Jamie exchanged looks. It was a good plan, but it was poorly executed.

"Bar wench," Colton exclaimed and pounded the table, vibrating their glasses of soda. "Another round for my brother and me."

Colton stumbled back to the pool table and reclaimed his pool stick.

"Did he just call me a bar wench?" Jamie demanded while eyeing Kasey.

"I assume so," Kasey replied, lacking emotion. "Because if he had called me that, I would have flattened him." She looked back at the pool table and shook her head. "Apparently, his threshold for alcohol was greatly exaggerated."

"I get the feeling he exaggerates about a lot of things," Jamie muttered.

Kasey smiled and chuckled. "You mean he's probably not as good in bed as he is on the dance floor?"

Jamie could barely hold her laugh in, and both had a good chuckle at Colton's expense. As Jamie walked toward the bar, Colton leaned on Hunter's shoulder and quietly said something. Both eyed Jamie. Colton then grinned deviously while Hunter hid his smile and shook his head. Kasey was curious about what was said but probably didn't want to know. While watching Colton head to the bar, she groaned softly.

"Oh, this was a mistake," Kasey muttered, now interested in the scene at the bar.

Colton sat on one of the stools and leaned on the bar while talking to Jamie. Kasey collected the cards and attempted to act disinterested, but she was dying to know what he was saying. The way Jamie looked at Colton indicated their plan had officially failed due to human error. Hunter sat on the pub chair alongside

Kasey, surprising her with his stealthy appearance. He finished the rest of his drink while watching the scene at the bar as well.

"It's absolutely none of my business, but I have to ask," Hunter announced, then indicated Colton. "How the hell did the two of you become friends with *that* one?"

"Well, he's usually not so--" Kasey began, then hesitated.

"Perverted?"

"Yeah, well, he's not usually like that," Kasey replied, then shrugged. "He's a good friend, and it's nice being friends with a guy who isn't only after one thing."

"I can see how you might think that, but I assure you, that's not how it is," Hunter replied and snorted a laugh. "And with the way his mouth is going, his hands won't be far behind. I suggest you don't turn your back on him tonight, or there might be some aggressive cuddling."

Aggressive cuddling? Maybe Colton was right. Maybe Hunter was drunk and was just better at hiding it. Colton approached their table with a devious and twisted drunken smile.

"I need my wing man. That one's not warming up," he announced, then glanced briefly at Kasey. "Oh, but I see you have your own game going with my girl, Kasey." Colton placed his hand on Hunter's shoulder and leaned closer. "Wasting your time, man. She's a virgin. Shh, don't tell."

Kasey stared at Colton, horrified that he'd actually said that to Hunter, although she may have already mentioned it to him last night. Still, it was quite the betrayal. Colton smiled at Kasey, blew her a kiss, and then returned to the bar. Hunter eyed Kasey and raised his brows in silent question, waiting for some sort of response.

Kasey glared back at him. "What?" she snarled as her cheeks reddened.

Hunter smirked and chuckled softly. "You don't remember much about last night, do you?" he asked, somewhat humored.

Kasey felt her cheeks become flushed and even hotter, no longer able to look him in the eyes.

Hunter suddenly raised his brows and straightened. "Oh," he announced. "So you do remember."

"I remember being drunk," she informed him. "People say and do things they wouldn't normally do after drinking too much."

"Yeah, I'm aware," he replied. "I've been drunk a time or two in my life."

"Obviously, anything I said last night shouldn't be taken too seriously," she informed him. "You should know that."

Hunter continued staring at her for a long moment in silence, almost as if attempting to read her thoughts. It made her very uncomfortable. A devious grin suddenly crossed his face, and it was enough to make her heart pound faster.

"Admit it," he announced, somehow pleased with himself. "You only invited me to join you and the *girls* tonight because you wanted to get me drunk and take advantage of me."

Kasey shot a horrified look at him and became flustered. "That was *not* my intention!"

"It's okay, Kasey," Hunter announced while standing, then leaned closer to her ear. "I'm all for being your *boy toy*."

Kasey suddenly shivered from his hot breath and his sultry tone, repeating what Jamie had said just a little while earlier. She was embarrassed that he'd overheard that private comment made in jest. Once Hunter resumed his pool game, Kasey finally snuck a peek at him. Kasey entertained the thought only briefly. Sadly, she'd have to put up with that shit-eating grin mocking her every day after, and then she'd end up killing him.

Chapter Twenty-one

A little while later, Kasey and Jamie sat at the bar and stared across the room in stunned disbelief while loud music blared from the old-fashioned jukebox. Colton danced bare-chested on the pool table and in his boxer shorts while swinging his shirt around. Despite having some awesome dance moves even while drunk, both women were shocked at Colton's drunken antics. He did, however, have a nicely toned upper torso, which was odd, considering neither woman figured Colton was the type who worked out. Apparently, he'd been holding out on them. Hunter stood behind the bar and poured himself another drink, then casually leaned on it and watched the show.

"I think it's time Gene Kelly went to bed," Hunter announced, then sipped his drink before eyeing them. "Are the three of you still sharing a room, because I'm thinking he's going to enjoy that threesome a little too much."

Hunter's words horrified Kasey and Jamie. They hadn't even considered Colton staying in their room with them.

"God, how do we get him off of there?" Jamie practically gasped.

"How do we keep him from taking off the shorts?" Kasey muttered.

"I recommend you stop him before he does that," Hunter insisted in all seriousness. "Because I'll probably shoot him if he does."

Taking the threat seriously, Kasey and Jamie jumped off their bar stools and hurried to the pool table, where they attempted to get Colton down. Hunter grinned, chuckled, and downed the entire contents of his glass. Kasey and Jamie finally got Colton off the pool table and attempted to collect his scattered clothing from the floor. When Colton felt Jamie's butt while she was bent over, Jamie jumped with a startled scream. Colton fell against Kasey and nearly knocked her onto the pool table. Being he was already there, he pulled Kasey into his arms, and she immediately attempted to push him off her.

"Hey," Colton suddenly cried out excitedly and placed his free arm around Jamie as well. "Bedtime!" He grinned lustfully and chuckled. "I'll be in the middle."

Kasey glared at Hunter behind the bar. "A little help here?"

"No thanks," Hunter replied with a low chuckle while seeming almost sober. "I'm not into that group stuff."

Hunter then winked at Kasey, further infuriating her, before refilling his glass and watching the show. When Colton's hand got a little too close to the side of Kasey's boob, Kasey firmly backhanded his groin. Colton gasped with surprise and some discomfort, although the hit wasn't meant to be hard. Colton gingerly rubbed himself, then held his hands up in the air.

"Point taken."

Hunter again chuckled, finished his drink, and approached them with a completely sober gait. All that alcohol, and he still didn't seem drunk. After being put in his place by Kasey, Colton was less cheerful as he attempted to put his pants on and failed twice. Hunter commandingly snapped his fingers, getting Colton's attention, and pointed at the door. Colton frowned and obediently stumbled from the game room in only his boxer shorts with his clothes in his hands. As Hunter herded Colton from the room, Kasey and Jamie leaned against the pool table and watched.

"Any more bright ideas?" Jamie scoffed while folding her arms across her chest.

"Never let Colton drink the hard stuff again, for starters," Kasey muttered.

"You know, I think that's the first time I've ever seen him drunk," Jamie remarked, then eyed Kasey and raised her brow. "I have to admit; it's not very attractive."

"Probably why he never drinks much when we go out."

"I'm ready to admit failure and call it a night," Jamie remarked and straightened, sighing in disgust. "I hope Hunter isn't putting him in our room because there's no way I'm staying in the same room with that pervert tonight."

"If he does put him in our room, we'll find another room," Kasey remarked. "There are plenty to choose from."

"Master bedroom?" Jamie suggested while raising her brows. "I don't know about you, but that garden tub was calling me."

Kasey suddenly grinned at the suggestion. "You're on."

"In that case, I'm taking a bottle of wine for the road," Jamie announced and headed to the bar. "May as well live it up before we buy it on this rock."

"I wish you'd stop talking as if we're going to die," Kasey remarked while approaching her. "It's kind of unnerving."

Jamie grabbed a bottle of wine and two glasses, then headed for Kasey and the game room door. "If last night taught me anything, it's live life to the fullest today. Tomorrow is not guaranteed."

Kasey again considered her own situation and her earlier conversation with Jamie. She couldn't believe she was actually considering seducing Hunter. She hated the thought of dying a virgin, but if she didn't actually die, she'd probably wish she had, having to look at Hunter's smug smile every day after that. He was definitely the type to drudge up past mistakes every chance he got and torment her with it. That was enough reason for Kasey to push the thought from her mind once again.

Chapter Twenty-two

Jamie soaked in the garden tub filled with bubbles while dance music blared through built-in speakers within the master bathroom walls. Her toes danced to the music just above the bubble-filled water while a glass of red wine set on the tub's edge within reach. The bathroom was almost entirely made of white and gray marble from the floor and walls to the vanity and the large garden tub. The tub was against the outer wall of windows, giving an incredible ocean view. The windows could even be opened for the full experience, although Jamie didn't open them, being the night air was a little cooler this evening. Instead, Jamie had lit several large candles strategically placed around the bathroom, lending a romantic setting despite only being a party of one.

The master bedroom wasn't much different than their original room but with a few more bells and whistles. There was a fireplace, a small bar, and a few extra plush chairs. Kasey was on her stomach across the large canopy bed, reading a book while wearing an oversized man's shirt as her nightgown. Despite the loud music from the bathroom, she attempted to concentrate on the book. When she thought she heard a clunk, Kasey looked up and listened, uncertain of what she'd heard due to the loud music. She didn't see or hear anything. The bedroom door then opened, surprising Kasey and revealing Hunter. She jumped into a sitting position with a startled gasp, pulled her nightshirt down over her panties, and stared at him.

"Try knocking," she scoffed as her surprise turned to hostility.

"I did," Hunter announced with a somewhat serious, stern look. "What's with the room change? I was concerned when I couldn't find the two of you."

Kasey quickly moved to the edge of the bed, uncomfortable with his presence, being she was on the bed wearing only a shirt and panties.

"We assumed you put Colton in our room, so we upgraded," Kasey informed him, then smirked. "I'm sure the admiral won't mind."

"Especially if he comes home in the middle of the night," Hunter replied. "He might be downright thrilled. Old guy might even enjoy it."

Kasey's discomfort increased, and something about Hunter's demeanor indicated he might very well be drunk, even if he didn't show it. She uncertainly stood and fidgeted.

"I'll be sure to lock the door," she remarked, then muttered, "although I thought I already had."

Hunter entered the room without being invited and approached the bathroom door. "What's with the music?"

Kasey immediately cut off his path to the bathroom door and stopped him from getting any closer in his drunken condition. She didn't need him walking in on Jamie while she was naked in the tub.

"Jamie's taking a bath," Kasey informed him. "If you don't mind, I'm tired."

Hunter looked from the bathroom door to Kasey, only a couple of feet away from him. She remained tense and stared back at him but didn't move from his path. Hunter casually placed his hands in his pockets and maintained his stare.

"You seem a little tense tonight," Hunter remarked, then cocked his head. "Is something wrong, or are you plotting something devious?"

"You're drunk."

He now appeared curious and smirked. "Wasn't that part of the plan?"

Kasey stared at him, feeling slightly alarmed. "I don't follow."

Hunter took a step closer to her and smiled deviously. Kasey backed up a step but kept her eyes on him.

"Colton confirmed that it was your idea to get me drunk," Hunter informed her while appearing almost humored. "I assumed it was so you could take advantage of me." His smirk cheapened. "Well, here I am."

"Colton has a warped sense of humor," Kasey informed him while feeling her heart race. "I don't know why he told you that."

Hunter took another step closer to her while maintaining his lustful smile. Kasey moved away from him and the bathroom door to avoid being trapped. Hunter casually turned and followed her, his hands never leaving his pockets.

"Am I coming on too strong for you?" he asked almost deviously. "Does that make you nervous?"

"Yes, you're making me nervous," she announced sternly. "I'd prefer we talk about this tomorrow when you're sober."

Kasey turned and again attempted to avoid him. He continued maneuvering around her, herding her as he had Colton but in a definite sexual manner. Kasey moved past him and to the open bedroom door. She paused near the door and indicated for him to leave. Hunter's hands finally left his pockets, and he casually shut the door. Now trapping her by the wall, he placed both hands on either side of her head and moved against her. Kasey felt a mixture of alarm and arousal sweep through her while instinctively bracing her hands against his shoulders, attempting to keep him back.

"Please leave," she whispered, almost unable to get the words out while lacking conviction, her eyes never leaving his.

As his left arm slipped around her waist, his right hand touched her face, and he offered his warmest smile.

"It's still your birthday for another half an hour," he reminded her in possibly the sexiest voice she'd ever heard. "That was the plan, wasn't it? Your first time on your birthday?"

Kasey tensed at the words coming from his mouth. Somehow her fantasy was suddenly turning into a nightmare. As Hunter lowered his mouth to hers while maintaining his smile, Kasey made a half-hearted effort to hold him back, but the anticipation was killing her. She didn't remember much about their little make-out session in the nightclub last night and desperately wanted a do-over.

"I'm *very* willing," he whispered with his lips close to hers while holding her against him. "And surprisingly passionate."

As his lips brushed past hers, Kasey felt her entire body tremble. Hunter met her gaze while keeping his mouth close to hers, which seemed to turn her on even more. Kasey couldn't help herself and eagerly kissed him. Hunter enthusiastically and aggressively returned the passionate kiss. His hand firmly slid down her body to her bare thigh and gently pulled her leg alongside his hip. Kasey gasped as he pressed his body against hers while bracing her against the wall.

She just about climbed him, feeling her body ache with desire. His hand firmly ran along her buttocks over her underwear as he grinded against her. Kasey had been convinced she came on to Hunter last night because she was drunk, but she still wanted him even sober. Kasey pawed his body and met his passionate kiss with her own aggression, willingly surrendering herself to him.

The bathroom music suddenly stopped, indicating Jamie was already out of the tub. Kasey jumped with a startled gasp, breaking off the kiss. Taking his cue, Hunter immediately released her and quickly stepped back. As the bathroom door opened, Kasey looked across the room and saw Jamie in her nightshirt while drying her hair with a towel. When Kasey glanced alongside her, Hunter was already slipping out of the room, shutting the door behind him. Kasey and Jamie both looked at the bedroom door with shared bewilderment. Kasey drew a deep breath, turned to the door, and fumbled with the lock. She placed her back to the door and appeared flustered.

"What was that?" Jamie asked.

"Just another one of my very bad ideas," Kasey replied while attempting to control her heavy breathing.

"What do you mean?" Jamie asked, then cocked her head while concerned. "You look all flushed. Did something happen?" She indicated the door. "Was that Hunter?"

Kasey nodded while attempting to compose herself after flirting with temptation. "He offered to fulfill my birthday wish," she announced while trembling over her moment of weakness.

Jamie's eyes widened in surprise. "You mean just now?"

"It was stupid, I know," Kasey cried out in frustration and started pacing the room. "But for a moment, I seriously considered going back to his room with him."

Jamie immediately smiled and chuckled. "Don't beat yourself up over it, Kasey," she remarked, then shrugged. "He definitely has a certain sex appeal--in a creepy, dominating sort of way." Jamie then flashed a smile. "I mean, if you're going to go for it, you may as well go all-in with someone like Hunter." She drifted into her own fantasies and groaned. "I'll bet he's amazing in bed."

Kasey stared at her friend a moment, then returned the smile and relaxed as they laughed.

Jamie indicated the door almost commandingly. "Go after him," she insisted. "You know you want to."

"Jamie, it's Hunter."

"Forget about that. He's a handsome, sexy man," Jamie informed her, then raised her brows. "You're obviously sexually attracted to him, and he's older with more experience."

"More like wild and aggressive," Kasey corrected while still trembling with sexual tension. "He scares me a little."

Jamie groaned and flopped onto the bed. "Hmm, you just described my dream lover."

"And maybe one day, I'll feel that way too," Kasey remarked. "But, right now, I want my first time to be with someone patient and gentle."

"You're right," Jamie replied while sighing with defeat. "I wasn't thinking. I dated my boyfriend an entire year before my first time, and he went out of his way to make it romantic and special." Jamie sprang up from the bed and placed her hands on Kasey's shoulders. "You should definitely wait until he's sober. Wise decision."

Kasey eyed her friend while cocking her head. "You honestly believe Hunter will be patient and gentle when he's sober?" she asked. "Have you even met Hunter?"

"Trust me," Jamie announced. "If he wants to get in your pants badly enough, he'll do just about anything you ask."

"And then what? He goes back to being a prick afterward?" Kasey asked, somewhat suspiciously.

Jamie shrugged and again flopped on the bed. "Pretty much. It's a major flaw in their DNA," she remarked. "I don't make the rules."

Kasey smiled and shook her head. "Well, at least you give better advice than Colton."

Chapter Twenty-three

Five-thirty the following morning, Kasey and Jamie slept peacefully in the king-sized canopy bed in the master bedroom. The heavy curtains blocked out any chance of the early morning light poking through. Kasey slowly woke to the sound of someone moving around in the hallway. She wearily rolled onto her back and listened a moment, uncertain of what she'd heard. The sound of someone up and about in the hallway was now distinct. Kasey quickly and quietly got out of bed, slipped into a pair of shorts, and grabbed her sword. She hurried to the door and opened it as quietly as possible. When she didn't see anyone, Kasey crept along the hallway and down the grand staircase with the sword slightly relaxed but in a ready position.

Kasey watched the open railing to the hallway below but saw nothing. When she reached the bottom, she crept along the main hall, glancing in each dark open doorway. She finally reached the kitchen door and paused to listen. Muffled voices were heard from the kitchen. Kasey considered her options and quietly hurried to the dimly lit dining room. The dining room contained hardwood flooring with a throw rug under the massive table that sat eight. Unlike the other rooms in the house, which were primarily white and bright, the dining room had orange walls, giving it a splash of color. Kasey crept past the table and paused near the kitchen entrance. As she listened by the side door, the conversation between the two men was more apparent now. One was Hunter, but the other was definitely not Colton.

"Don't start with me," Hunter scoffed. "I'm tired and cranky."

"What's wrong?" the male voice responded. "Haven't banged either of them yet?"

"Fuck off!"

There was a low, mildly familiar chuckle. "I'll take that as 'no'," the male voice remarked.

Even though the man's chuckle sounded familiar, Kasey couldn't place his voice. It couldn't have been anyone she knew. At least now she had proof that they weren't alone. Unfortunately, it meant that Hunter was in on the deception. She frowned while looking around, contemplating her next move. Kasey gently propped her sword alongside the wall next to the connecting door, then quickly and quietly hurried out of the dining room. She approached the kitchen door from the main hallway, drew a deep breath while pushing the door open, and entered. Hunter stood by the island counter with a cup of coffee and looked at her with some surprise.

"You're up early," Hunter casually remarked as if he hadn't been secretly meeting with someone in the kitchen.

"I could say the same about you," Kasey announced while briefly scanning the empty kitchen, somewhat surprised when she didn't see anyone.

"Shouldn't you be sleeping off your bender right about now?"

"Unfortunately, alcohol has the opposite effect on me," he informed her, then flashed a tiny grin.

Kasey approached him and casually leaned her back against the main counter in the corner. "About last night--"

"Yeah, it's a bit of a blank," Hunter easily lied, not letting her finish the sentence. "I hope I didn't do anything stupid or more offensive than usual."

She wasn't buying it. He knew exactly what happened in the master bedroom but hoped to avoid being called out on it.

"Nothing nearly as stupid as what I almost did," she muttered, unamused at the irony, and then eyed him. "You honestly don't remember?"

Kasey's gaze was transfixed upon his as she took a step closer. Hunter watched her closely, possibly attempting to gauge her mood. She placed her hands on his chest, allowing her left hand to run up to his shoulder, then gently touched his beard. Hunter groaned softly while attempting to hide his smile and lowered his mouth to hers while slipping his arm around her waist.

"It's coming back to me," he replied, pleased with her reaction.

Kasey brushed her lips past his as her right hand slipped under his jacket. She swiftly removed the gun from his shoulder holster, jumped back, and aimed it at him. Hunter stared at her with surprise and held his hands up defensively.

"Whoa, hey," he announced with some surprise but not particularly concerned. "I'm sure I didn't do anything to warrant this sort of reaction."

Kasey glared while keeping the gun aimed at him. "Save it," she snarled, then shouted. "Come out now, or I'll use him for target practice!"

"Kasey--"

Kasey kept her back to the corner of the cabinets and watched both doors to the kitchen. She kept the gun aimed at Hunter more than arm's length away so he couldn't easily disarm her.

"You may want to stand very still, Hunter," she snarled at him. "I may get nervous and accidentally shoot you."

"There's no one here, Kasey," Hunter explained in an unusually calm tone. "Now put down the gun, and let's talk about this."

"I stood by the door and listened to the two of you having a conversation," she informed him. "About me, I believe. No one got *banged*, but I'm pretty sure Jamie, Colton, and I got fucked." Her anger now consumed her, easily hiding her fear. "Now, call your friend out because I'm just desperate enough to shoot you."

Hunter stared at her for a moment in silence. While his look was hard to read, he appeared unusually calm. When the satellite phone on the counter rang, Hunter frowned.

"Please, Kasey," he pleaded. "Give me the gun. No one needs to get hurt."

"Aren't you going to answer that?" she snapped while raising an arrogant brow.

"I have three more rings," he informed her. "Just give me the gun."

As the phone rang again, his words concerned her. What would happen if he didn't answer the phone? Kasey stared at Hunter while keeping the gun aimed at him without flinching.

"Call him out--now!"

"I can't," Hunter announced gruffly, then relaxed. "That's him on the phone."

Kasey eyed Hunter and then the phone with an odd look of concern. "Why is he on the phone?" she asked, now suspicious.

The satellite phone rang a fourth time, now alarming Kasey.

"One of us has to answer it before the next ring," he informed her.

Kasey hesitated only a moment, then indicated for him to answer it. Hunter stepped closer to her and the main counter then pressed a button without picking up the phone.

"Confirm," the male voice on the phone snarled.

Hunter kept his eyes on Kasey while speaking at the phone. "Tango."

"Roger that," the male voice replied.

Hunter continued to stare at Kasey, who was now tense. There was a thunderous crack over the phone, followed by Jamie screaming. Kasey gasped in horror. The man was in the bedroom with Jamie! In that split second of vulnerability, Hunter grabbed Kasey's wrist and twisted it, causing her to drop the gun. He then twisted her arm behind her back and swiftly threw her face forward over the main counter. As Hunter stood behind her while holding her arm pinned against her back, Jamie could still be heard screaming over the phone's speaker.

"Delta foxtrot!"

Jamie still screamed.

"I said *delta foxtrot*, you stupid mother fucker!" Hunter shouted at the phone.

"I heard you, you prick," the voice shouted back. "She's fine. She's not exactly happy to see me." There was a pause as Jamie was still heard screaming over the phone. "We're coming down."

Hunter looked at Kasey in the vulnerable and compromising position in which he had her bent over the counter. He leaned over her while keeping his hips firmly against her buttocks from behind.

"You heard him," he remarked close to her ear. "She's fine, and he's also coming out now. So I guess you got what you wanted."

"Get off me," she cried out and made an effort to free herself, which only resulted in grinding against him.

"I might be mistaken, but I'm pretty sure you're in no position to give orders," Hunter informed her matter-of-factly. "You may want to remember that when dealing with my partner. He doesn't have my sense of humor or my compassion." Hunter kept his mouth close to her ear while firmly pressing against her from behind. "And if you had pulled his gun on him, I'm pretty sure you'd have a broken wrist and dislocated shoulder."

Kasey stopped struggling and held her breath, allowing his words to register. She was completely at Hunter's mercy, and although she may have been mistaken, his pelvis against her backside might have aroused him.

"Now, I'm going to release you, and you're going to try really hard not to piss me off," he announced close to her ear, causing her to shiver from his warm breath and chilling tone. "Do we have a deal?"

Kasey was already regretting her suspicious nature. It's what got them to this point. Perhaps, if she'd played dumb and hadn't confronted him--? When he spoke again, she realized too much time had passed without a response from her.

"Okay, I want you to carefully consider your position and decide how you want this to play out," Hunter informed her. "Because I'm starting to enjoy my dominance over you."

Kasey was already aware of that, but his pointing it out made it a little more frightening. "I won't piss you off," she huffed.

Hunter released her wrist, backed away, and picked up the discarded gun as Kasey slowly straightened and turned. She gingerly rubbed her wrist and glared at him.

Hunter flashed the gun at her and smirked. "Hands off my toys."

As Hunter replaced the gun in his shoulder holster, Kasey glared at him with a wildly unpredictable look.

A strange and twisted smile crossed his face. "I'd love to read your mind right now."

"It would only piss you off," she scoffed.

Hunter casually leaned against the island counter behind him and studied her. "If you and your friends behave, no one has to get hurt," he informed her. "If you hadn't been so damned curious, you wouldn't even have realized you were being held against your will." He shook his head and frowned. "We could have had fun playing house, and all of this could have been avoided."

Kasey frowned and looked away. Part of her wished she'd pulled the trigger, ending Hunter and his smug, devious smile. The other part of her wished she'd remained blissfully ignorant of his betrayal. Jamie was heard screaming in the hallway moments before the kitchen door burst open, revealing a large, muscular man carrying Jamie over his shoulder. The man was taller than Hunter and with more muscles. His dark hair was buzzed close to his head, and he had dark scruff that possibly constituted a beard. Jamie beat her handcuffed fists against the man's back while screaming and cursing. Kasey appeared horrified at the familiar man from her recent past.

"Jughead?" Kasey gasped.

The large man glared at Kasey, having heard the name. "Juggernaut," he snarled, correcting her.

Hunter turned, saw the spectacle, then frowned and shook his head. "Really, Diesel?"

Kasey had almost forgotten that Jughead had an actual name. Diesel pulled the angry woman, dressed only in her nightshirt, from his shoulder and released her. Jamie fell to the floor with a scream, landing roughly on her buttocks. Diesel smiled and laughed at Jamie's expense. There were three lightly bleeding scratches across his neck from Jamie's fingernails. When he reached down and pulled Jamie to her feet, she kicked and beat him with her cuffed hands, increasing his amusement. Kasey just stared at the man with horror. Diesel laughed and tossed Jamie into Kasey. As she caught her friend, Jamie immediately clung to Kasey, genuinely frightened by their new nightmare.

"If the order comes down," Diesel announced and grinned while indicating Jamie. "I call dibs on hurting that one."

"What about the other one?" Hunter asked without reacting to the comment.

"He's still out," Diesel replied. "I'll deal with him, don't worry." He then chuckled in a somewhat evil manner. "I can't believe she didn't shoot you." He then indicated Jamie. "That one would have. I forgot how feisty she was." His grin increased as he cast a sweeping look over Jamie. "Kind of turned me on. Reminded me of that really wild ride she took me on in the back of the limousine."

Jamie sneered and attempted to lunge for him with rage in her eyes. Kasey held her back, putting some distance between her and Diesel.

"You are so dead!" Jamie screamed.

"Okay, I think Jamie needs a time out," Hunter announced, then looked at Kasey while remaining calm. "You may want to explain to your friend that she and Colton are leverage over you. Their only value to us is to keep *you* in line. And, honestly, we only really need one of them to do that, which means one of them is expendable."

Jamie looked at Kasey with fear and once again clung to her. Kasey held Jamie and glared at Hunter with the same look from moments earlier.

"I don't know, Hunter," Diesel announced and chuckled in his throat. "The next time you let her take your gun, I think she's going to pull the trigger without blinking."

"Get those cuffs off her," Hunter ordered without reacting to the comment.

Diesel flashed a smile, approached Jamie, and unlocked the handcuffs. Jamie glared at him as he removed the cuffs and again clung to Kasey. When Diesel smiled and winked at Jamie, she turned her head into Kasey's shoulder to avoid looking at him. Diesel maintained his smugness as he turned and walked past Hunter.

"And, Romeo--" Hunter announced.

Diesel eyed Hunter.

"If you know what's good for you," Hunter remarked, "you'll keep it in your pants."

"You have nothing to worry about," Diesel announced and again eyed Jamie. "Been there; done that."

Diesel smiled while laughing as he left the kitchen. Hunter returned his attention to Kasey and Jamie.

"I'm sure the two of you are eager to see your new accommodations for the remainder of your stay," Hunter announced, then indicated the kitchen closet.

Kasey and Jamie were concerned by the action. Hunter opened the closet door and pulled a lever, popping a secret panel away from the wall. There was a hidden staircase behind the panel.

Chapter Twenty-four

Hunter forced Jamie and Kasey down the tight dark staircase and into the secret basement, which was more like a dungeon. He stopped them before an old-fashioned, iron cell door. Hunter unlocked it with an old brass key and then pressed a code into the modern security panel, which was an alarm for added protection. He pulled open the door that creaked loudly and ushered them inside. Both frowned and entered. The windowless living room had a large, plush sectional sofa with a coffee table, carpeted floor, and a large television with a DVD player. A kitchenette was beside a door leading to the bedroom and the only bathroom. As Kasey and Jamie looked around, Hunter remained by the door.

"There's a camera in the living room and the bedroom, but none in the bathroom," Hunter informed them while pointing out the cameras. "We've childproofed the place for our comfort. You'll find snacks and drinks in the frig." He then eyed both women still in their nightshirts. "Don't worry. We'll bring your clothes and your playmate down later today."

"Think you can tell us what this is about?" Kasey demanded while cautiously approaching Hunter and the cell door.

"I thought we'd already covered that," Hunter replied with little emotion. "Your uncle has an endless supply of enemies, my boss being his biggest one. Once we get what we want from your uncle, you'll be free to go."

"And if he doesn't pay?"

"It won't come to that," Hunter assured her. "In case you're wondering, our orders are to hold you here for as long as it takes." He drew a deep breath and sighed. "You'll probably be here a couple of weeks, so you may as well make yourselves comfortable." Hunter stared into Kasey's eyes, but she didn't back away from him. "As long as you play nice, no one will get hurt. This is a vendetta against your uncle, not you or your friends. We don't need to hurt you to make our point."

"What about the innocent people you killed on the ship?" Kasey demanded. "Are we supposed to believe you'd kill them in cold blood but somehow have a conscious about harming us?"

"Those men weren't working for us," Hunter informed her. "I don't know who they were, exactly, but they were out to get you as leverage on your uncle too." He frowned and shook his head. "Their attack in the nightclub forced us to move ahead of schedule. Believe me when I tell you; if they had gotten you instead of us, Colton *never* would have made it off the ship alive, and if they hadn't killed Jamie onboard, she certainly would have wished they had. And you? You'd be missing a finger, which would be sent to your uncle."

"So we're supposed to be grateful to you?" Kasey demanded while folding her arms across her chest.

"I think you should," Hunter replied, then sighed, "but that would be expecting too much."

"Okay. You want grateful? Fine," Kasey snarled, regaining some of her arrogance. "Tell the admiral I'm willing to make any deal he wants if he'll let Jamie and Colton go."

"He's not going to give up his leverage over you," Hunter informed her without even thinking about it. "He's smarter than that."

"Fine," she scoffed. "You said you don't need both of them. Let Jamie go. Same deal."

Jamie looked at Kasey with some surprise.

Hunter studied Kasey for a long moment. "Just for shits and giggles, I'll tell him you'd like to make a plea deal, but don't expect anything," he remarked, then hesitated while studying Kasey. "You must really care about your friends. I respect that."

"Remember that the next time I piss you off," she muttered.

Hunter snorted a soft laugh and left the room, shutting and locking the cell behind him. He punched a number on the security alarm pad, and it beeped as he left. Kasey approached the cell door and looked at the basement corridor a moment before finally turning toward Jamie.

"We need to work on a really good plan to get out of here," Kasey remarked.

"Does that camera have volume on it?" Jamie asked while indicating the camera in the corner of the room.

"No, it's just a basic security camera like at the supermarket," she replied.

"I'm all for escaping, Kasey," Jamie informed her while rubbing her chilled shoulders as she looked around the prison suite before meeting Kasey's gaze. "But even if we did get out of this prison, we're still stranded on this island."

"There might be a boat or that helicopter," Kasey informed her. "They might have them hidden somewhere."

"That's a big *might*," Jamie muttered insecurely.

"The satellite phone," Kasey announced with renewed enthusiasm. "We just need to get that phone, and we can call someone."

"Colton's pretty techy," Jamie remarked. "I'm sure he'd know more about it."

"We'll need to wait for them the bring Colton down anyway," Kasey reminded her. "The two of you are leverage against me. If we're getting out, we're getting out together."

Chapter Twenty-five

Kasey and Jamie sat huddled on the sofa while talking softly and privately. Even though the video cameras had no volume, they weren't taking any chances. Diesel appeared at the cell door, almost startling them as he turned the old key in the lock. He opened the door and tossed Colton inside. Colton was barely awake and was still only wearing his boxer shorts. Diesel locked the door and eyed them with a devious smile.

"The bellhop will be along with your luggage," Diesel remarked, then chuckled. "Enjoy your stay." He then walked away.

Kasey and Jamie jumped off the sofa and hurried to Colton, who stood silent and confused in the middle of the cell's living room.

"Are you okay?" Jamie asked while affectionately rubbing his bare arm.

"Uh, yeah. What the hell happened?" Colton asked while looking around the strange room. "What month is this?" He then pointed back at the door. "I mean, that was Jughead, wasn't it?"

"Yeah, that was Jughead all right," Jamie muttered and patted his shoulder. "It's a long story."

Both women hugged Colton while he remained confused about what had happened.

"What happened to Hunter?" Colton asked. "Did they get him?"

"No, but they got *to* him," Kasey scoffed and started pacing the living area. "He's been working against us the entire time."

Colton was genuinely surprised. "What?" he asked. "You mean, on the ship? That was him?"

"He says not," Kasey replied. "According to him, he's just one of many interested parties looking to use me against my uncle."

"Oh, that's just terrific," Colton muttered while running his fingers through his hair. He then frowned, appearing ashamed. "If I hadn't gotten drunk last night, I might have somehow prevented this from happening."

"There's nothing you could have done," Kasey remarked with a defeated sigh. "This is all on me. I was too curious for my own good. Even so, if I hadn't acted when I heard Hunter talking to Diesel, we could have kept up the illusion until we had some sort of plan to take them down."

"No one here is to blame," Jamie insisted. "Not you and not Colton. This is because of your uncle and his bad decisions. We're just pawns."

"Unfortunately, that makes us expendable," Kasey muttered.

§

After an uneventful afternoon in their new prison suite, Diesel arrived at their cell and announced it was time for dinner. He handcuffed Jamie and Kasey together and escorted them from their basement cell.

The pair entered the kitchen and saw Hunter setting dinner plates on the table. When Diesel unlocked the handcuffs binding them together, Hunter eyed them and then indicated the table. For now, they had little choice but to do as instructed by their captors. Both sat down at the table alongside each other with some apprehension.

"Why isn't Colton here?" Kasey asked, revealing little emotion. She wouldn't give either man the satisfaction of witnessing weakness in her.

"As long as the three of you aren't together outside of your suite, there's less chance of you doing something stupid," Hunter informed her in a less confrontational tone. "Alternating who comes out is the best solution. Believe it or not, we're trying to be nice."

"*He's* trying to be nice," Diesel informed them. "I don't give a fuck."

When Jamie sneered at Diesel, Kasey felt increasing concern for her friend. Jamie's intimate encounter with Diesel made for an uncomfortable situation. It made Jamie angry and gave Diesel the upper hand as well as leverage against her.

"Let's all be nice," Hunter announced, scolding all three. "We're going to do this dance for several weeks, so we may as well try to get along."

"A couple of weeks turned into several pretty quickly," Kasey muttered.

"As long as it takes, remember?" Hunter reminded her.

Hunter set a platter of grilled chicken and bowls of mashed potatoes and string beans on the table before joining them at one end. Diesel sat at the opposite end of the table and immediately dived into the feast before him. Kasey and Jamie remained quietly seated and took none of the food. While scarfing down his food, Diesel eyed the women, then looked at Hunter and offered a humored smile.

"I told you this was a waste of time," Diesel announced. "More for me, though."

"I'm not that bad of a cook," Hunter informed the women.

Neither woman responded.

"We could just as easily allow you to stay in your suite your entire stay," Hunter informed them. "I'd think you'd appreciate being brought out and allowed to see a little sunlight."

"And maybe after dinner, we can play fetch on the beach," Kasey scoffed.

"I'm trying to make this as pleasant as possible," Hunter informed her. "But you're just going to insist on making things unpleasant."

Kasey casually pushed her empty plate away, leaned on the table closer to Hunter, and looked into his eyes.

"If the tables were turned and you were the one being held captive, would you be so appreciative and sociable?" Kasey asked. "Or would you be sitting there waiting to strike with deadly force?"

Hunter released a sigh and leaned back in his chair. "The last time I was held captive, I was tied to a chair with wire and beaten so badly I didn't even know my name," he informed her. "I would have preferred this over what I went through." He finally leaned forward on the table and met her gaze. "You can't get away, and even if you did, where would you go? There's no way off this island."

Kasey sat back in her chair, looked away, and folded her arms across her chest. "I'm ready to go back to my cell now."

Hunter straightened and silently watched her, but she refused to look at him. He groaned and cast his napkin on the table.

"Fine," Hunter scoffed, then glared at Diesel. "Take Jamie back to the suite. I've got this."

Diesel stood, possibly disgusted that his meal was interrupted, and glared at Jamie. Jamie uncertainly looked at Kasey, who appeared a little less confident now.

"Now, babe," Diesel snarled.

Jamie slowly stood and left the room with Diesel. Kasey still refused to look at Hunter, although she couldn't deny she was a little worried about her friend being alone with a man like Diesel. Just because Hunter told him to behave, that didn't mean he would listen. Hunter was unusually silent, and Kasey was sure he was looking at her, but she kept her eyes locked on her empty plate. Kasey felt her tension rise with Jamie's absence. Hunter pushed his empty plate away and stood, making Kasey twitch slightly at his movement.

"Okay, let's go," Hunter announced.

Kasey stood from the table and still avoided looking at him. Hunter removed the pair of handcuffs from the island counter.

"Right hand."

Kasey eyed him and attempted to hide her concern. She extended her right hand to him while trying not to tremble. He placed the handcuff on her wrist and then attached the other to his left wrist. Once she was secured to him, he showed her the key to the handcuffs before slipping it down his pants. He jumped slightly.

"Oh, that's cold," he gasped, then smirked. "I'm sure you'll think twice before going for the key."

Without any further comment, Hunter headed out of the kitchen, forcing Kasey to follow him.

Chapter Twenty-six

As they left the mansion and headed onto the beach, Kasey felt her tension rising. Being handcuffed to Hunter didn't make her feel any better, either. She had so many conflicting emotions regarding this man she didn't even know how to sort through them. He started as her protector, and now he was her captor. She resented him for doing his job, then found herself attracted to him the moment they set foot on the cruise ship. When he saved her and her friends from the nightclub attack, she used him as a security blanket, and her feelings for him intensified. Now, she was back to hating him.

"What are we doing out here?" she asked timidly, not wanting to provoke him more than she already had, especially since they were now alone.

"I wanted to show you something," he announced with little emotion.

"I prefer you showed me my cell," she replied, almost instantly regretting her smart remark.

Hunter stopped her in the sand halfway to the surf and pointed across the ocean. "The mainland is about two hundred miles that way," he informed her. "It's a very long swim." He turned his head and looked at her. "There's nowhere to go, Kasey. You may as well make the best of your situation. You could be in worse hands."

"And, surprisingly, that doesn't make me feel any better," she replied.

Hunter continued to walk along the beach, tugging mercilessly on her cuffed hand. Kasey winced from the pain and gently rubbed her wrist with her free hand.

"Nothing in my orders says I have to be nice to you or your friends," Hunter informed her. "In fact, nothing says I have to keep you and your friends together." He cast a look at her. "I'm actually on a fairly long leash. If Diesel were in charge, you might realize just how nice I'm being."

"I'm glad you think you have the upper hand, Hunter," she announced and instantly regretted it. Why couldn't she keep her mouth shut?

"I do have the upper hand."

"Not if I'm dead, you don't," Kasey reminded him.

"No one's going to kill you."

"I want to see the admiral," she demanded.

"He's not here, and I don't think he'll be coming around any time soon," Hunter informed her. "If anything goes sideways, there's nothing to tie him to us."

"Oh, so you two idiots are left holding the bag?" she asked. "How convenient. I guess someone's being paid big bucks. Either that, or you're just really stupid. Sounds like the perfect setup for a double-cross." She glared at him as they walked. "When my uncle pays the ransom, your admiral could easily order us all killed--including you. No loose ends and nothing to connect him to the kidnapping or murders. He gets away with everything."

"Nothing could be further from the truth," Hunter informed her.

"So that's a 'no' to talking with this mysterious admiral, huh?"

"Correct."

Kasey stopped and immediately felt the cuff bruising her wrist. She winced slightly from the pain but held her ground. Hunter stopped and turned to face her with a curious look.

"I don't think I have anything left to say to you, Hunter," she announced. "So why don't we make your job really easy for you? Put me back in my cell and forget about me until you're either ready to let me go or kill me. Otherwise, I'm just going to end up pissing you off."

"Is that what you really want?" he demanded as his anger increased.

"What I really want is to put a bullet in your head," she shouted angrily. "Which I should have done this morning!"

"Walking on the dark side, are we?" Hunter scoffed as his anger increased. "Fine, I'll return you to your cell. Maybe a little solitude will soften your mood."

Hunter turned and pulled her toward the mansion. Kasey winced again from the pain of the handcuff pulling against her wrist. She had to hurry to keep up with his long, fast strides. Having had enough, Kasey suddenly grabbed the handcuff chain with her left hand and threw herself into a sitting position on the sand. Hunter was pulled off balance but didn't fall. As he turned toward her, Kasey swept his legs out from under him. He fell roughly to the sand, nearly pulling Kasey with him. Kasey jumped on top of him, dug her fingernails into his throat, and stared into his eyes while hovering over him.

Hunter stared back at her with little reaction. It was an empty threat at best. She wasn't going to cut his throat with her fingernails. Hunter casually removed her nails from his neck and sat up. Kasey frowned while attempting to move backward and off him, but he grabbed her wrists and kept her from moving, putting them only inches apart.

"Was that supposed to be an attack, or were you initiating foreplay?" he demanded.

Kasey stared into his eyes without emotion and didn't respond. Although she was frightened by how angry she had made him, she tried not to react. Hunter raised his brows along with a tiny smile.

"Oh, I'm supposed to decide?" he asked with a snarl. "That's fine by me."

Hunter released Kasey's left wrist, slipped his right arm around her hips, and aggressively slid her hips closer to his. Kasey refrained from moving or reacting, but the action was enough to surprise her. As she kept her eyes on him, his aggression and hostility seemed to vanish while staring into her eyes. Hunter lowered his mouth and warmly kissed her neck. Kasey still didn't move, but she tensed from the sensation. As he moved his cuffed left hand to her face, Kasey placed her cuffed right hand on his. He warmly kissed his way across her neck and toward her throat. Kasey still didn't move or react, although her breathing became noticeably heavier.

Hunter lifted his head with his mouth close to hers and hesitated only a moment before warmly and gently kissing her on the lips. Kasey couldn't help herself and returned the kiss. Hunter groaned softly as the kiss turned more aggressive. Kasey gasped softly, realizing what she was doing, and pushed on his shoulder with her left hand in an attempt to hold him back. Hunter broke off the kiss and, in one swift motion, moved her off him, dropping her into the sand. He avoided looking at her, although it was apparent he was annoyed. Hunter grabbed her right, cuffed hand, stood, and pulled her to her feet.

"Lucky for you, I don't do little girls."

Hunter didn't release her hand as he forcibly pulled her toward the house with disgust and possible frustration.

Chapter Twenty-seven

Hunter roughly stopped Kasey in the corridor just outside the cell door, then reached into his pants in an attempt to retrieve the key. He cursed softly, turned his back to her, and made another effort to find the key. Kasey took a deep breath and leaned back against the wall while shutting her eyes. Hunter turned with the key in his hand and unlocked the handcuffs. Kasey gently rubbed her sore wrist, which was already red and bruised. Hunter eyed her bruised wrist and seemed to lose some of his hostility.

"There should be an ice pack in the freezer," Hunter informed her in a gentle tone.

"It's fine," she snarled.

Jamie and Colton approached the cell door as Hunter unlocked it. As Kasey entered the cell, Hunter locked the door behind her and left without comment. Colton and Jamie hurried toward Kasey and embraced her.

"Are you okay?" Jamie asked, then pulled back and looked her over. "Did he hurt you?"

"No, surprisingly, he didn't," Kasey replied, then eyed them. "Are you guys okay?"

"I'm fine, but Colton has to watch himself a little more carefully around Diesel," Jamie remarked with a disgusted huff. "Jughead is just waiting to pop him in the mouth."

"Hey, he might be big, but I'm not going to stand by and allow him to talk to you like that," Colton remarked.

"Yeah, better he breaks your face than berate me about our limo escapades," Jamie remarked and shook her head. "If you're going to get yourself killed, Colton, at least save it for when it really matters."

Kasey and Jamie crossed the living room and sat on the sofa while Colton sat on the arm of the nearby chair.

"Are you going to tell us what happened?" Jamie asked while rubbing Kasey's arm. "You were gone almost an hour. We were worried sick that he was doing something horrible to you."

"I think he's just trying to intimidate me," Kasey informed her, then managed a tiny laugh. "And it's working, but he doesn't need to know that."

"Why?" Colton asked, then turned angry. "What did he do?"

"Nothing. It's not worth mentioning," Kasey replied, then hesitated. "Well, maybe it *is* worth mentioning." She shifted uncomfortably. "There's something off about Hunter's behavior. He puts on a big show to intimidate me, but it's almost as if he doesn't really want to do it. I'm starting to believe he doesn't want to hurt us."

"I'm pretty sure Diesel does," Jamie remarked. "His look tells me he'd just love to make me scream some more."

Kasey remained lost in her thoughts a moment longer.

"I'll be honest with you, Kasey," Jamie remarked. "You're not exactly making any impact by trying to intimidate them. We would be better off just playing submissive toward them for now. Honestly, I don't see how we'll ever be able to get the drop on them anyway."

"Not without some serious firepower," Colton remarked.

Kasey glanced at her friends. "Do you think it's possible to convert Hunter to our side?" she asked. "I mean, if there's a way off this island, he'd know it. Would it be worth it?"

"Exactly what do you have in mind to 'convert' Hunter to our side?" Colton asked, now curious.

"He's been very, well, sexual toward me," Kasey replied.

"What do you mean sexual?" Colton demanded while fidgeting and appeared ready to lunge. "Did he try something? I'll kill him!"

"Calm yourself, Colton," Kasey announced. "You wouldn't last two minutes." She hesitated a moment, then clarified the situation. "I don't think he'd do anything without my consent." She eyed both her friends. "Do you think he'd help us if I, well, 'took one for the team'?"

Colton stared at her with something resembling horror.

"I don't know, Kasey," Jamie remarked somewhat sympathetically. "Diesel isn't exactly playing nice with me, and we had a wild time in the back of the limousine. You'd probably just be giving it away for nothing."

"I'm with Jamie," Colton announced while shifting uncomfortably on the arm of the chair. "Hunter isn't some average, horny guy. The way he took on those guys on the ship, he's definitely professional, possibly military. I think he'd gladly take whatever you offer and leave you hanging."

Kasey sank into thought and shook her head. "I just have this nagging feeling there's something else," she muttered.

"I'm with Jamie on this one," Colton informed her. "It's not going to hurt us any to play nice with them for a while. In your case, not too nice with Hunter, but if they do have something more sinister planned, gaining their sympathy will make it harder for them to harm us willingly."

"You're absolutely right," Kasey remarked with a sigh. "The two of you need to be as nice as possible to Diesel and Hunter. You're their leverage over me. If you play your cards right, you can get in good with them. That way, they're less likely to harm you if I do something stupid."

"I hope you're not suggesting I cozy up to Diesel," Jamie gasped. "Because the way I feel about him right now, I'd probably bite it off."

"Okay, enough sex talk," Colton announced and turned animated. "Neither of you is *taking one for the team,* so let's just forget about that. End of conversation."

§

Jamie sat on the bed in her nightshirt while watching a movie on the television. Their prison bedroom was nothing spectacular. It had a plain king-sized bed with an uninspiring comforter, two chairs, and two nightstands. The floor was carpeted throughout the suite, and there was a television in the bedroom armoire as well as one in the living room. There was also another dresser in addition to the drawers beneath the armoire. Jamie attempted to get into the movie, although remaining restless due to their situation. Despite being bedtime, Kasey appeared from the bathroom, still fully dressed.

"What are you watching?" Kasey asked while standing alongside the bed.

"Oh, some old movie on DVD," Jamie replied, then indicated the cabinet. "There's an entire drawer full of DVDs in the armoire. Apparently, the admiral is into Alfred Hitchcock."

"So is my uncle," Kasey remarked, then sank into thought. "Kind of ironic, don't you think?"

"Aren't you changing for bed?" Jamie asked while indicating she was still dressed. "Are we expecting company?"

"I'll change in a little while," Kasey informed her. "I want to do an experiment first."

"Oh, that can't be good," Jamie announced with a groan. "Your last experiment landed us on house arrest."

"Not funny," Kasey muttered.

Jamie cringed. "Too soon?"

Kasey managed a tiny smile while shaking her head. At least Jamie still had her sense of humor intact. Kasey turned and approached the camera in the upper corner of the bedroom. She pulled a chair beneath the camera, stood on it, and rubbed a bar of soap over the lens. Jamie watched her work, now curious.

"What are you doing?" Jamie finally asked.

"A thick layer of soap will make it impossible for them to spy on us," Kasey informed her.

"What exactly are you trying to accomplish?" Jamie asked, then turned concerned. "You're only going to piss them off."

"Let's call it creating the illusion of a conspiracy," Kasey informed her friend.

"You have one evil, devious mind, girl," Jamie replied. "I hope it doesn't come with an equally evil punishment."

Kasey climbed down from the chair and remained optimistic. "I have my reasons," Kasey informed her. "I want to see how long it takes them to figure out that they've lost visual."

"What purpose will that serve?"

"Maybe they're not watching us at all," Kasey suggested. "The cameras may not even be functional. Maybe they're playing games with us." She then smiled somewhat deviously. "I also have plans for the cell door."

"Oh, you are bad," Jamie remarked while adding a tiny smile. "Where do you get this stuff?"

"Nine years of Embry."

"Embry?" Jamie asked with surprise. "He's about as passive as they get."

"He may be passive, but he's also very devious," Kasey informed her. "Get on his bad side, and he would do little things as pay back. Once, he let the air out of the limo tires when the chauffeur irritated him. Sometimes, he'd fiddle with the heat and the air-conditioning to annoy my uncle." A grin crossed her face. "But the most epic was the time he'd convinced one of the maids that the second floor was haunted." She shook her head while grinning. "God, I love that odd little man."

Jamie eyed her somewhat suspiciously. "He told me the chauffeur was gay."

"Yeah," Kasey announced with a sigh. "He didn't want you sleeping with the chauffeur."

Jamie's eyes widened, and she gasped, "That little prick!"

Chapter Twenty-eight

Morning. Colton slept soundly on the sofa in the quiet prison living room as if he didn't have a care in the world. The old key was heard turning in the cell door with a distinctive clatter, barely waking Colton. A loud metallic bang was followed by cursing.

"What the hell--?" Diesel cried out.

Colton abruptly woke, sat up disoriented, and looked at Diesel outside the cell door. He struggled with the key in the lock.

"Don't tell me the key broke in the lock," Colton muttered while running his fingers through his mussed hair.

"No one's talking to you, dick head," Diesel snarled.

Colton muttered under his breath, casually lying back on the sofa, and attempted to return to his slumber.

"Son-of-a-bitch!" Diesel cried out and again slammed his palm against the cell door.

A slightly humored smile crossed Colton's face, even though he didn't open his eyes.

§

A little while later, Kasey casually leaned against the wall just inside the cell by the door and watched Hunter and Diesel working on the lock from the other side. Hunter kneeled before the lock while Diesel hovered over his shoulder. The two men were like an old-time Abbott and Costello show.

"Careful not to break the key," Diesel announced from over Hunter's shoulder.

"I know what I'm doing," Hunter snarled in response, becoming irritated with the bigger man. "Stop hovering over me!"

"Maybe it's the wrong key," Kasey added with little emotion, then eyed Hunter. "Did you check your underwear?"

Hunter glared up at Kasey through the bars. Kasey offered a slightly mocking smile. Diesel appeared baffled by the comment while Hunter returned to the lock.

"You're going to break the key," Diesel continued with a groan.

"I'm going to break something else if you don't get away from me," Hunter snarled back.

Jamie appeared from the bedroom, dressed and drying her wet hair after her morning shower. She eyed the scene by the door.

"They still didn't get that thing unlocked?" Jamie asked, then appeared curious. "Did they break the key in the lock?"

Hunter glared at Jamie across the room. Jamie had to turn away in order to hide her smile.

"Twenty bucks says he breaks the key before opening the door," Colton announced.

Diesel snickered at the comment, but Hunter wasn't amused and jabbed his elbow behind him, lightly striking Diesel in the groin. Diesel jumped with a slight yelp and gingerly rubbed his groin.

"Prick," Diesel scoffed.

Hunter groaned with disgust and glared at Kasey. "What did you do to the lock?"

"Me?" Kasey demanded while giving him an insulted look. "You're the brilliant boys with the century-old lock and key."

"And what did you do to the cameras?" Hunter snarled, his irritation increasing.

"What cameras?" Kasey asked with a perfected look of innocence.

Hunter glared at her from his position on the floor just outside the door. Kasey casually tilted her head and raised her brows with an innocent look. Hunter returned to the lock. The key suddenly snapped. Kasey gasped, placed her hand to her mouth with surprise, and tried not to laugh. Hunter groaned with disgust, then reached through the bars and grabbed for Kasey's ankle. She jumped back a step and continued to hide her smile.

"Nice going, prick," Diesel scoffed, redirecting his hostility.

Hunter stood and kicked the bars just hard enough to rattle the door. He glared at Kasey, who stood back several feet with a mocking grin.

"I'm glad you're amused," Hunter launched, clearly annoyed. "You've got your wish. You get to stay in there until you're released." He then muttered, "--or I kill you."

"We could blow it," Diesel suggested.

"Brilliant," Hunter replied while glaring at his cohort. "And where to you propose we keep them when we have no cell door?"

"We'll handcuff them to the furniture," Diesel replied, then shrugged. "Or to us." He then smirked at Jamie. "That could be fun. You can keep me company while I drain my snake."

Jamie looked away with disgust.

"It would be chaos with the three of them," Hunter informed him.

"So we'll shoot the runt," Diesel announced with a shrug, then indicated Colton. "We don't need him."

Diesel removed his gun from his shoulder holster and aimed it at Colton through the bars. Colton cried out, jumped off the sofa, and ran into the bedroom. He peeked around the door as Diesel chuckled softly and replaced his gun.

"You can't buy entertainment like that," Diesel announced.

"No imagination," Kasey muttered, then glared at Hunter. "Do you have a pack of gum and a metal coat hanger?"

Both men eyed her.

"It's not rocket science, boys," she announced with a groan.

"How about you tell us what you did to the lock so we don't break the last key?" Hunter demanded.

"It's an old lock," Kasey informed him. "Ever think about trying some lubricant?"

Hunter looked at Diesel with a frown. "She rusted the lock."

"How the hell--?"

"Don't ask," Hunter muttered and quickly waved him off. "Just get the spare key, some gum, and lubricant."

Diesel shook his head and walked away while Hunter leaned against the cell door, eyeing Kasey.

"You think you're so clever, don't you?" Hunter demanded.

"Actually, I am very clever," Kasey informed him while grinning. "I had an excellent teacher, and I'm highly motivated."

"You've also been nominated to remain in your cell alone for the rest of the day," he informed her. "Maybe the rest of the week. That should be long enough for you to start playing nice." He raised his brows with a slightly arrogant look. "Of course, your friends will be locked in a twelve by twelve concrete cell down the hall with absolutely no comforts whatsoever while constantly being reminded that you're the reason they're pissing in a bucket." His sly smile increased. "I'm sure they'd be more than thrilled to return to this cell and keep you in line for me."

Jamie quickly approached Kasey and leaned over her shoulder. "I love you, Kasey, but I don't want to be locked in a cell for a week with Colton with only a bucket of piss between us," she begged. "For my sake, please make up with him."

Kasey didn't take her eyes off Hunter but appeared to consider what Jamie had said. She glanced back at Jamie and motioned her away. Jamie uncertainly walked away and nervously joined Colton near the bedroom door. Colton placed his arms around her and held her. Kasey stared into Hunter's eyes as he casually looked down at her.

"You win," Kasey replied in defeat. "No more soaping the camera lenses, rusting the locks, itching powder in your shorts--" She frowned, admitting defeat. "Can we call a truce?"

"Are you going to be a good girl and behave for a change?" Hunter demanded.

"I don't seem to have a choice."

"Good. Remember that," Hunter replied, then straightened. "Will you be joining us for dinner tonight?"

"I'm not hungry," she informed him. "Take Jamie and Colton. They'll be better company."

"You have to eat something," he insisted.

She considered the comment and then shook her head. "No, actually, I don't."

"So a hunger strike is the answer?" Hunter demanded.

"Only because I'm not desperate enough to slit my own wrists just yet," she casually replied.

Hunter's reaction to the comment was a mixture of surprise and concern that she was even somewhat serious.

"Stop being overly dramatic," Hunter scolded. "No one's hurting you. Consider all of this as a minor inconvenience."

"You don't know that, Hunter," she informed him. "You don't know what the admiral is capable of doing. My friends are expendable. That means he's perfectly willing to kill anyone who gets in his way, which includes me." Kasey shook her head. "I'm not stupid enough to believe he won't kill me after he gets what he wants."

Hunter stared at her for a long moment in silence before finally responding. "That won't happen," he informed her while staring into her eyes. "I won't allow it."

As Hunter turned and walked away, Kasey watched him until he was gone. Colton and Jamie approached her with matching looks of concern.

"What was that about?" Colton asked.

Kasey glanced at her friends and offered a tiny smile. "I think he can be converted to our side," she informed them.

Chapter Twenty-nine

Around six o'clock that evening, Diesel took Colton and Jamie upstairs to dinner, which was what Kasey had requested. There was no reason why her friends should starve alongside her. Kasey knew she was becoming a liability to Jamie and Colton. They were in danger because of her, and she couldn't stop harping on that fact. While left alone with her thoughts, Kasey paced the living room portion of the basement cell. She heard movement in the corridor, alerting her that someone was coming. Kasey jumped on the sofa, curled up, and pretended to be asleep. She listened to the distinctive clatter as the cell door was unlocked. Hunter entered with a covered dinner tray and set it on the coffee table.

"I know you're awake," Hunter announced with little emotion. "You soaped the camera lenses again after you promised you wouldn't."

Kasey didn't respond and continued pretending she was asleep. Hunter approached her and slapped her on the ass. Kasey cried out with surprise and eyed him.

"That hurt!"

"That's what you get for ignoring me," he informed her, then smirked. "Lord knows you need a good spanking."

Kasey slowly pulled herself into a sitting position with her legs partially under her. "When do I get to slap you around?"

"Put on a leather bodice and three-inch stiletto heels, and I'll consider it."

Hunter collapsed onto the opposite end of the sofa and casually reclined in the corner with one leg on the couch and his arm draped over the back. Kasey eyed him and his sexually provocative pose.

"I thought you were entertaining Colton and Jamie?" she remarked.

"They were bickering like an old married couple from the moment they sat at the table," Hunter informed her. "It was then that I realized how much I missed you giving me the silent treatment, so I brought you some dinner."

"Thanks, but I'm not hungry."

"You have to eat."

Kasey considered the comment and then shook her head. "Actually, I don't. We covered this earlier," she informed him, then smirked somewhat deviously. "Be sure to lock the door on your way out. There are a lot of sketchy characters running around this neighborhood."

"You promised you'd be nice."

"This is me being nice."

"It needs some work."

"Promising to be nice doesn't include whatever little plan of seduction you have in mind," she remarked.

"What plan of seduction?" he asked with some surprise. "You've lost me."

"You waltz in here and cast yourself on the sofa with that sexy, come-hither pose," she announced, then raised her brow. "There's so much testosterone in this room; it's almost as bad as Colton at the dance clubs at two in the morning, prowling for overnight company."

Hunter studied her a long moment, then smiled. "This is a sexy, come-hither pose?" he asked, appearing curious. "And here I thought this was my 'I just want to watch football' look." His grin then cheapened. "What else do I unintentionally do that you find sexy?"

Kasey groaned, rolled her eyes, and looked away. She wasn't touching that comment. Hunter sighed and stood.

"Well, I hate to disappoint you, but you've exhausted me enough for one day," Hunter announced. "Is there anything else you need before I lock you in for the night?"

She considered the question and then looked at him. "I could use a book."

"Are you asking me to do something nice for you?" Hunter asked.

"No, I'm just asking for a book," Kasey informed him. "Something nice would be you letting me and my friends go home."

"That would be a hell of a lot more than nice," Hunter insisted.

"Now, you're the one exhausting me," she informed him. "Goodnight, Hunter."

Hunter extended his hand to her. "Come on," he announced. "We'll take a little field trip together to the library."

Kasey eyed him with some surprise, then uncertainly accepted his hand and stood. He smiled and held her right hand in his left.

"Now, see, that was being nice on your behalf," he announced.

"What do you mean?"

"You actually took my hand," Hunter informed her. "Yesterday, you would have bit it."

He guided her to the open cell door and passed through it.

"What? No handcuffs?"

"Believe it or not, Kasey," he announced. "I want to trust you almost as much as I want you to trust me."

"Oh, so you're a dreamer?"

"I've been called worse."

"I'll bet."

"Locking the three of you in this cell was a last-resort option," Hunter reminded her. "Everything would have been so much easier if you had just trusted me and left well enough alone."

"But you couldn't be trusted," she reminded him.

"Not the point."

"Kind of is."

Chapter Thirty

Hunter closed and locked the library door before finally releasing Kasey's hand. He showed her the old-fashioned key before slipping it down his pants. One of these times, she would shock him and go for the key. Kasey managed to ignore him and looked around the impressive room. The library was on two levels with ten-foot tall bookcases along three walls and a rolling ladder on a rail to reach the higher shelves. The room had hardwood flooring, many throw rugs, a few plush chairs, two heavy desks, a sofa, and a long window seat. As Kasey walked around the library, Hunter remained close, keeping an eye on her. She ignored him as she looked at the different titles filling the extensive library.

"Obviously, these are for show," Kasey remarked. "No one reads this much crap. A bit like my uncle's library. Probably isn't a single book under one hundred years old."

"I don't know what you're hoping to find," he remarked.

"At least one book by someone who's still living," she remarked, then eyed him. "Must you follow me? You look like a panther ready to pounce."

"I'm pretty sure that's my job."

Kasey pulled out a book and eyed it. "Just a few days ago, your job was to protect me," she reminded him. "Ironic that you were the one I needed protection from."

"Not true."

"And just so we're on the same page," Kasey informed him matter-of-factly. "I'm officially firing you as my bodyguard."

Hunter chuckled while grinning. "You don't have the authority," he remarked, clearly mocking her.

"Under the circumstances, I'm pretty sure my uncle would agree with my decision," she informed him.

Kasey replaced the book while Hunter remained just on the other side of her and continued to stalk her. She eyed him and casually turned in the opposite direction, which he followed. Kasey turned the other way, and he continued to follow. She again returned her attention to the shelves.

"You will warn me before you pounce, I hope," Kasey remarked.

"If I pounce, it'll be because you forced me to do so," he informed her. "So, yes, you'll have fair warning."

Kasey eyed him and smiled somewhat slyly. "I think we both know you're looking for any opportunity to pounce," she announced. "You enjoy it just a little too much."

"That might be a bit of a reach."

Kasey walked past the shelves of books while watching him and seductively ran her fingers along the dusty spines. She maintained a tiny, almost lustful smile. Hunter continued to follow and watched her with an intrigued grin. Kasey passed by one of the library tables with some writing material on it. She ran her hand along the desk while he followed a couple of feet away on the other side. A small, stiletto letter opener vanished as her hand slid across the top of the desk. Kasey turned toward the next wall of bookshelves and continued to search the titles, the sexual tension quickly fading. She removed a book, eyed it a moment, and turned back toward Hunter while flashing the book along with a smile.

"Found one," she announced cheerfully. "I know you were looking for an opportunity to pounce, but I'm sorry to disappoint you."

Hunter remained still and watched her. Kasey casually set the book down on a nearby table and smiled at him.

"Too bad," she informed him. "I kind of like the way you pounce."

Hunter stared at her a moment. Despite the lack of reaction on his face, his body tensed slightly at the comment. Kasey smiled slyly.

"I'll bet you won't be able to sleep tonight if you don't get to stop me from one escape attempt," she remarked. "I'd really hate to think you're not earning your keep."

Kasey maintained her smile and darted several feet toward the door. Hunter bolted after her. She stopped, smiled, and paced in the opposite direction. Hunter now smiled and followed her. Whatever their game, he was enjoying it just as much. Kasey ran her hand along the bookshelf ladder as she passed it. She suddenly turned, jumped on it, and rode it down the bookshelves toward the door. As it crashed to a stop at the end, Kasey used the forward momentum to toss herself on top of a nearby table. Hunter darted for her to cut off her path. Instead of running, Kasey stood on the desk, towering over him, and smiled slyly.

"Maybe you're not so much a panther as an alley cat," she remarked. "You'll need to do better."

Hunter grinned while extending his hand to help her down. She ignored his hand while seemingly lost in her own world.

"My mother, God rest her soul, wanted me to be a dancer," she informed him, then laughed at the thought. "Ballet."

Kasey placed her arms above her head and did a little ballet action while standing on the desk. As she landed flat on her feet, she suddenly leaped over his head, somersaulted, and landed on her feet on the floor behind him. Hunter whirled around with surprise by the swift action. Kasey then did a round-off back handspring away from him and landed in a graceful seated position on the desk across the room. She crossed her legs and smiled seductively.

"Ten grueling years of gymnastics," Kasey informed him.

Hunter cautiously approached her but now kept his distance. The way she sprang over him must have been cause for concern.

"My father, well, stepfather, wanting me to be the perfect lady," she informed him. "He insisted I take ballroom dancing classes."

Kasey sprang off the desk and did a princess bow, pretending to hold her long gown.

"So he could dress me up as a little princess and land me that prince," she remarked, then smirked. "Can you ballroom dance?"

"I can fake the waltz," he replied as his grin increased.

"Embry and I swing dance when no one's home," she informed him.

Hunter appeared surprised by the admission. "Embry can swing dance?"

"Yes, he's very good," she informed him. "He's quite bendy for a fifty-year-old man. He does yoga too."

Kasey moved into a yoga position that was noticeably tai chi. Hunter watched while intrigued, realizing that her moves were clearly karate.

"He taught you that?" Hunter asked with some surprise.

"Yeah."

"And how long has he been teaching you *yoga?*" Hunter asked.

"Eight or nine years."

Hunter hid his smile and laughed while shaking his head. Kasey stared at him while taking offense to his amusement.

"What's so funny?"

"Just trying to imagine you and the butler swing dancing and doing yoga between tea and dusting," Hunter remarked.

"Don't knock Embry," she scoffed. "He's the greatest man I've ever known."

"And what makes him so great?" Hunter asked while cocking his head, clearly amused.

"He saved my life, and he's my best friend," Kasey insisted. "I watched him pull a knife from his leg and stab a man in the throat with it. How many men do you know that could do something like that without barely flinching?"

Hunter studied her for a long, silent moment. "He actually did that?" he asked. "Your uncle didn't mention that."

"That's because Embry didn't want to sound like the hero that he was," she replied. "He wanted me to tell everyone there was a struggle for the knife, and he didn't intentionally kill the guy." She shook her head. "But what he did was next to shocking." Kasey considered the comment and reflected on that night. "If he had wanted to, I think he could have taken the man alive, but he chose to finish it, you know, for me." She raised her brows. "He wanted to ensure that man would never come after me again."

"That's quite a bit of rage for a seemingly quiet guy like that," Hunter remarked. "I'd never imagine him capable of something like that."

"Well, the killer tried to force himself on me," Kasey informed him. "Having seen that, I think that's what pushed Embry over the edge."

Hunter silently stared at her for a moment, then appeared uneasy as he stiffened. "I didn't hear about that either," he announced in a tone that conveyed a hint of anger.

"I only ever told Jamie about that," she informed him. "It wasn't essential for the investigation, and repeating it made me violently ill."

Hunter was silent for a long moment while studying her. "You know I'd never do anything like that, right?"

"You have your faults, but I don't think that's one of them," she informed him.

"What brought you to that conclusion?" he felt compelled to ask.

"That night when you were drunk," she replied, then shrugged. "You walked away when you didn't have to."

"Yeah, I wasn't drunk," he told her with a tiny mocking smile. "If I had actually gotten drunk, Diesel would never have let me live that one down."

"I should have guessed," she muttered.

Kasey returned to the bookshelves and again walked along them, heading back to the library door. Hunter once more followed. Kasey casually eyed the books while running her fingers along them as she passed.

"Your boss, the admiral, doesn't live here, does he?"

"No one does."

Kasey didn't look at him but continued to scan the books. Hunter casually followed while now observing her.

"But he's here now, isn't he?"

"No."

Kasey eyed him with a smile. "Liar."

"What makes you think he's here?" Hunter asked while hiding his humored grin.

Kasey returned to the books and paused by the ladder on the other side of the room. She casually leaned her back against the ladder in a somewhat sexual manner and smiled at him.

"There's a third person among you," she informed him. "Someone's keeping an eye on our cell through those cameras."

Hunter watched her and the seductive way she leaned against the ladder. "No, it's just Diesel and me."

"You wouldn't have known about the cameras as quickly as you had without a third eye," Kasey informed him. "I think I know why the admiral won't show himself."

"Because he's not here."

"It's all adding up real fast," she informed him. "You don't give me enough credit for intelligence, Hunter, but I've listened to the things you've said and what I've seen, and it all makes sense now." Kasey casually approached him and placed her hand on his chest. "He won't show himself or talk to me because I already know him, and he doesn't want me to know it's him."

Kasey walked past him and toward the door. Hunter followed, casually cut off her path, and walked toward her. Kasey turned and walked away from him while he continued to follow her.

"Your assumption is incorrect."

Kasey snorted a soft laugh, returned to the bookcase, and leaned seductively against it. "No? Those spy cams aren't there to keep an eye on me; they're there to keep you and Diesel in line," she informed him. "You aren't allowed to harm me, and I'm guessing you're forbidden from any and all sexual activity where I'm concerned as well because *he* doesn't want you touching me." Her smile increased.

"The taste in books and movies; my favorite shampoo and soap; the fact that the clothing is my size." She snorted a laugh. "Hell, even the drinks in the mini-frig are what I drink. He knows me very well." She stared into his eyes. "I know who the admiral is, so it's probably time you called him out and got this over with."

Hunter's expression never changed as he continued to stare at her. "You're so far from the truth on almost everything you've said; I don't even know where to start."

"Then you'll just have to prove me wrong," she replied. "I'm guessing the monitors for the security cameras are in the servants' quarter just off the kitchen. That's the only place I haven't been, so that's probably where the admiral has been hiding." She maintained her devious smile. "So we're just going to take a walk over there and have a look."

Kasey headed toward the library door. Hunter casually cut her off, blocking her with his body, keeping her from leaving even though she didn't have the key to unlock the door.

"You seem to be mistaken about who's actually in charge here," Hunter informed her. "I decide where we go, and you're not leaving the library until I say you can."

"I'm ready to test that theory," she announced while cocking her head and then extended her hand. "Give me the key to the door."

Hunter smirked and snorted a laugh. "Take it," he casually replied. "You know where it's hidden."

"Fine."

Kasey took a step closer to him and wasn't too surprised when he didn't back down, his smile clearly mocking her. He knew she wouldn't go through with her threat. While keeping her eyes locked on his, she grabbed his belt buckle with her left hand and slipped her right hand down his pants. A startled Hunter grabbed her hand, stopped her, and quickly stepped back.

"You could at least buy me dinner before grabbing my pocket rocket," he announced, still somewhat playful.

While he held onto her right wrist, she unbuckled his belt with her left hand, startling him. His playful smile quickly disappeared as he released her hand and buckled his belt.

"Stop that," he insisted, scolding her. "We both know you're not actually going for that key."

Kasey again took a step closer while maintaining her devious smile. "Oh, really?" she asked. "And you're going to stop me?"

Hunter stared at her a moment, grinned, and regained some arrogance. He held his hands up and his arms out, calling her bluff.

"Fine, go ahead," he replied. "Cop a feel. I don't mind."

Although she was aware that he was trying to intimidate and embarrass her, Kasey knew she had to go through with it. If she wanted to prove her theory, she needed to test him and force his hand. If she were right, he wouldn't do anything to hurt her. Kasey forced herself to reach for his belt, but she had to abort her mission between his arrogant smile and his arousal pressing against his pants. She frowned and shook her head.

"You're a real prick, you know that?" she scoffed while folding her arms across her chest and avoiding looking at him.

Hunter maintained his smile while taking a step closer to her. When she looked up to meet his gaze, he affectionately pulled her into his arms. Kasey immediately braced her hands against his chest but didn't actually push him away. She had to at least pretend to protest his arms around her. He gently brushed the hair from her face while staring into her eyes.

"You don't trust me," he remarked while grinning. "I get that." Hunter studied her a moment. "But you also know I'd never hurt you. So where does that leave us?"

Kasey relaxed her hands against his chest and lightly cocked her head. "Where do you want that to leave us?" she asked while searching his eyes.

He considered the question only a moment. "Just you and me, all alone on a moonlit beach," he replied while lowering his mouth to hers.

"That can be arranged," she whispered, warmly kissing his lips.

Hunter groaned and returned the kiss with added passion while Kasey placed her arms around his neck and sank against him. Hunter swiftly guided her to the sofa and lowered her to it without breaking off the kiss. He maneuvered himself on top of her and kissed her neck while gently caressing her body. Kasey ran her fingers through his hair and briefly enjoyed the moment before speaking.

"Although I do have a few conditions," she cooed softly.

Hunter chuckled softly while kissing her neck. He didn't even bother lifting his head and continued working his way down her neckline.

"Of course you do," he warmly replied between kisses. "I'm fully aware of your conditions. Don't worry; I'll come up with something that'll get us both what we want. You just have to trust me."

Kasey drew a deep breath while clinging to his head and sighed softly as she smiled. "I trust you," she whispered.

Hunter groaned while lifting his head and met her gaze with a grin. "I love hearing you say that," he announced, then sought her lips.

As they kissed and caressed each other on the sofa, the library door was jolted, startling them. Hunter jumped off Kasey and leaped to his feet while Kasey sat up on the couch. Hunter was slightly ruffled and turned away to adjust himself. A key rattled in the lock only seconds before the door was thrown open. Diesel stood in the doorway with an annoyed look on his face.

"What the hell are you doing here?" Diesel demanded, then cocked his head. "Taking her out on a date?"

"No, she wanted a book," Hunter remarked while resuming his tough-guy role.

"And you just let her run around?" Diesel demanded as he shook his head.

"I locked the door," Hunter snarled in response, then removed the handcuffs from his jacket pocket. "She wasn't going anywhere."

"I don't give a fuck," Diesel scoffed, then motioned in anger. "Get the princess back to her cell. We have work to do."

Hunter approached Kasey, cuffed her right wrist to his left, and pulled her to her feet before glaring back at Diesel.

"I know what I'm doing," Hunter insisted, turning angry. "Go away."

"Oh, my book!" Kasey announced, then pulled Hunter to the nearby desk and grabbed her discarded book.

Once she had her book, Hunter escorted her to the door and Diesel.

Diesel shook his head while watching them. "She already has your balls in her purse," he scoffed. "You're such a push-over when it comes to women, you little mama's boy."

Hunter sneered at Diesel as he left the library with Kasey in tow. Kasey wasn't sure what had happened between him and Diesel, but she could see Hunter easily turning on him. It was obvious the two were bucking heads over who was in charge, neither willing to back down, which worked in her favor.

Chapter Thirty-one

Hunter and Kasey entered the empty prison living room through the cell door. Jamie and Colton could be heard in the bedroom watching "Psycho" beyond the open bedroom doorway. The sound of the rattling key in the lock must have alerted them. Colton appeared in the doorway and eyed them, obviously concerned for his friend.

"You okay, Kasey?"

As Hunter unlocked the handcuffs tethering Kasey to him, Kasey smiled at Colton and his concern for her welfare.

"Yeah, I'm fine," she replied, then held up the book. "Just went to the library for a book."

Colton nodded, glared at Hunter, and then returned to the bedroom. Hunter stepped into the corridor and turned to close the door. Kasey paused before him in the open doorway and smiled.

"Goodnight, Hunter."

Hunter stared at her a moment and returned the smile. "Goodnight, Kasey."

As Hunter shut and locked the door, Kasey casually leaned her shoulder against the wall and smiled lustfully.

"And for the record," she announced. "I like the way you pounce."

Hunter stared at her a moment, then groaned softly. Kasey flashed a smile, blew him a kiss, and headed toward the bedroom. As she entered the bedroom, she saw Jamie and Colton partially reclined on the bed together while watching the movie. Colton patted the bed alongside him while he and Jamie made room for her. Kasey couldn't resist joining them on the bed.

"What you got there?" Colton asked, indicating the book.

"A little "Poe"."

As the creepy music played, ending the movie, Colton looked at Kasey and Jamie on either side of him and grinned.

"You know, I should stay here tonight for safety," Colton informed them.

Kasey flipped through her book while speaking simultaneously with Jamie.

"Okay."

"No way!" Jamie eyed Kasey with surprise and possible horror. "Did you just say okay?"

"The bed's big enough," Kasey informed her with a casual shrug. "What's he really going to do?"

"Spoon all night," Jamie huffed under her breath.

"Is that such a crime?" Kasey asked.

Colton suddenly clung to Kasey's arm while grinning. "I love you."

Jamie stared at her friend in silent disbelief. "Who are you?" she demanded.

Kasey shut her book and sighed. "We've all been under a great deal of stress," she remarked. "We should support each other. And if Colton wants to poke me in the hip all night, I think he's entitled."

Colton smiled and rubbed his head against Kasey's shoulder. "You're the best friend ever!"

Jamie groaned and rolled her eyes. "She's up to something again."

"Are the lenses still soaped?" Kasey asked.

"Yeah, Diesel didn't even look," Jamie replied. "He just tossed us in here."

"Good," Kasey announced, then grinned at her friends. "I know who the admiral is."

Colton and Jamie stared at her with surprise, giving her their full attention.

"You saw him?" Colton asked.

"No, but I didn't have to," Kasey replied. "It was right in front of us the whole time. The admiral is my uncle."

"Your uncle?" Jamie gasped.

"Not harming us, all of the same interests as my uncle, knowing what shampoo I like, the clothing in my size," Kasey announced. "It makes sense. His enemies killed my aunt and the staff, but they didn't get me." Her smile increased. "He had these guys take me to make it look like I was abducted. He wants me safely hidden."

"But if it's your uncle, why not come right out the first day?" Jamie demanded with some distrust. "Why hide?"

"Maybe he doesn't want me to know it was him, even if it was for my own good," Kasey remarked.

"So we're safe then?" Colton asked and appeared relieved. "End of story. We can go to bed now."

"I have to be sure."

"How?" Colton asked. "He's not here, and they're certainly not going to admit it."

"I'm working on that."

"Well, I, for one, feel better now," Colton announced with some relief. "If it's your uncle, we're all safe."

"That would make me feel better, too," Jamie replied, finally relaxed. "If we got them to admit it, they could let us out of here because we'd stay willingly."

"Enough of that talk for tonight," Colton announced and eyed both women. "The real question. Can I sleep in my shorts?"

Jamie rolled her eyes and groaned.

Chapter Thirty-two

Midnight. All three slept in the large bed with Colton in the middle. He clung to Kasey from behind and appeared to be smiling in his sleep. Kasey woke from her light sleep, looked at the bedside clock, and gently wiggled free from Colton's python grip. After she'd freed herself, Colton turned over and immediately spooned up against Jamie from behind. Kasey quickly changed from her nightshirt and shorts, slipped into her shoes, and grabbed her book from the nightstand. She quietly left the bedroom, shutting the door behind her, and crossed the living area while opening her book. The stiletto letter opener fell from the book's spine. She tossed the book aside, approached the cell door, and worked on picking the lock with the letter opener.

Within minutes, the lock gave, and the door sprang open. Kasey immediately stepped through the doorway and punched the code into the security panel. When the code was accepted, she breathed a sigh of relief. She was confident she had the correct code, but she could have been mistaken, which would have cost her dearly. Kasey then returned the letter opener to the book's spine for safe keeping, set it on the coffee table, and left through the cell door, partially shutting it behind her.

§

One o'clock in the morning. Kasey quietly crept around the dimly lit kitchen, collecting things she would need. She had a well-thought-out scheme and even had a backup plan in case things went sideways. Just because she was almost one hundred percent convinced her uncle was the mysterious admiral calling the shots, she needed a fallback in case she was mistaken.

§

Two o'clock in the morning. After the failsafe of Kasey's plan was in place, it was on to her master plan. She crept along the bland, dimly lit corridor within the staff wing just off the kitchen. She paused by several staff bedroom doors and listened for sounds of life. When she heard any sound that indicated the rooms were occupied, she secretly marked the door with a permanent marker. Kasey counted the three marked doors out of six and considered what she now knew. She had been right; there was a third person among them, which had to be the admiral. Kasey heard movement from one of the rooms, which sounded like someone getting up. She didn't know whether the rooms had their own bathrooms and couldn't risk being caught.

Kasey quickly darted into one of the known vacant rooms and cracked the door open so she could watch the corridor. Hunter walked down the hallway in his boxer briefs, looking half asleep, and entered the kitchen. An opportunity had presented itself, and at the risk of getting caught, Kasey decided it was worth it. She hurried across the hall and entered Hunter's bedroom. The staff bedroom was small and bland, with only hardwood flooring, but it did have its own bathroom. There was a double bed, a nightstand, and a small armoire that probably contained a television. Kasey approached the no-frills bed in the dimly lit room, slipped her hand under the pillow, and removed one of the two guns Hunter had taken off the men in the nightclub. She then hurried back for the door and peered out.

When she saw Hunter returning, she panicked and ran back for the bed, quickly sliding under it. There were a lot of dust bunnies under the bed, possibly not having been swept out in years. She watched them roll and held her breath, hoping they wouldn't roll out from under the bed and give her away. Hunter entered the bedroom, shut the door behind him, and climbed back into bed. In the tight area, Kasey remained quietly under the bed and mouthed a curse.

§

Three o'clock in the morning. Kasey had patiently remained under Hunter's bed for over an hour, giving him plenty of time to fall back to sleep. Despite her racing heart and her spike of adrenaline, she quietly slid out from under the bed, preparing to make her escape. Hunter groaned softly and turned on the bed. Kasey slid back under the bed and remained silent, listening to the man moving around on the mattress above her. The bed bounced slightly, and Hunter was heard hitting his pillow before groaning in disgust. When the television came on, partially brightening the room, Kasey shut her eyes and mouthed another curse.

§

Six o'clock in the morning. The floorboard creaking woke Kasey from her uncomfortable position on the floor beneath Hunter's bed. She saw Hunter's bare feet as he walked across the floor while returning from the bathroom. She could hear the faint sound of the shower running, which meant it would soon be her time to evacuate. Kasey watched and waited for her chance to escape when she saw his boxer briefs fall to the floor. She attempted to sneak a peek and saw Hunter's bare backside as he headed into the bathroom. Kasey couldn't deny he had a nice ass. The door only partially closed behind him, but he would soon be in the shower, so she needed to move. Kasey was about to slide out from under the bed when the bathroom door opened again, and Hunter walked back out.

Kasey remained still while looking out, tilted her head, and admired Hunter's full frontal nudity, complete with morning wood. She mouthed the word 'wow' and knew that image would be burned into her mind for the rest of the day. Hunter returned to the bathroom and partially closed the door again. This time, the shower curtain was heard sliding into place. Sore and stiff, Kasey slid out from under the bed and hurried for the bedroom door. She quietly scurried along the staff wing corridor and paused before the kitchen door. She listened for a moment but didn't hear anything. One of the bedroom doors opened behind her. Kasey withheld her gasp and quickly slipped into the kitchen to avoid getting caught.

As she hurried across the kitchen, out of the corner of her eye, she noticed someone standing near the counter. Kasey spun with surprise while aiming the gun at the man. Embry stood by the counter facing her. Although dressed in black combat fatigues, there was no mistaking it was Embry. Unable to move, they stared at each other with the same shocked expressions for a moment. Kasey slowly lowered the gun at the sight of her dear friend standing in the kitchen of her island prison.

"Embry--?" she gasped as her mind raced, processing the new information.

With the way he was dressed, he looked more like a mercenary than a butler. A look of horror suddenly swept over her, and she aimed the gun at him with realization.

"Oh, God, no!" she cried out.

Embry just stared at her with a stunned look. He didn't even lift his hands from the counter.

"Kasey, I--"

"How--how could you?"

Embry stared at her and just shook his head, appearing unable to speak. When the servants' wing door opened, Kasey spun and fired twice without aiming or even looking. Diesel dove back into the staff wing corridor.

"Jesus Christ," Diesel cried out.

Kasey turned the gun back on Embry, who still hadn't moved. "Talk!" she screamed. "Talk or so help me, God, I'll shoot you!"

"I'm sorry, Kasey," Embry just about whispered. "I'm so sorry!"

Tears streaked Kasey's face as she cried out before repeatedly pulling the trigger. Embry shut his eyes but didn't move. Several bullets flew past him and splintered the cupboard behind him near his head. He opened his eyes and again looked at her. Not a single shot had hit him. Kasey kept the gun aimed at him with a hateful look on her face. The door to the servants' wing partially opened, revealing Diesel down low with his gun aimed. Embry looked at the door, saw Diesel, and panicked.

"No!" Embry cried out while waving his arm. "Leave us!"

Diesel kept his gun aimed at Kasey from his position near the floor but didn't fire. Kasey turned and ran from the kitchen. Once she was gone, Diesel appeared from the corridor and ran across the kitchen after her.

Embry leaped over the island counter and stopped him, despite that Diesel towered over him. "Let her go."

"But she--" Diesel began.

"She's not going anywhere," Embry informed him. "Get down to the basement and make sure Jamie and Colton are still locked up."

Diesel nodded without comment and hurried to the secret basement entrance in the closet.

§

Kasey sat on the beach, hugging her knees to her chest while staring at the ocean shortly after sunrise. The gun was draped casually from her hand while she was mentally a million miles away. Hunter walked across the sand and approached with extreme caution.

"Kasey?"

Kasey didn't respond or react to his words or his presence. Hunter moved closer to her and joined her on the sand, sitting alongside her. Kasey casually handed him the gun dangling from her index finger and thumb without looking at him.

"Out of bullets."

Hunter took the gun and slipped it down the back of his pants. "Jamie and Colton are in the kitchen waiting to have breakfast with you," he informed her. "They're concerned about you."

"Is *he* in there?"

"Yes."

"I'm fine here," she scoffed, lacking emotion.

"That wasn't a request," Hunter informed her. "We have to go inside."

"Yeah, well, right now, I don't give a fuck," she muttered and waved him off. "Do what you have to do." She then cast an evil, hateful look at him. "You knew about him." She looked back at the ocean. "I'm finished with you too."

"Look, either I bring you in or Diesel will," he informed her in a gentle tone. "And just so you know, you shot Diesel, so he's not exactly crazy about you right now."

"Take me back in there, and I'm going to kill that bastard, Embry," she remarked, then glared at Hunter. "And, just so we're clear, you might be next."

Hunter took her hand and gently caressed it as she looked away, showing no emotion. The handcuff clicked as it gently connected to her wrist and then his.

"You're safe here, Kasey," Hunter gently reassured her. "He would never hurt you, and if he'd try, I'd kill him."

Kasey looked at Hunter and his reassuring look. "He hurt me," she informed him without emotion. "Kill him."

"You don't want him dead."

"Reload the gun," she casually announced. "Let's find out."

Chapter Thirty-three

Colton and Jamie sat at the table with their wrists cuffed to each other as Kasey and Hunter entered the kitchen. Kasey's friends looked up and stared at her, but neither said a word. Diesel stood by the island counter while Embry patched the bullet graze wound on his upper arm. Diesel glared at Kasey with a vengeance, then sneered, slipped into his bloodstained shirt, and approached the coffeepot, putting some distance between them. Embry eyed Kasey's wrist cuffed to Hunter's.

"Was that really necessary?" Embry asked.

"She's very upset," Hunter remarked, then raised his brow, "and she wants to kill you. So, yes, it's necessary."

"I'll take my chances," Embry replied, then indicated her wrist. "Remove the cuffs."

Hunter sighed and removed the handcuffs. Kasey refused to look at Embry and let Hunter guide her to the table. When she didn't sit, he pushed on her shoulders, guiding her into the seat. Embry approached Kasey, moving alongside her with a cup of tea.

"I made you some tea."

Kasey still refused to look at him. As he set the cup down before her, she elbowed him in his groin. Embry immediately clutched himself and doubled over in moderate agony. Diesel lurched forward, but he was too far away. Hunter swiftly moved between Kasey and Embry, giving Embry time to move before she could strike again.

"Okay, regretting teaching her that," Embry muttered with some discomfort.

Without a second thought, Hunter took the vacant chair alongside Kasey. Despite what had just happened to Embry, Hunter didn't appear concerned for his own welfare.

Jamie slowly leaned across the table while studying Kasey's transfixed expression. "Are you okay?" she whispered.

Kasey didn't look at her friend and didn't respond, making everyone nervous. It was the calm before the storm, and one hell of a storm was brewing beyond Kasey's eyes.

Jamie sat back in her chair as her eyes widened. "Oh, that's not good," she muttered.

Hunter slid Kasey's tea across the table closer to her. Kasey picked up the cup and whipped it across the room at Embry. Jamie and Colton ducked with surprise at the flying teacup. Embry barely avoided the cup as it shattered against the cupboard where his head would have been.

"Let's just lock her up until she calms down," Diesel announced while dropping into the chair at the head of the table.

Embry placed large plates of French toast and sausage on the table, but even Diesel and Hunter were too tense to eat with enthusiasm. Colton sipped his coffee and nervously watched the exchange. He was her friend, and even he was frightened. Embry brought Hunter some coffee and set it on the table before him. Hunter eyed his cup and casually slid it to the side furthest away from Kasey. Embry returned to the main counter, sitting on it rather than joining them. He eyed Kasey, frowned, and looked away. Hunter, Diesel, and Colton finally started to eat while Jamie sipped her tea and nervously watched Kasey. The table was unusually silent.

Kasey finally looked at Embry across the kitchen. "Why?" she demanded.

"I'm trying to keep you safe," Embry replied.

"Bullshit," she scoffed. "You're after my uncle's money."

"That's not true," Embry insisted. "Your uncle has enemies who want to harm him. They were planning to use you to do that. We stopped that from happening."

"You lying mother fucker!" she cried out in rage.

"Hey," Embry launched in a stern tone. "Watch your language!"

"Come over here and make me, you cocksucker," Kasey shouted back at him.

"Breakfast in the Navy," Diesel announced with a chuckle. "She's not without her charm."

"Relax, Kasey," Hunter announced in a calm, gentle tone.

Kasey looked away and resumed her silence. Embry eyed Hunter with a strange look.

"You two suddenly seem awfully chummy," Embry scoffed.

Hunter glared at Embry across the kitchen. "I'm running damage control," he snapped back. "She's turning into an emotional wreck. Maybe you can live with what you're doing to her, but I'm getting a little tired of sitting by and watching it."

Kasey looked at Hunter with surprise that he defended her while Embry stared at Hunter with something resembling betrayal.

"Exactly what's been going on between you two?" Embry demanded.

"Nothing," Hunter snapped back. "And I resent the accusation!"

Jamie, Colton, and Diesel watched the exchange with astonishment. Was Hunter switching sides? Had Kasey successfully converted him?

"Relax," Diesel announced to Embry with little interest. "He hasn't touched her."

Embry didn't seem to believe either of his men and glanced at Kasey. "Kasey, is that true?"

She continued to ignore Embry. Hunter shifted uncomfortably as all eyes were now on Kasey. She caught the looks she was receiving and then glared at Embry.

"They're both a couple of dickless, mama's boys, without a brain between the two of them," Kasey snarled in response. "If the pussies didn't have guns, they'd be fucking useless."

"I'm getting a little turned on here," Diesel remarked while grinning.

"Where did you learn such language?" Embry demanded.

Jamie and Kasey pointed at Colton.

Colton appeared stunned and quickly looked around. "Hey, she was corrupt long before I met her," he insisted. "It had to be that one." Colton pointed at Jamie.

Jamie appeared offended. "Yeah, look who's talking," she huffed. "You're like a drunken sailor on shore leave when we go out."

Diesel was amused and chuckled at the breakfast table conversation. Hunter glared at him, clearly not humored.

"Just trying to imagine that pussy in the military," Diesel announced while indicating Colton. "Pretty funny. He wouldn't last a week."

Colton sneered at Diesel.

"Look at all that French toast still left," Jamie announced, attempting to shift their focus to the remaining food. "You guys need to eat more."

The comment appeared to work, with all three men helping themselves to more French toast. As Embry served the guys more coffee, Kasey glared at him. Once he was away from the table, she resumed looking at nothing. Embry remained quiet while leaning against the island counter. He occasionally looked at Kasey with sadness.

Diesel groaned softly and appeared bewildered while holding his stomach. "I think there's something wrong with the sausage," he remarked.

"The sausage was fine," Embry scoffed. "You just eat too fast."

Diesel swayed slightly, placing his hand on his forehead before collapsing on the table. Wanting to check on him, Hunter attempted to stand but was unable to make it to his feet. He clutched the table and immediately sat back down. Without warning, Colton suddenly fell against Jamie. Jamie cried out with surprise and alarm. Hunter held onto the table while looking bewildered and unsteady. Kasey casually moved his plate away as he looked at her emotionless expression and appeared surprised.

"What did you do?" Hunter gasped.

Kasey placed her arm around his shoulders from the front and helped lower his head to the table, keeping him from hurting himself. Embry bolted away from the counter with alarm and hurried toward the table. Kasey swiftly removed Hunter's gun from his shoulder holster and aimed it at Embry. Embry stopped only a couple of feet away when he saw the gun aimed at him. Jamie remained alarmed while lowering Colton's head to the table, then looked around at the unconscious men.

"What's wrong with them?" Jamie gasped.

Kasey slowly stood while keeping the gun, and her eyes locked on Embry. Embry stared with concern and possible horror.

"What did you do to them?" he gasped.

"Drugged their coffee," Kasey casually replied. "Nothing that will kill them. They'll just be napping for a while."

"The coffee?" Embry gasped. "How?"

"I've been out of my cage since midnight," she informed him. "I've had many hours to wreak havoc on this place." She cocked her head while glaring at him. "I learned from the master of deceit." Kasey then looked at Jamie. "Get the handcuff keys from Diesel's pocket."

Jamie stood while still cuffed to Colton and attempted to find the keys on Diesel not far from her. Kasey moved slowly around the table for a clear line of sight on Embry.

"Now, I'm a little low on bullets," she informed Embry. "So you'll understand if I don't purposely try to miss you this time."

Jamie found the handcuff keys and unlocked the cuffs from her and Colton.

Kasey maintained her glare at Embry. "You and I are going to play a little truth or dare," she informed him, then looked at Jamie. "Place the handcuffs on the island counter and move away from him."

Jamie set the handcuffs on the counter and quickly moved away from Embry.

Kasey indicated the cuffs to Embry. "Put them on."

Embry eyed the handcuffs and picked them up while showing little emotion.

Kasey shifted her attention to Jamie. "Check Diesel for a gun."

Jamie hurried to Diesel and searched him. She looked up and shook her head. "None on him."

"He had one on him earlier," Kasey assured her. "It's in the kitchen somewhere. Find it."

Jamie nodded and mistakenly passed between Kasey and Embry. Embry seized the opportunity and grabbed Jamie while she was blocking the shot. In that split second, he cuffed her wrist to the drawer handle. As he darted behind the island counter, Kasey pulled the trigger. The gun clicked empty. Hunter's gun wasn't loaded? Kasey cursed and darted across the kitchen. She jumped onto the wheeled kitchen armchair and rode it across the floor as Embry leaped over the island counter to block her path to the servant's quarter. The chair plowed into him. As Kasey rolled off the chair and across the floor, Embry tossed the chair off him and sprang to his feet. He lunged for Kasey and caught her around the waist from behind, pinning her arms.

Kasey stomped on his foot and rammed her elbow back into him. He gasped slightly and released her out of reflex. She then spun and threw a punch for his face. He blocked her fist, caught her wrist, and slammed her backward into the wall with his body. Slightly surprised, Kasey breathed more heavily than Embry did as he held her immobile. He looked into her eyes and immediately turned docile.

"The last thing I want to do is hurt you, Kasey," Embry assured her. "I'll make us some tea, and we'll talk about this." His eyes pleaded with hers. "Please, Kasey--"

"Will you let my friends go?" she asked in the same cold tone.

"I can't," Embry informed her. "They're in just as much danger as you because they know where you are."

"Then we have nothing to talk about," she snarled.

With her free hand by her side, Kasey suddenly grabbed Embry in the crotch. He cried out and released her with pain and surprise. Seeing what was happening, Jamie struggled with her hand cuffed to the drawer. She stopped, considered something, and pulled the drawer all the way out, dumping the contents onto the floor. Kasey again ran for the servant's wing doorway, but Embry recovered from the groin shot and darted after her. He managed to stop her from leaving, but she bolted away before he could grab her. Kasey ran for the kitchen table, tossed herself on top of it, and leaped to her feet just as Embry attempted to grab her. She jumped from the table to the island counter.

As Embry turned and bolted to the counter, Kasey kicked several plates at him, which he easily dodged. She then ran two steps, somersaulted off the counter, landed on her feet, and immediately threw herself into a forward roll. Embry stopped momentarily and stared, surprised at what he'd just witnessed.

"Amazing."

When Embry bolted after her, Kasey whirled around while low to the ground, attempting to sweep his legs out from under him. As he leaped over her leg, Kasey sprang up and kicked to the side, turning her slow Tai Chi yoga movement into its official karate kick. Embry deflected her kick and appeared almost surprised by her move. She sank to the floor and again attempted to sweep his legs. He once more jumped her leg. As she attempted to spring back up, Embry kicked out, struck her in the shoulder, and knocked her onto her back. She attempted to strike him several times as he jumped on top of her, but he blocked each move. Kasey broke free and tried to get to her feet, but he grabbed her from behind and pulled her back against him.

Embry locked one arm around her shoulders and held her arm to her waist with the other, forcing her to more or less sit on his lap while holding her from behind. Kasey struggled but had no leverage. Embry held her tightly against him until she stopped struggling. He kept his face next to hers and spoke softly.

"It's okay, darling," Embry whispered. "No one's going to hurt you, I promise. I'm going to take care of you."

He gently rubbed his cheek against hers and rocked her in his arms as he clung to her.

"I love you more than anything, you know that," he informed her. "No one will ever hurt you again."

"You betrayed me," she snarled. "Nine years I've trusted you. How could you?"

"Eight years," he casually corrected her. "You can trust me. Everything I did, I did for you. I just want to be with you. That's all I've ever wanted." He then hesitated and sighed. "I needed to get you away from your uncle, from all of his enemies who wished you harm. I had to take you someplace safe. We're safe here, and I can take care of you. Let me take care of you."

Kasey gently caressed his hand on her lower arm. "Okay--"

Embry sighed with relief, kissed her cheek, and hugged her. "Everything is going to be okay now," he assured her.

Jamie appeared behind Embry and hit him with the empty drawer on the back of the head. When he released Kasey and fell to the floor, Kasey sprang to her feet, eyed the unconscious man, and then looked at Jamie.

"What took you so long?"

"His words were touching," Jamie remarked, then shrugged. "In a disturbed psychotic sort of way. It was only polite to let him finish."

Kasey rolled her eyes and groaned. "It's time to get these guys to talk."

"What do you intend to do?"

"A little torture with a pleasant sugarcoating," Kasey replied.

Jamie eyed her with concern. "You know, you're starting to scare me."

Kasey ignored the comment. "Let's tie them before they wake up."

Chapter Thirty-four

Kasey and Jamie rolled the three unconscious men tied to kitchen chairs into the nearby library. Embry was out cold, slumped in the arm chair with his wrists duct-taped to each arm and his ankles duct-taped together, while Diesel was bound with duct tape in the same fashion. On the other hand, Hunter was in an armless chair with his wrists handcuffed behind the back of the chair, and his ankles were duct-taped to the chair legs. They rolled Colton in last and gently moved him from the chair onto the sofa. Jamie sat on the sofa next to their unconscious friend and affectionately brushed his hair away from his face. After finding a first aid kit, Kasey tended to the bleeding cut on the back of Embry's head. Although she currently hated him, that didn't alter the fact that she'd spent nine years idolizing the bastard.

"Are you sure they'll be okay?" Jamie asked while doting over Colton.

"They're fine," Kasey insisted. "I used those sleeping pills I found in the desk drawer the other day.

I ground them up and put them into the coffee grounds." She then frowned. "I didn't know the admiral was Embry. He doesn't drink coffee. He drinks tea."

"And if you did, I'm sure I'd be out cold with the rest of them," Jamie muttered.

"True, but you wouldn't be tied to a chair," Kasey remarked while grinning slyly.

"I suppose not," she muttered, then looked back at Colton, studied him, and grimaced slightly. "We kind of accidentally 'did it' this morning."

Kasey stopped dabbing Embry's cut and looked at Jamie with surprise. "You and Colton?"

"Yeah," Jamie replied, then glared at Kasey and turned stern. "It was all your fault."

"How do you figure?"

"You're the one who invited him for a sleepover," Jamie remarked, then shrugged and smiled almost timidly. "He was spooned against me, humping me like a cute little puppy. I couldn't resist."

"Sorry."

"Don't be," Jamie replied and offered a tiny laugh. "He wasn't exaggerating, you know. He is as good in bed as he is on the dance floor." She sank into her own fantasy. "I hope to get him out on the open road and really take him for a test drive."

Kasey rolled her eyes and groaned. "I'm going to be violently ill."

"You'd better get over that real fast," Jamie informed her. "If you're that squeamish, I don't know how you think you're going to torture Embry into talking."

"Leverage, Jamie," Kasey replied. "Know your enemies' weakness and exploit it."

Jamie stood and approached Kasey with a slightly humored smile. "Oh?" she asked. "And what's Embry's weakness?"

"Me."

Jamie stared at her for a moment with a puzzled look. "So you're going to torture *yourself?*" she asked while raising a brow.

"Maybe a little."

"Is this going to make me puke?" Jamie asked with noted concern.

"Quite possibly."

§

Hunter slowly regained consciousness while groaning softly. It only took him a few seconds to realize he was handcuffed to the chair, and he immediately thrashed around to free himself. He looked like a wild animal caught in a snare. Kasey approached, kneeled alongside his chair, and touched his knee while offering a somewhat sympathetic smile. He attempted to control his emotions and stopped struggling.

"How are you feeling?" Kasey asked.

"Fuzzy," he snarled in response. "What did you give me?"

"Prescription sleeping pills in your coffee," she replied matter-of-factly.

Hunter looked around, saw Diesel and Embry were still out, and then looked back at Kasey.

"I promise not to hurt you if you let me go," Hunter insisted.

"I have no intention of hurting you," she informed him while maintaining her smile. "You're safe, I promise. You just need to trust me." Her smile then increased. "I bet that doesn't make you feel any better than it did for me. There's a bit of irony to that, don't you think?"

"Show a little mercy," he remarked with a little less hostility. "You know how I feel about being tied to chairs."

Kasey offered a warm smile and gently rubbed his leg. "You'll be fine, I promise," she informed him.

"Jesus Christ!" Diesel cried out.

Kasey straightened and paced between the three men tied to their chairs. Embry woke as well, possibly having been alerted by Diesel's outburst. Diesel fought the duct tape to no avail.

"Okay, gloves off," Diesel cried out. "I'm beating up both of them."

"Shut up, Diesel," Embry snarled, then looked at Kasey while slightly disoriented. "What the hell did you hit me with?"

"A kitchen drawer," Jamie replied.

There was a moment of silence as Embry surveyed their situation. "What now?" he asked.

Kasey and Jamie casually leaned against the back of the sofa and watched the three men.

Kasey shrugged, showing little emotion. "That all depends on you boys," she announced. "One of you three will tell me what is happening around here and what you're after. This time, I'm demanding the truth."

Jamie flashed the satellite phone and grinned. "I'm thinking the FBI as my first phone call," she announced.

"I've told you the truth," Embry insisted while eyeing both women. "We're protecting you from Vincent's enemies."

"So why not just come out and say so when we arrived?" Kasey demanded while straightening, then shook her head. "No, you're hiding something, and I want to know what it is." A strange smile crossed her face. "And if one of you doesn't spill it, things could get a little *wild* in here."

"Oh, great," Diesel scoffed with increasing agitation. "We're going to be tortured by Girl Scouts." He then glared at Embry. "How the hell do two women get the drop on three Marines?"

"Just keep your mouth shut, Diesel," Embry snarled.

"Marines, huh?" Kasey remarked. "Well, *Admiral*, that does explain some things."

Colton slowly sat up on the sofa with a groan. He held his head a moment and then looked at the three tied men.

"Did I miss something?"

"Your girlfriends are planning on torturing us," Diesel snarled at him. "Try talking some sense into them."

"Don't be such a wuss," Colton scoffed back. "You deserve whatever you get. You don't mess with my girls."

Jamie smiled sweetly, leaned down, and kissed him quickly. He returned the smile while giving her a quick once-over.

"If it's not asking too much," Colton announced a little too cheerfully. "Could I bitch slap Jughead around a little?"

"Ask Kasey," Jamie replied with a shrug. "This is her party."

"It's covered, Colton," Kasey informed him. "But thanks."

Colton slowly and weakly stood and joined them on the other side of the sofa. Jamie gladly helped steady him.

"So?" Kasey announced while eyeing the three men. "No one's willing to talk?"

Embry looked away and frowned. Diesel struggled a little more than grunted and gave up. Kasey paced before the three men while eyeing each one. All three now avoided looking at her and seemed to flip a switch, turning emotionless. Apparently, this wasn't their first rodeo. Kasey paced behind the three men, attempting to work some sort of intimidation on them, not that it would work. She placed her hand on Hunter's shoulder as she moved around him, then stopped and looked down at him. He didn't look up, and neither did the other two. Colton, on the other hand, watched with nervous anxiety and chewed on his fingernail. Kasey placed both hands on Hunter's shoulders, swung her leg over his, and sat, straddling his lap while facing him.

Hunter's eyes suddenly met hers, surprised by her interesting tactic. She offered a tiny, come-hither smile and gently ran her hands along his shoulders and chest. Embry and Diesel now looked and stared with their mouths hanging open. Colton was motionless with his finger still against his lips, equally surprised by what he was witnessing. Jamie bit her lip and had to look up to keep from laughing at Kasey's idea of torture. Kasey seductively opened the buttons on Hunter's shirt and then ran her hands along his bare chest. Diesel was more interested in watching than Embry. Embry was obviously possessive over Kasey, quite possibly jealous, and she was using that against him.

"Torture me instead!" Diesel cried out while just about bouncing in his chair to free himself.

"Shut up," Embry snarled.

Embry looked away and appeared lost in thought. Hunter continued staring at Kasey with some anticipation as her hands traveled his chest. He was fighting the urge to smile at her torturous method, although his breathing became heavier. Kasey leaned down and began warmly kissing his neck. Hunter shut his eyes, and a soft groan escaped his throat while Embry silently raged. Diesel and Colton continued to watch with anticipation.

"That's so hot," Colton announced, then leaned closer to Jamie. "Will you do that to me later?"

"You're on."

Kasey lifted her head, brushed her lips past Hunter's, and passionately kissed him. Hunter groaned and eagerly returned the kiss. As Kasey slowly grinded against his lap, Hunter fought the handcuffs binding him in an attempt to reach her. Kasey broke off the kiss, then moved off his lap and kissed her way down his bare chest to his abdomen with her hands leading the way. Hunter groaned and shut his eyes, apparently enjoying being tortured. Kasey hovered over his lap and ran her hands firmly along his thighs near his crotch. Hunter again groaned with anticipation, and his breathing became even heavier. As Kasey continued to caress his thighs, getting closer to his crotch, Hunter writhed sharply within the chair and now watched her.

When her hand ran over the pronounced bulge in his pants, he shut his eyes and groaned, enjoying the sensation. Kasey looked up at him, met his gaze with a smile, and lustfully raised her brows. In that brief moment, she was able to capture a glimpse of Embry. He still stared straight ahead and refused to watch while his hands tightly gripped the arms of the chair, and his knee bounced furiously. As Kasey began unbuckling Hunter's belt, Hunter's head tilted back while he groaned. When she unbuttoned his pants, Hunter's eyes suddenly opened, and he looked at Kasey with alarm.

"Please, Kasey, stop," Hunter just about gasped.

Kasey was surprised Hunter was the one protesting and eyed him before checking Embry's reaction. Embry's head was back, his eyes were closed, and he clawed into the arm of the chair.

"You can't do this," Hunter announced, returning her attention to him. He then released his breath and groaned softly. "Not in front of your father."

Kasey appeared stunned by his words and looked back at Embry. Embry turned his head away, unable to look at her.

Hunter also turned his head away, unwilling to look at Embry, and frowned. "Sorry, Finn."

"You did the right thing," Embry replied, barely getting the words out.

"No, that's impossible," Kasey remarked while straightening and staring at Embry. "My father died before--"

Kasey's thoughts raced a moment before she approached Embry and stared at him while he avoided looking at her.

"Is it true?" she gasped.

"Yes," Embry replied softly without looking at her. "It's true."

Chapter Thirty-five

Kasey sat on the lower steps of the grand staircase while lost in thought. Her mind was racing with the new information about Embry. It didn't seem possible, but she knew it was conceivable. Her mother said her birth father was in the military, they had a brief fling before he was called back to duty, and he died overseas. Her mother never mentioned him by name, and she had no pictures. Her stepfather married her mother before she was born, and he was the only father she'd ever known, which was why Kasey never questioned it. Perhaps her mother lied about her biological father's death, being it was just a fling with a soldier. And maybe she thought he *had* died.

All the questions she had could be answered by the man sitting in the library, tied to a chair. Jamie approached the stairs from the library and leaned on the banister, studying her friend.

"Are you okay?"

"Yeah, just a little shocked, that's all," Kasey replied and finally looked up. "I'm not sure what I'm feeling right now."

"Relief that Embry's not secretly in love with you?" Jamie questioned.

Kasey snorted a laugh and actually smiled. "I guess that *is* a good thing," she replied.

"Colton thinks we should untie them," Jamie informed her. "Under the circumstances, we should probably consider that."

"They've been tied an entire fifteen minutes," Kasey muttered. "They can stay tied a little while longer. I still want more answers. Even if he is my father, that doesn't mean I should trust him."

"But it's Embry," Jamie reminded her. "You've known him almost ten years."

Kasey finally stood and groaned. "Let's have a talk with dear old Dad first," she announced. "Then we'll consider untying them."

Both walked back to the library. As they entered, it wasn't surprising the men watched them, including Colton.

"Can we untie them now?" Colton asked Kasey.

Kasey looked at Embry, meeting his gaze. "I'd like to discuss current events a little first," she replied and cocked her head. "Are you ready to have an open and honest discussion?"

"I'd rather do it over a cup of tea on the terrace," Embry remarked, "but if this makes you feel more comfortable--"

"Anyone care about my comfort?" Diesel scoffed from his chair.

"Shut up," Embry and Hunter snarled in unison.

The faint sound of a helicopter was heard in the near distance, possibly closing in on the beach. All six looked around and listened to the sound, unsure what to make of it. Embry, Diesel, and Hunter suddenly appeared alarmed.

Embry looked at Kasey with horror in his eyes. "Who did you call?" he gasped.

"No one," Kasey replied, then looked at Jamie, silently questioning her.

Jamie shook her head, denying she had called anyone either.

"Untie us, or we're all dead," Embry announced, now fighting the duct tape binding his wrists to the chair.

Kasey, Jamie, and Colton exchanged looks and silently considered their options. Hunter looked at Kasey, pleading with his eyes.

"Please, Kasey," Hunter begged. "If you've ever trusted me, untie us."

Kasey stared at him for only a moment before removing the keys and swiftly unlocking Hunter's handcuffs. Colton hurried toward them and cut the duct tape holding Hunter's ankles to the chair before moving to Embry.

Kasey removed the loaded gun from the back of her pants and looked at Colton, who briefly glanced at her while busily working.

"Keep an eye on them," Kasey announced. "Hunter, Jamie, and I will check out the helicopter."

§

Kasey, Jamie, and Hunter hurried along the hallway toward the front door. Hunter remained alongside Kasey, stride for stride.

"That gun's not loaded," Hunter informed her matter-of-factly while searching his jacket pockets.

"It is now," she informed him. "I found the full magazine in your pocket. Why wasn't it loaded?"

"I was afraid you'd shoot me," Hunter remarked, then snatched the gun from Kasey while attempting to keep them behind him.

"You mean the other day in the kitchen--?" she asked with surprise.

"Empty magazine," he informed her.

"You're a bastard; you know that?" Kasey scoffed.

"Why keep it loaded? I certainly wasn't going to shoot you," Hunter remarked, then gave a nod. "Stay behind me."

Just before they reached the door, it was suddenly kicked open. Hunter aimed the gun at the door as two heavily armed men entered and aimed their weapons at him. Hunter was possibly considering how heavily outmatched he was and debating his next move when he saw Vincent in the doorway just behind the armed men. Although Hunter didn't shoot, he also didn't lower his weapon.

When Vincent saw Kasey, Jamie, and Hunter, he cried out, "Stand down!"

"Uncle Vincent?" Kasey gasped.

There was a tense moment while Hunter and the armed men had their weapons aimed at one another. Several armed men rushed down the hallway from the kitchen as well and approached them from behind. Hunter had five assault rifles aimed at him, yet he seemed reluctant to lower his puny semiautomatic pistol. One of the men approached and took his gun from him without a fight. Once everyone seemed to relax, Kasey released the tense breath she'd been holding. She couldn't believe her uncle had found her on the remote island.

Vincent appeared relieved and held his arms open to her. "Kasey," he gasped.

Kasey hurried toward him, and they hugged happily. He pulled away almost as quickly and looked over her for any signs of injuries.

"Are you okay?" Vincent asked, then met her gaze while clutching her shoulders. "What happened? We were told people were killed on the ship, and no one could find you or your friends."

"It's a long, complicated story," she replied, smiling with relief. "I'm just glad you found us."

Her cousin Dillon poked his head into the open doorway from the porch and looked around. "Is it safe?" he asked.

"Yes, it's safe," Vincent replied with a moderately amused chuckle.

Dillon entered the foyer and saw Kasey. "Kasey," he announced and approached, pulling her into his arms.

Kasey hugged her cousin in a long, warm embrace. "You came along," she gasped with some surprise, knowing her cousin wasn't exactly the run-into-danger type.

"Of course I did," Dillon replied while holding her. "I was worried sick about you." He then chuckled close to her ear. "Bet you're wishing you'd brought me along on the cruise, huh?"

"You wouldn't have liked it," Kasey reported, then pulled away, forcing him to release her.

Most of the men, dressed in black combat fatigues, looked very similar to one another. Young, tall, and beefy with steely cold eyes. As the men scattered and searched the rooms like a well-formed militia, Kasey and Jamie saw one of the men hurry into the library. The women feared what they'd find and how they'd explain it. Kasey held her breath and was about to speak when the man returned and gave the all-clear sign. Kasey looked at Hunter, who still had one man holding a rifle pointed at him.

"Sir, what about this one?" the armed man asked, indicating Hunter with his aimed weapon.

Dillon rolled his eyes while muttering under his breath, "Shoot him."

Kasey was the only one who heard the comment and glared at her cousin.

"It's okay, Davy," Vincent replied, waving him off. "That's just Kasey's bodyguard."

Davy was about the same height and build as Hunter. His dark hair was buzzed close to his scalp, and he had a few days' worth of facial stubble, although not enough to constitute a beard. He wasn't a bad-looking guy, but he was definitely a tough-looking guy. Davy lowered his rifle but still appeared untrusting. With little emotion, Hunter extended his hand to the man. Davy reluctantly returned the gun he'd confiscated, and Hunter casually replaced it to his shoulder holster.

"The place seems secure," another man remarked. "No one else down here. We'll check the second floor."

"Anyone else with you?" Vincent asked Kasey while looking around.

"Uh, Colton's around somewhere," Kasey replied, then hesitated. "Embry too."

Dillon snorted a laugh, clearly amused at the comment. "That man's got more lives than a cat," he announced.

Vincent approached Hunter and eyed him while smiling. "I'm sure I have you to thank for saving Kasey."

Hunter gave him an acknowledging nod. Kasey approached Jamie and Hunter while casting several glances at the library doorway. Jamie remained tense and bewildered while putting on a brave front as she looked at Kasey.

"Uh, where do you suppose Colton and Embry went?" Jamie asked, silently conveying her concern over what the men *didn't* find in the library.

"Your guess is as good as mine," Kasey muttered to her friend while nervously folding her arms across her chest.

"I'm sure they're around," Vincent replied with little concern, having overheard them. "The men I hired won't shoot them without provocation. They're not as frightening as they look."

Kasey noticed the doubt in Hunter's eyes. He wasn't convinced of that.

Dillon joined them while looking around the impressive mansion. "Whose place is this anyway?" he asked.

"It was abandoned when we got here," Kasey replied. "Looks like it's been that way for a least a month or longer, but the pantry was full, so we haven't exactly been roughing it."

"Well, why don't we see if there's some coffee while we wait for Embry and Colton to surface," her uncle announced, then offered a smile. "I'm sure you're eager to return home."

"More than you know," Jamie muttered.

"The kitchen is a bit of a mess," Kasey informed her uncle while internally fidgeting, then clutched Jamie's arm. "Why don't Jamie and I clean up from breakfast a little first and make some fresh coffee? We'll call you when the coffee is ready."

"Are you sure?" Vincent asked.

"Yeah, there's a fully stocked bar in the game room," Kasey informed him. "Maybe the guys want a drink after their little shock and awe."

"It's a little early for drinks," Vincent remarked.

"That's your opinion, Dad," Dillon eagerly announced while clapping his hands together. "I'm always up for a drink or two."

"It's this way," Hunter replied, motioning for them to follow him to the game room.

Vincent, Dillon, and four others followed Hunter to the game room, giving Jamie and Kasey a chance to hurry back into the kitchen. Hopefully, the men who entered through the kitchen didn't think much of the mess left behind.

Chapter Thirty-six

Kasey and Jamie quickly entered the kitchen and gathered the dishes and scattered items from the floor. They had to clean the place so it didn't look like a domestic dispute had occurred. Jamie remained tense and eyed Kasey.

"What are we doing, Kasey?" Jamie asked, practically trembling from her rising anxiety. "Colton is missing. There's no telling what Diesel and Embry intend to do to him. Shouldn't we tell your uncle what really happened?"

Kasey quickly tossed the leftover food from the plates into the garbage and glanced at Jamie. "This is all moving too fast," she insisted. "I'm not ready to throw Embry under the bus just yet. If he's right, we might still be in danger."

"They *took* Colton," Jamie protested while pointing at the kitchen door. "If we don't say anything, we may never get him back."

Hunter entered the kitchen with all four rolling chairs from the library. Kasey and Jamie both jumped when they saw him. After placing the chairs in their proper places at the table, he casually removed a small patch of duct tape from the arm of one chair.

"Well, this has been a productive morning," Hunter remarked as he threw the duct tape in the garbage.

"What have they done with Colton?" Jamie demanded while approaching him, displaying her anger.

"Don't worry about Colton. He's fine," Hunter insisted, turning moody. "We have bigger concerns right now."

Jamie wasn't happy with Hunter's response, but she resumed cleaning the mess, although remaining tense about the whole situation. Kasey approached Hunter, stopped directly in front of him, and looked into his eyes.

"Hey, you should be grateful I didn't sell you out," Kasey snapped in response. "The way I see it, you've got a clean slate, so you're in no position to give orders."

"How can you be so suspicious one minute and so naive the next?" Hunter demanded while attempting to keep his voice down. "Who are those heavily armed men with your uncle? Did he just find them in the yellow pages under mercenaries? You can't trust him."

"No, I can't trust you," Kasey snarled back at him. "You're the one who's been holding us prisoner for the last two days."

"And I was working on rectifying that, per our *conversation* in the library last night," Hunter informed her. "Before you went all Lizzy Borden on us this morning."

"Lizzy Borden hacked her parents into little pieces with an axe," Kasey informed him. "I hardly think there's a comparison."

"Psycho chick analogy," he grumbled. "Point made."

Kasey folded her arms across her chest while glaring at him. "And who turned me into a psycho chick?" she demanded, then raised her brows. "As for that little seduction scene last night in the library, that was all bullshit. I just wanted you on my side." She immediately regretted the lie but didn't want to walk it back and appear weak. She waved him off. "It's not important. We're going home. End of story." Kasey stared at him a moment while raising her brows. "I'm giving you the choice to come with us, but no one's forcing you. I'm sure you have your own way off this rock." She then indicated the kitchen. "If you want to keep your freedom, stop complaining and help us clean this mess."

Hunter frowned, then helped Kasey and Jamie clean up the last of the mess. He replaced the slightly mangled utensil drawer while Jamie gathered the utensils scattered across the floor. Hunter finally approached Kasey and watched her dump the tainted coffee down the drain. When she set the coffeepot down, he grabbed her around the waist and pulled her against him. Kasey gasped with surprise, braced her hands against his chest, and stared into his eyes. His motive concerned her, but she didn't fight him.

"I *am* grateful that you covered for me," Hunter replied in a less confrontational tone. "Despite what you say, I know you trust me, and I know our conversation last night wasn't bullshit." He stared into her eyes, searching for any indication that he was right. "Don't let your uncle's hired men with the big guns give you a false sense of security. I believe you're still in danger, and I need you to trust me as if your life depends upon it."

Kasey relaxed her hands against his chest while staring into his eyes. "And I believe you, but I don't want to be here," she gently informed Hunter while subconsciously caressing his chest and shoulders. "No matter how good your intensions were, you put my friends and me through hell with your elaborate scheme." Kasey then focused on her hands, which continued to caress his shoulders. "You're very lucky I have a weak spot for you, Hunter, or this day might have turned out a lot differently for you and your friends."

Kasey forced herself to pull out of his arms despite his refusal to release her. He captured her hands and held them. She was reluctant to pull her hands from his but maintained a serious look while raising her brows.

"I want Colton returned," Kasey announced in a stern tone. "You and Embry have your own choices to make. This is a one-time offer, Hunter. You two can either return to life as usual before the abduction, walk away, or try to remain in power and have a showdown with those men out there."

Jamie cast a nervous glance at Kasey and Hunter, anticipating his response. As Kasey pulled her hands from his, Hunter stared into her eyes and was reluctant to comment. Embry appeared on the back stairs, now changed into more appropriate and familiar clothing.

"I'd very much like to return to life as usual," Embry announced in a docile tone, unable to look her in the eyes. "If you'll let me."

Hunter shut his eyes as if in pain and looked away. Kasey looked at Embry by the back stairs. He met her gaze with a lost and sad look.

"Just because I haven't turned you in, that doesn't mean I've forgiven you for what you've done," Kasey informed him.

"I know, and I'm willing to live with that," Embry replied. "I just want to remain in your life as much as possible. Even if you do hate me."

Kasey stared at him a moment in silence, then finally groaned. "I don't hate you, Embry," she reluctantly replied. "And I'm willing to give you a second chance."

Embry smiled gently and nodded his appreciation. Hunter looked back at him with a hard-to-read expression.

Embry fidgeted. "Sorry, Hunter," he announced. "I have to do what's best for my daughter and me. You're not obligated to stick around if you don't want to."

"It's a big risk," Hunter informed him. "Either one of them could have a change of heart at any time and turn us in."

"I'm willing to risk that," Embry replied, then drew a tense breath while staring at Hunter. "I don't expect you to take that risk blindly, so you can leave with Diesel as soon as it's safe."

Hunter looked back at Kasey while indicating Jamie. "Does Jamie share your sympathies toward her abductors?" he asked.

Kasey looked at Jamie, who now watched them closely with anticipation. "Are you willing to stick to the story I gave my uncle?" Kasey asked. "Will you agree to being stranded and never repeating that we were held against our will?"

"Well, no one actually got hurt," Jamie remarked, then shrugged. "And Hunter did save us from those men on the ship. I suppose I could pretend the rest didn't happen." She then hesitated, and her look turned stern. "On the condition that someone bitch slaps Diesel for breaking into my room and carrying me caveman style down the stairs."

"I'm sure someone would be willing to do that for you," Embry replied.

"Okay," Jamie announced with a defeated sigh. "But if anything happens to me, Kasey, or Colton, I promise you, there will be a letter implicating the three of you."

"Naturally, you're entitled to some added insurance," Embry assured her.

Kasey and Embry glanced at Hunter, curious about his decision.

Hunter groaned softly while scratching his bearded chin, then met Kasey's gaze. "I'm in," he replied with a sigh. "I'll happily hold your purse while you lingerie shop."

"Oh, that ship sailed," Kasey announced boldly. "You've got more than enough pockets to carry all my stuff. I'm leaving the purse behind."

Jamie suddenly grinned but withheld her laugh. "You're going to make him carry tampons in his jacket pocket as punishment, aren't you?"

"Oh, definitely."

Chapter Thirty-seven

A few of Vincent's hired men sat at the bar in the game room and had a couple of drinks while Embry played bartender to them. While Vincent played a game of pool with Hunter, Kasey sat at the nearby pub table with Dillon and alternated watching the men play pool and Jamie and Colton slow dancing to a song on the jukebox. She had her own concerns and doubts, and they weren't going to vanish now that they were rescued.

Dillon watched her and appeared curious. "Are you okay?" he asked.

Kasey snapped out of her thoughts and looked at her cousin. "Yeah, I'm fine," she replied, then smiled tensely. "It's just been a long, rough couple of days."

"Dad said you were in the nightclub when it was shot up," Dillon remarked, then cringed slightly. "That must have been terrifying."

"Yeah, it was pretty intense," Kasey replied, then shuttered slightly.

"Did you want to talk about it?"

"Jamie and I were pretty wasted when it went down," Kasey timidly informed him, not wanting to get into any details for fear of slipping up. Dillon and her uncle couldn't know Embry wasn't with them during the attack, or his being on the island wouldn't make any sense. "It's all kind of a blur for us." She then focused on Hunter lining up his next shot at the pool table. "If it hadn't been for Hunter, there's no telling what would have happened to us."

Dillon followed Kasey's gaze to Hunter. Just before Hunter made his shot, his eyes flicked up and met Kasey's gaze. Even though he showed no reaction, Dillon cocked his head and noticed the look they seemed to share.

"Did I miss something?" Dillon asked while studying her.

She looked at Dillon, feeling her cheeks redden slightly. "What do you mean?"

"Before you left for the cruise, you couldn't stand the guy," he remarked. "Now, you're looking at him, well, *differently.*"

Kasey immediately shook her head and shifted uncomfortably. "You're reading too much into it," she informed her cousin. "I'll admit; he could be a real prick at times, but when all hell broke loose in that nightclub, he took charge of the situation and got us out of there. It's hard to hate the man who saved your life."

"Yeah, you're probably right," Dillon remarked, then managed a smile. "Everything will go back to normal once we return home." He then hesitated. "Well, Dad will probably want you bubble-wrapped for a few months, but that'll eventually wear off."

Kasey snorted a laugh. "I'm sure I'll be a little gun-shy myself," she remarked.

"Then I guess you won't mind if I hang around a little more," Dillon remarked, then smiled almost timidly. "For your protection."

"You don't need to worry about me so much, Dillon," she insisted. "I have Hunter watching over me.

You can't stop living your life because you're worried about me."

"My life has been a parade of stupid parties and drunken flings," he insisted while raising a brow. "I think it's time I became the responsible, dependable type, don't you think?"

Kasey placed her hand on Dillon's lower arm and met his gaze. "I think you need to do what makes you happiest," she insisted. "Don't alter your life because of me."

Dillon nodded with conviction. "You know," he announced. "You're absolutely right. I should do what makes me happy. Sometimes, Dad gets in the way of that."

Kasey snorted a laugh and had to smile. "Yes, Uncle Vincent sometimes does do that," she replied. "But, he's not always wrong."

"Maybe, but he's always done whatever made him happy over the years," Dillon informed her. "No one could tell him what to do." He held up his empty glass and indicated the bar. "I'm going to get another drink. Did you want something?"

"No, I'm going to get a cup of tea and relax before we leave," she informed him.

"We'll talk more on the helicopter ride home," he insisted, then headed to the bar.

Kasey's cousin was only gone a moment before Vincent approached the table and offered a slightly humored smile.

"Dillon being the overly protective brother type?" Vincent asked.

"I'm used to it," Kasey replied with a sigh. "He's been that way ever since Aunt Nat died. I guess he's never moving back to his own apartment now. I wish he didn't worry about me quite so much. I think it's affecting his social life."

"It's complicated," Vincent remarked, somewhat defeated. "The night his mother died, and you were attacked, he was at a party trying to pick up girls. I think he feels guilty for not being there for you and Natalie."

"He shouldn't feel guilty," Kasey informed him. "He didn't even live at home when that happened. No one expected him to be there."

"Maybe it's me who feels guilty then," Vincent replied, frowning. "I should have been home that night." He then looked at her. "I also wish I'd gone on that cruise. Maybe I could have prevented what happened."

"I doubt that would have changed the outcome any, and you can't watch over me twenty-four seven," Kasey reminded him. "That's why you hired Hunter, remember?"

"I suppose," he replied, then seemed to sink into thought while watching her. "I don't mean to pry, dear, but is something wrong?" He placed his hand on her shoulder. "As close as the two of you are, you seemed a little cool toward Embry ever since he came into the room."

Kasey tensed that her uncle noticed her mood toward Embry but managed a smile.

"Well, you know Embry," Kasey replied, attempting to remain lighthearted. "He's always been so protective over me."

"And you've never seemed to mind before," her uncle pointed out.

"The attack on the ship pretty much rattled all of us," Kasey informed him, "and sometimes you do things you may not otherwise do."

"What are you trying to say?" Vincent asked, now curious.

"Nothing," she replied with a low groan, then hesitated. "Well, nothing that really matters. I may have gotten a little closer to Hunter than Embry would have liked, and I may have told him to mind his own business."

Vincent appeared slightly surprised and eyed Hunter by the pool table. Hunter had finished his shot and now watched them, possibly realizing they were discussing him.

Vincent looked back at Kasey and raised his brow. "How close?"

Kasey laughed softly while hiding her smile. "Not *that* close."

"I'm glad to hear that," Vincent replied, somewhat relieved. "I'd hate to seem ungrateful and have to fire the bastard. He knows you're off-limits, and I was very specific about that when I hired him."

"Well, that would explain why he kept his distance," Kasey remarked.

"Even better yet," Vincent replied and appeared pleased. "After that last one, I was reluctant to hire another bodyguard." He then indicated the pool table. "Well, let me finish getting my ass kicked in this game, and we can be on our way. These guys I've hired aren't cheap, and I don't want to pay for them to be hungover."

As Vincent approached the pool table, Hunter glanced at Kasey. They exchanged looks longer than they should have before Kasey finally looked away. She felt her entire body tense with all that had happened the last few days. Her sultry interrogation of Hunter also crept into her mind. Honestly, she was a little surprised by her own actions. She wouldn't have guessed she had that in her. Kasey quickly pulled herself together and left the game room. As she entered the hallway, she glanced at the front door. One of her uncle's men was smoking a cigarette outside the open door. He eyed her, then minded his own business. Something about the way he looked at her sent a shiver down her spine.

Kasey headed down the hallway and entered the kitchen. Another one of Vincent's men stood just outside the back kitchen door. Something seemed off about her uncle's hired men. The way they looked at her made her uncomfortable. Maybe that was just because they were creepy men. Kasey approached the counter and leaned against it while sinking into thought. When the inner kitchen door opened, Kasey jumped with a tense gasp and looked toward the door. Hunter entered and casually approached her while eyeing the man just outside the kitchen door. He paused near Kasey and nodded at the man standing guard.

"Your idea of freedom feels a lot like being held captive to me," Hunter remarked.

"I'm sure they're just being cautious," Kasey replied, although her words didn't comfort her. "I mean, if my uncle could find us, so could those men who were trying to kill us."

"Yep, and the world just suddenly got a lot smaller, didn't it?"

"Makes me wonder what would happen if I tried to walk out that door," Kasey remarked, now curious.

"I'm recommending you don't find out," Hunter informed her.

Kasey looked at him with some concern. That's exactly what got her into trouble in the first place, and he knew it. Hunter nodded toward the back stairs while holding his hand out to her. Kasey placed her hand in his without hesitation and followed him.

Chapter Thirty-eight

Hunter led Kasey along the second floor hallway without releasing her hand. As they headed for the master bedroom, Kasey suddenly questioned her willingness to follow this man blindly. After everything that had happened, she must have been insane to trust him. Hunter led Kasey into the master bedroom and locked the door behind them. Kasey looked back at Hunter, curious about his motive. Perhaps his mind was still on her little interrogation scene. While releasing her hand, he indicated the large window alongside the window seat. Kasey crossed the room, placed one knee on the padded seat, and leaned closer to the window to peer out past the sheers.

Kasey saw two large helicopters on the beach with two armed men standing nearby, possibly guarding them. Two more men appeared to be milling around the area just before the main entrance below. Kasey continued to stare out the window with mixed feelings of concern while Hunter paused directly behind her and admired her back side.

"Are they still out there looking all military efficient?" Hunter asked.

"I see four of them," Kasey replied without taking her eyes off the guards. "Two by the helicopter, two covering the front of the house--" She then hesitated. "And you covering my rear."

Kasey looked back at him where he stood behind her with a devious smile and his hands just inches from her hips.

"I enjoy covering your rear."

Kasey rolled her eyes and then continued staring out the window. "Is that what they teach in the Marines?" she asked.

Hunter smiled and chuckled softly at the burn. Kasey backed up without straightening and purposely bumped against his pelvis with her buttocks. He groaned softly and placed his hands on her hips, attempting to hold her against him in that position. Kasey easily moved off the bench seat and away from him. She walked across the room, then turned to face him and backed up while eyeing him with a playful smile.

"Why is it you seem incapable of rational thought whenever we're alone?"

"Limited blood flow to the brain," he replied while grinning.

Kasey backed against the tall bedpost and seductively leaned against it while watching him.

"You do realize my uncle will skin you alive if he catches you prowling around me," she informed him, then raised a skeptical brow. "That is, providing Embry doesn't catch you first."

"I've noticed you're in no hurry to tell either about my inappropriate behavior toward you," Hunter remarked, humored. "Guess I'm lucky you like the way I pounce."

"And yet you still haven't managed to catch me," she insisted.

"I've caught you plenty of times," he replied while grinning. "I'm just polite and let you go."

"Maybe you should stop being so polite."

Hunter's grin increased. As he moved toward her, Kasey grabbed the bedpost and used it to jump up on the bed. Hunter made a motion to lunge onto the bed after her, but she jumped off on the other side of the post. To her surprise, Hunter suddenly backtracked and cut her off. Kasey released a startled, playful scream and jumped back onto the bed to avoid him. Hunter dove on top of her, tackling her face down on the thick comforter. Kasey attempted to escape from under him, but he was reluctant to let her go. While straddling her thighs, he placed his mouth near her ear and groaned softly.

"I'd rather you were facing the other direction, but this works too."

"God, you're like a mutt in heat," she informed him.

When they heard movement in the hallway, both became still and silent while listening.

Hunter placed his mouth close to her ear and smiled. "This would look really bad if someone walked in and saw us," he remarked.

"Yes, so you'll probably want to get off," she informed him.

"That's my intention, but you keep squirming," he remarked with a devious chuckle.

Hunter moved to his knees while straddling her thighs, letting her pull herself up to her hands and knees. Once she made it to all fours, Hunter skillfully flipped her onto her back and again pounced on her. He caught her hands and pinned them to the mattress alongside her head.

"This way's much more fun," he announced with a smile that made her heart race.

Hunter warmly kissed her neck as he leaned closer while holding her down. Kasey attempted to hide her smile.

"And this doesn't look bad?" she asked as a giggle escaped.

"It's okay," Hunter replied between kisses. "I'll just explain that you squirm too much." He chuckled warmly against her skin. "It'll be fine."

Kasey managed a tiny laugh. "Okay, big boy," she announced. "Off."

Hunter ignored her command and continued kissing her neck while releasing her hands. His hands immediately ran along her sides and slipped beneath her buttocks, pulling her hips firmly against him. Kasey placed her hands on his shoulders and enjoyed the sensation of his kisses as well as his arousal, firmly poking against her.

"I can't take advantage of you if you keep squirming," he informed her.

Kasey hesitated only a moment, then slipped her legs out from under him and placed them alongside his hip on either side, allowing him unobstructed access. He lifted his head and met her gaze with a devious, lustful smile.

"You do realize," he announced. "Encouraging my bad behavior is not recommended."

"You're such a little tease," she announced while running her hands along his chest.

Hunter groaned softly and eagerly kissed her. Kasey immediately returned the kiss and attempted to slip his jacket off. Hunter more than willingly shed his jacket the rest of the way and tossed it across the bed without breaking off the kiss. When Kasey's hand ran along his shoulder holster with the gun still in it, Hunter broke off the kiss and stared into her eyes with a devious smile.

"You just can't keep your hands off my weapon," he remarked.

"I would think you'd want my hands on your weapon," she announced.

Hunter groaned, slipped out of the shoulder holster, and allowed it to fall to the bed alongside them. He immediately resumed kissing her and running his hands along her backside. Kasey writhed beneath him and let out a soft groan at the sensation, despite being fully clothed. Her mind was made up. This was the moment, and Hunter was the man. She would give herself to him, allowing him to do whatever he wanted with her. Wishing to convey her submission to him without words, Kasey began unbuttoning his shirt. Hunter tensed slightly, broke off the kiss, and eyed her while she unbuttoned his shirt. To clarify any confusion about her intentions, Kasey kissed his neck while undoing his buttons. Hunter stopped her hands from undoing any more buttons and groaned softly.

"If you keep undressing me, I might get the wrong idea," he remarked.

Kasey's hands returned to his buttons as she continued to kiss his neck. "I want you to get the wrong idea."

Hunter shut his eyes and groaned softly but still didn't move. He again stopped her hands from further unbuttoning his shirt. Kasey stopped kissing him, pulled her head back, and met his gaze with some surprise.

"Aren't you supposed to be the easy one out of the two of us?"

"Definitely," he replied while fidgeting. "But I wasn't expecting you to go along with it."

Kasey stared at the strange look on his face and immediately felt a flood of concern sweep over her. She became instantly annoyed.

"Get off me!"

Hunter jumped off Kasey and sat on the bed alongside her with a low, frustrated groan while running his fingers through his hair. Kasey quickly sat up and glared at him.

"You're married, aren't you?" she demanded.

Hunter stared at her with some surprise. "What?" he gasped. "No, of course not."

"Well, you can't be gay," she huffed, then eyed him. "Can you?"

"You've got to be kidding," Hunter demanded, then groaned softly while nervously scratching his beard as he looked away. "I've known Embry, well, Finn, thirteen years. He was my commanding officer." He sheepishly looked at her. "If he had any idea I'd even touched his daughter, he'd be devastated and very disappointed in me." He then frowned and shook his head. "But he'll never forgive me if I have sex with his little girl. That man had saved my life more times than I can even count. You can't just betray someone like that."

"I understand."

"You do?" he asked with surprise, then released the breath he'd been holding. "Thank God."

"Your loyalty to him is commendable," she remarked, then sneered at him. "Although, you're a prick for initiating something you knew you couldn't finish."

"Oh, come on. That's not fair," Hunter informed her. "Women do it all the time. Besides, you're supposed to be a virgin." He raised his brows. "I have the right to expect a solid protest until the wedding night."

Kasey slid off the bed with a low groan and spun to face him. "I don't know what I was thinking anyway," she snarled at him. "After everything you'd put me through, I'd have to be insane to even consider having sex with you." She held her head up proudly while folding her arms across her chest. "I deserve better than a one-night stand with a questionable character like you anyway. I deserve to be with a man who loves me." She allowed her hands to fall to her sides. "Keep your hands and everything else of yours off me. I'm officially off-limits to you."

As Kasey turned and headed for the door, Hunter rolled across the bed, jumped off the other side, and cut off her path.

Kasey stopped and glared at him. "I'm not in the mood."

"That's pretty obvious, but you're going to listen to me now."

"Hmm, no, I don't think so," she casually replied, then sneered at him. "You're not in control anymore, and I don't have to listen to you." She shook her head and grumbled under her breath. "I should have gone after Colton. At least he wouldn't have disappointed me."

As she attempted to move past him for the door, Hunter placed his hand on the door and blocked her path with his body. He appeared slightly annoyed and didn't take his eyes off her.

"Colton?" he demanded. "Seriously?"

"Think what you will," Kasey scoffed in anger. "But he's a great guy. Any girl would be happy with him as her first, and that's how I had planned it." She then sneered at him. "But then you had to start being all nice at the night club and make me reconsider my whole plan." Kasey shook her head. "I don't know what I was thinking."

"I don't know why you're so mad about this," Hunter demanded, turning angry. "You should be fucking thrilled that I'm willing to wait until you're ready." He then turned commanding. "Don't you think I haven't thought of a thousand ways I wanted to violate you? I'm trying to do the right thing here, and you're treating me like I'm the bad guy."

There was a tense moment as they stared at each other in silence. Hunter finally straightened and stared down at her.

"You want me to choose between you and my loyalty to Finn?" he asked. "Fine, I choose you. You win hands down over Finn every time." He drew a deep breath and attempted to collect himself. "I want you, Kasey, and I've wanted you from the moment I first laid eyes on you. Whatever you want, my loyalty is to you."

Kasey stared at him a moment, surprised that he had those sorts of feelings for her even before the cruise ship.

"Even if it pisses off Embry?" she asked in a softer tone while taking a step closer to him.

Hunter pulled her into his arms and smiled as he searched her eyes. "I'll deal with him," he replied as he gently brushed the hair from her face and then warmly kissed her.

Kasey returned the kiss that quickly turned aggressive. As Hunter's hands eagerly traveled her body, Kasey broke off the kiss and met his gaze.

"Choosing me over Embry is gesture enough," she replied, then sighed with some frustration. "If you consider it betraying him, I'll respect your decision to wait."

Hunter smiled and chuckled. "Now, you're just messing with me," he remarked, kissing her quickly before firmly caressing her backside while holding her close. "Lucky for you, I don't want to get caught with my pants down with all these hired guns running around."

"Is that so?" Kasey cooed while running her hands along his chest, no longer attempting to hide the lustful look in her eyes. "What would you do if we were all alone?"

"Hmm, verbal foreplay," Hunter remarked with a low chuckle. "I can get into that. Probably arrange a bath for two because you are a dirty girl."

Kasey blushed and buried her face against his chest as she giggled. "You're bad," she replied.

Hunter continued caressing her backside. "Yes, but you knew that, which is probably why you wanted me over Colton."

She lifted her head and met his gaze. "Actually, I wanted the most qualified man for the job," Kasey informed him.

Hunter groaned while grinning. "Oh, that one tickles me right where it counts," he replied, warmly kissing her.

They heard movement further down the hallway and broke off the kiss. Both fell silent and listened a moment. They then heard a nearby bedroom door open and listened to someone moving around within the room.

"I don't think we should be caught together like this," he informed her.

"Like what?" she asked with some surprise. "We're not doing anything."

"Please, just this once."

"Fine," she replied with a sigh. "What do you suggest? Hide under the bed?"

Hunter took her hand and hurried her across the room, grabbing his jacket and shoulder holster as they passed the foot end of the bed. When he pulled on a lever near the fireplace, Kasey was surprised to see the bookcase pull away from the wall, revealing a secret passageway. Kasey stared at the secret passage with surprise and awe. He indicated for her to enter. Kasey considered it only a moment before the bedroom doorknob jiggled. Hunter again pointed for her to enter. Kasey hurried into the passageway with Hunter only a step behind her, shutting the bookcase behind them. Kasey looked around the dimly lit passageway that was even creepier now that there was no light from the bedroom.

Hunter positioned himself against Kasey, keeping her pressed against the wall as both remained silent and listened. They heard knocking on the bedroom door. Only a moment passed before the door was broken open. Kasey eyed Hunter with some surprise. Why were they breaking down the door? And what were they looking for? They heard movement within the room. It was obvious by the sounds that the room was being searched, but why? As the footfalls got closer to the passageway entrance, Kasey placed her hands on Hunter's shoulders and nervously clung to him. While she shivered with anxiety, he warmly kissed her neck. Kasey shoved his shoulder, forcing him to stop kissing her.

When they heard the footfalls walk away from the passageway entrance and eventually leave the room, Hunter removed a tiny flashlight from his pocket and shined it toward the passageway staircase. There were cobwebs along the passageway walls, but it was obvious someone had been through recently.

"We'll take the secret passageway," he informed her. "Keep out of sight for a while. See how this plays out."

"What about my friends?" she asked.

"We'll catch up with them," Hunter replied. "They'll be fine."

Chapter Thirty-nine

Hunter held Kasey's hand while quietly leading her down the stairs within the dimly lit secret passageway. The old steps were narrow and on a steep incline, making them difficult to negotiate in near darkness. The walls were just framework with drywall separating the secret stairs from the mansion rooms.

"Why was someone searching the rooms?" Kasey asked while attempting to keep her voice down. She wasn't sure if anyone could hear them through the walls. "Why break down the door?"

"I told you something wasn't right," Hunter informed her.

"Where does this lead?"

"To the library and then to the game room," he replied.

"So that's how Diesel, Colton, and Embry vanished from the library," she remarked.

"There are several passageways in this old place," Hunter informed her.

Kasey stopped Hunter on the stairs just short of the bottom. "What do you really think is going on?" she asked.

"Best guess?" he asked. "I think your uncle hired the wrong men to rescue you. They probably haven't acted yet, because a few of them aren't in on it, and they're probably the ones drinking in the game room. If that's the case, they'll kill those men to get them out of the way."

"What should we do?" Kasey asked with concern. "Wait for them to attack?"

"Well, we could, but there's a good chance we'll all be dead once they do."

"You've already plotted a counterattack, haven't you?" she asked with surprise.

"And it would run much more smoothly if you worked with me rather than against me this time," he informed her.

"You do realize that every time I trust you, I end up handcuffed or locked in a cell."

"Your uncle is a bad man, Kasey," Hunter informed her gently while caressing her hand. "He's surrounded by bad people--both friends and foes. Embry is convinced he was responsible for the attack on you and your aunt."

"That's insane."

"Have you ever known Embry to be wrong?" Hunter asked.

"Well, no," she replied. "But he's also not really Embry, is he?"

"Well, Finn is never wrong either," Hunter informed her. "He hears and sees everything. His little, devious mind can put together plots you couldn't even imagine. You can't even lie to him and expect to get away with it."

Hunter wasn't wrong. Kasey knew how sneaking Embry could be, and it now made a lot more sense. To think an Admiral in the Marines had spent the last nine years passing himself off as a butler. And, yet, that sounded like something Embry would do.

"And he thinks my uncle had my aunt killed and is trying to kill me?" Kasey asked, then shook her head. "I find that a little hard to believe."

"Well, it has to be better than his first theory," Hunter remarked. "Where he had your aunt murdered so he could put the moves on you."

Kasey was somewhat shocked that Hunter would even suggest something so absurd. It almost made her ill.

"Yeah, that's even more ridiculous," Kasey insisted. "He's my uncle."

"Not blood relation, and there are sick freaks out there molesting their own children," Hunter replied. "It's not completely out of the question."

"What if you're wrong about those men?" Kasey asked. "You're going to end up killing a bunch of innocent men." She shook her head. "I don't think I can let you do that."

"We'll make sure we have proof before anyone gets shot," he insisted. "But the objective is to get you and your friends out of the crossfire before it happens."

"Is this the part where you want to lock us back in that cell?"

"No, this is the part where you help sneak your friends to safety," Hunter informed her. "I guarantee that once you and your friends are MIA, his men will react differently than a rescue team. They're obviously looking for you already. It won't be long before they show their true colors, and your friends turn into live bait to get you back. You'll have your proof, but your friends will suffer."

"What about my uncle?"

"If he doesn't try to kill us, we'll protect him," Hunter informed her. "But I don't think that'll be the case."

"Okay, but I want a gun."

"Fine, I'll get you a gun."

They continued down the stairs and stopped near the library exit. Kasey was a bit surprised to see there were several assault rifles in a case along the wall. The panel was accessible from one of the library shelves as well. Hunter removed a semiautomatic handgun, checked the clip, and cocked it. He showed her the safety lever.

"Safety on," he announced, then flicked it. "Safety off." Hunter flicked it again, so the safety was on before handing it to her grip first. "Try not to shoot yourself--or me."

"I know how to use a gun," she informed him matter-of-factly. "I shot at Embry five times and didn't hit him once."

"You fired twice at Diesel and hit him once," Hunter reminded her.

"I was actually trying to hit him," she casually replied.

Hunter eyed her with some surprise, but she didn't bother looking at him.

§

Vincent's hired men were still drinking at the bar and relaxed after their uneventful shock and awe. They weren't the type of men who cared if they drank the hard stuff in the morning. Vincent and Dillon now played a game of pool together, having a heated debate over something. Playing his role, Embry remained behind the bar serving drinks while Colton and Jamie sat in a chair together near the back wall. Now that they were able to relax, Jamie was on Colton's lap, and they shared a passionate kiss or two. After serving another round of drinks, Embry glanced across the room at Colton and Jamie, but both had mysteriously vanished. Embry stared at the empty chair a moment while drifting off into thought. His eyes strayed to the nearby secret passageway entrance a moment before coming back to life. Embry looked across the game room at Vincent by the pool table.

"Perhaps I should serve some coffee before we leave," Embry suggested to his boss.

Vincent straightened from the pool table and nodded in agreement. "Yes, we should be heading out soon." He then glanced at the guys. "That's last call, gentleman."

Embry casually walked out from behind the bar and left the game room, but it was obvious he had his own mission.

Chapter Forty

The bedroom door within the secret room opened to reveal Hunter, Kasey, Jamie, and Colton. The hidden secret bedroom looked the same as the rest of the staff bedrooms. Bland and uninspiring. As they entered the small bedroom, Kasey, Jamie, and Colton looked around.

"Our cell just keeps getting smaller," Kasey remarked.

"So there's a passageway that leads from the game room to the servant's wing?" Jamie asked, then cocked her head. "What's to stop them from just walking back here from the kitchen?"

"This section of the wing is part of the secret passageway. It's sealed off. Like a secret wing," Hunter informed them. "There are four bedrooms only accessible from the passageways."

Diesel entered the bedroom. "Finn's made his exit," he announced. "The mansion is officially our playground."

"What next?" Kasey asked.

"We spy," Hunter replied, then opened the armoire to reveal monitors from hidden cameras throughout the mansion. He attempted to use one of the remote controls, but nothing happened. "Didn't you label these things?"

"On the back, numbnuts," Diesel scoffed.

Diesel snatched the remote from Hunter and searched through several cameras on one of the four televisions.

"There were cameras in all the rooms?" Jamie asked, horrified.

"Not in the bedrooms and bathrooms," Hunter informed her.

"Finn wouldn't allow them," Diesel remarked, then smiled and snickered. "But these cameras have speakers, so we can hear all the good stuff."

Kasey, Colton, and Jamie grimaced slightly at the admission. They might have heard parts of their plan to get Hunter drunk and other more embarrassing things.

Hunter stared at the camera view of the beach outside the house and tensed at the image. "Huh?" he muttered almost more to himself. "When was that one installed?"

"Don't worry," Diesel announced without taking his eyes off the security screens. "Finn didn't catch your shock and awe on the beach." He then snickered. "I got a kick out of it, though."

Hunter glared at Diesel while Jamie and Colton eyed Kasey somewhat suspiciously. Diesel grinned and chuckled, then looked at Kasey as well.

She immediately held her hands up. "Hey, I was just along for the walk," Kasey announced. "Literally handcuffed to him."

"Although I did hear he caught the little seduction scene in the library," Diesel remarked.

Jamie and Colton eyed Kasey in silent question while Diesel chuckled and appeared pleased with himself. Hunter frowned and glanced at Kasey, realizing they'd been caught.

"Okay," Kasey announced and nodded. "That one I had a part in."

"Yeah, I heard you slipped your hand down Hunter's pants," Diesel remarked while grinning, then indicated the dent in the armoire door. "Finn just about put his fist through the cabinet."

Embry appeared in the bedroom, looking stern and official. "Coffee break's over," he announced to his men. "We have a mess to clean up."

"What sort of mess?" Jamie asked.

"Kasey's not the only one who knows how to spike a drink," Embry replied, then nodded for them to follow.

§

Five men lie unconscious and scattered along the game room floor. Embry emerged from the secret passageway and hurried for the main door, quietly shutting it. Hunter, Diesel, and Colton quickly entered and dragged unconscious men into the passageway. Diesel carried one over his shoulder and pulled the other by his shirt collar without breaking a sweat. Kasey and Jamie stood just outside the passageway and watched the efficiency of the men.

"Five down," Diesel announced while grinning. "Seven to go."

"What happened to Dillon and my uncle?" Kasey asked, now curious.

"I only had enough drugs for five men so I chose the hired guns," Embry replied. "Your Uncle Vincent, Dillon, and Davy were 'called away' before the drugs affected the men."

"Called away?" Jamie asked.

Embry didn't elaborate but maintained his sly grin. It was best that they didn't know.

"What are you going to do with them?" Kasey then asked while watching them drag the unconscious men across the game room. "I mean, we really don't know if all of them are involved in what's happening around here. Some may be innocent."

"None of them are innocent," Diesel remarked while passing them. "They're mercenaries."

"We'll put them in the prison suite in the basement," Hunter informed her. "We can sort out the good from the bad later."

"In that case, grab my book," Kasey informed him. "I don't want them finding my stiletto letter opener and freeing themselves."

Hunter eyed her, then cocked his head. "Is that how you got out?" he asked. "You swiped the letter opener from the library in that book?"

"That trip to the library wasn't all pleasure," she informed him, then smiled and winked.

"It was for me," Hunter muttered while hiding his grin.

Diesel overheard the comment and rolled his eyes. "Will the two of you get a room and get it over with," he scoffed.

Chapter Forty-one

Secret room. Less than an hour later, Kasey and Jamie sat on the foot end of the bed and flipped through the different security cameras while Colton paced the bedroom not far from them. After a private discussion, Diesel, Embry, and Hunter finally returned to the room. Honestly, Kasey didn't like that they needed to have private conversations. She was still anxious that they were conspiring against her and her friends, but she wanted to trust Embry and Hunter. Embry removed a heavy duffel bag from under the bed and dropped it on the bed behind Kasey and Jamie. Both looked back to see what the three conspirators were up to. Embry unzipped the bag and removed a small kit containing tiny earbuds, which intrigued Kasey.

"What's that?" Kasey asked.

"Micro ear transmitters so we can communicate with one another," Embry informed her.

"To coordinate our attacks," Diesel added.

Jamie lightly tapped Kasey's arm and indicated the security monitors. "Look, your uncle and Dillon are in the kitchen with that guy; what's his name? Davy."

"How do you turn up the volume?" Kasey asked while indicating the security cameras.

Hunter took the remote and turned up the volume on the kitchen camera, where Vincent was seen talking to Dillon.

§

Vincent paced the kitchen while Dillon leaned against the island counter and watched his father's meltdown. Vincent finally spun to face Davy, turning angry.

"They have to be here somewhere," Vincent insisted, shouting. "Keep looking. I want them found!"

"The men searched all three floors and even looked outside," Davy informed him. "Unless they went inland--"

"Did you search the basement?" Vincent demanded.

"It's a tropical island," Davy reminded him. "There is no basement."

"The first floor is twelve steps above ground level with a concrete foundation," Vincent reminded him. "There has to be something beneath the first floor. If not a basement, then a very large crawl space. Look for a door."

"Do you actually think they're hiding?" Dillon now felt compelled to ask.

Vincent spun to face his son. "Five of my men are missing," he announced as his anxiety bubbled over. "Perhaps they betrayed me, or they could be working for my enemies. I seem to have no shortage of men willing to betray me these days. If Kasey and her friends aren't hiding, they've been taken."

Dillon folded his arms across his chest while suspiciously eyeing his father. "Your concern over

Kasey is borderline creepy, Dad," he remarked while somehow seeming casual. "I mean, I don't see you hiring a bodyguard to protect me, and you certainly didn't hire someone to look after your wife while you were away on your *business* trips."

Vincent stared at his son with a surprised look. "I don't think I like your tone," he scoffed, then cocked his head. "Exactly what are you getting at?"

Dillon shrugged almost as if he were disinterested. "Just wondering why you're so concerned over Kasey, who isn't even your own flesh and blood."

"You're more than capable of protecting yourself," Vincent informed him while remaining irritated by the entire conversation. "And she may not be my biological niece, but I love her like a daughter nonetheless. She was nearly killed last year, and I don't want someone with a vendetta against me going after her again."

Dillon chuckled, somewhat amused at the response, then shook his head. "Admit it, Dad," he remarked, then raised his brows. "You've got a hard-on for Kasey."

Vincent was stunned by the comment and immediately turned defensive. "That's disgusting and disturbing!"

"Yeah, so were the videos I found saved on your laptop of Kasey in her bikini out by the pool," Dillon remarked. "You went out of your way to make copies of them from the security cameras."

"I have access to the security cameras on my laptop," Vincent informed him. "I'm sure that's just a coincidence."

Dillon casually shrugged. "Yeah, sure," he replied. "Security footage of Kasey in her bikini just happened to download to files in your computer. Two entire summers' worth of poolside footage. Nothing from the other cameras. Just footage of Kasey. In her bikini. Saved in neatly marked files."

Vincent instantly became flustered. "I didn't put those there," he insisted. "Someone else must have done that. Embry has access to my laptop to pay bills. He must have downloaded them."

"You gave Embry a laptop for finances a little over two years ago," Dillon informed him. "I remember; I was there. It was almost as if you didn't want him accessing your personal laptop anymore." He then raised his brows. "On an interesting side note. Embry approached Mom with a spy cam Betty had found in Kasey's bedroom, which she practically accused me of putting there." Dillon cocked his head. "When I told her it wasn't me, she was too easily convinced. Almost as if she just wanted to confirm it hadn't been me. Two weeks later, she was murdered."

Vincent glared at Dillon, turning angry. "Are you actually accusing me of killing your mother, Betty, and Abby all because you think I was spying on Kasey?" he demanded. "Do you have any idea how insane that sounds?"

"I know it sounds insane," Dillon replied while shrugging, then smiled. "Especially since I was the one who installed the hidden camera in Kasey's bedroom."

"What?" Vincent gasped while staring at Dillon, attempting to understand what he'd just heard.

"Sorry, Dad," Dillon announced while grinning. "You weren't the only one dogging Kasey. Dear old stepmom was already considering divorcing you before I threw you under the bus with that whole spy cam lie. Unfortunately, I didn't realize that little lie would push her over the edge."

Vincent stared at Dillon with a strange, horrified look. "What are you saying?"

"I'm saying I had to kill her before she divorced you," Dillon replied with little emotion. "If she had gone through with the divorce, you'd get nothing per the prenup you signed, which meant I'd also get nothing. She had already cut off my allowance. At least if you got all her money, I knew I'd still have a steady income."

"You killed your mother?" Vincent gasped, stunned by what he was hearing.

"No, I killed my *stepmother*," Dillon corrected. "That woman was never my mother. When I asked for an increase in spending money, she said no, forcing me to work for you at the real estate office. And I know she's the reason you cut off my allowance."

"You graduated college," Vincent scoffed. "It was time for you to earn your own money." He shook his head in stunned disbelief. "I can't believe you were responsible for the deaths of three people. And Kasey. You actually hired those men to kill Kasey?"

Dillon snorted a laugh and shook his head. "You're unbelievable," he remarked. "You just can't stop sniffing around Kasey for two minutes, even after I told you I had your wife killed." Dillon's smirk turned into a sneer. "No, I didn't order a hit on Kasey. Of course, I didn't. She wasn't even supposed to be home until one or two in the morning." His sneer turned into a grin. "Of course, I didn't want Kasey dead. I had other plans for her."

"What plans?" Vincent demanded, attempting to understand everything being thrown at him.

Dillon appeared slightly humored. "I know you were trying to keep the details of her inheritance from her after her aunt died, but once she turned twenty-one, the estate lawyers would hand her the deed to the house along with her trust fund. I don't think she even realizes how wealthy she will become. That's why I arranged the attack on the cruise ship under the guise of your enemies out to harm her. Killing Kasey's bodyguard and abducting her would be my 'in' with her. I'd come to her rescue, and she'd fall madly in love with me." He shrugged while grinning. "I'll get Kasey, the mansion, and the millions from her trust fund." Dillon cocked his head. "There's really only one thing standing in my way of getting everything I want."

Vincent stared at his son with shock and horror while shaking his head before turning angry. "There's plenty standing in your way if you think for a minute you're going to get away with killing all those people," Vincent snarled, then glared at Davy while angrily indicating Dillon. "Davy, put my son under house arrest. The police will deal with him when we get back home."

Davy seemed to be following the conversation but was hesitant to react.

"You weren't really paying attention, Dad," Dillon informed his father, then cocked his head. "The only thing standing in my way is *you*."

Vincent eyed Dillon, attempting to make the connection, then looked at Davy. Davy casually raised his handgun and shot Vincent in the abdomen without hesitation. Vincent gasped while clutching his bleeding mid-section and looked from Davy to Dillon with betrayal and horror in his eyes.

"All those men you thought you hired," Dillon casually informed his father, who now clutched the counter for support while staring at him. "They all work for me. You were never in charge of this rescue mission. It was the perfect opportunity to get you someplace remote where no one would ever find your body." He then looked at Davy without emotion. "Finish it."

Davy shot Vincent twice in the chest, instantly dropping him.

Chapter Forty-two

Within the hidden bedroom, Kasey and Jamie suddenly cried out when they saw Vincent shot for the first time. When they witnessed Davy shooting him twice in the chest, they screamed again as Vincent dropped to the kitchen floor. Embry, Hunter, and Diesel were also slightly surprised, although they were expecting some sort of double-cross. Kasey turned to Jamie, who immediately pulled her into her arms and held her.

Colton stared at the security screen with a dumbfounded expression, then shook his head. "I didn't see that coming," he remarked, still somewhat stunned.

"Dillon was the ring leader?" Diesel demanded, stunned. "I thought for sure it was Vincent."

"I don't know what's worse," Jamie announced under her breath to Kasey while consoling her. "Your cousin wanting Colton and me dead, or your cousin just *wanting* you."

Kasey slowly pulled away from Jamie, sniffed, and looked at the security monitor again. "My uncle wasn't behind any of the murders," she just about whispered.

"Finn was right, though," Diesel remarked to Kasey. "Your creepy uncle *was* sniffing around you, and he also knew his dirty dealings put your life at risk."

"He lied to you about everything," Colton scoffed, showing less sympathy than Jamie and taking Diesel's side. "Including your inheritance. Probably wanted to keep it from you so you wouldn't leave him. The pervert."

"I'm not sure how I feel right now," Kasey muttered, unable to look away from the screen. Her friend made a valid point, yet she wasn't sure her uncle deserved execution for it. As Kasey witnessed Davy dragging Vincent's lifeless, bloody body from the kitchen, she shivered slightly and shook her head. "I can't believe Dillon killed Aunt Nat and his own father."

"I'm sorry you had to see that, Kasey," Embry informed her while affectionately placing his hand on her shoulder.

Kasey drew a deep breath and held it for a moment. Given everything she'd just learned and what she knew about her uncle's marriage to her aunt, she realized Vincent wasn't a very good person, and he was at least partially to blame for everything that happened to them and himself.

"I guess there's just one thing left to say," Kasey announced while shaking her head, then looked back at the guys. "Happy hunting."

"Time to clean house," Embry announced, reinvigorated by Kasey's approval of their actions. "Lethal force is authorized on all targets."

Embry handed assault rifles to Hunter, Diesel, and Colton. When Colton masterfully cocked the rifle, Jamie and Kasey stared at him in stunned silence.

Colton suddenly tensed and looked at his two friends, realizing what he'd done and how it looked.

"Oh, God," Jamie cried out, her eyes wide with shock. "Not you too!"

"That figures," Kasey groaned while frowning.

Colton's expression immediately dropped as he turned defensive. "I can explain," he announced.

Kasey and Jamie stared at him with matching frowns of disappointment.

Colton tensed and shifted uncomfortably, unable to look his friends in the eyes. "I can explain later," he announced, quickly leaving the room.

"Oh, man, he is so pussy whipped," Diesel remarked, then eyed Hunter. "He's practically in your league."

Hunter glared at Diesel, not humored.

Diesel chuckled with amusement and lightly smacked Hunter on the arm. "When I was watching the security cameras, and you mentioned the time Colton shot you in the ass right there in front of the girls, I nearly pissed myself," he announced. "That was too funny."

Now that Diesel mentioned it, Kasey remembered a few times the guys said things that seemed to get under Colton's skin, and they were finally starting to make sense.

Hunter maintained his glare at Diesel. "Remember the time I shot *you* in the ass?"

Diesel cocked his head, somewhat bewildered. "You never shot me in the ass."

"Day's not over," Hunter snarled.

Diesel's smile faded, and he hurried from the back room. Embry watched the doorway a moment, then shook his head, obviously disgusted with his men.

"So you were *all* in on this?" Jamie practically demanded while folding her arms across her chest. "Colton didn't just happen to find the raft and satellite phone on the ship, did he?"

"Diesel hid the life raft and satellite phone onboard before we boarded," Hunter informed her. "It was our emergency exit."

"We'd planned on evacuating you at the first port," Embry remarked. "The attack at the nightclub forced us to act ahead of schedule, putting us further from this island than we'd intended. Hunter called Diesel, who then flew out to your location and towed your raft to shore. I disembarked at the first port, following through with our original evacuation plan. I arrived by private boat later that first afternoon."

Jamie rolled her eyes and shook her head. "You guys are the worst," she scoffed.

"I won't deny that," Embry replied.

Kasey frowned and shook her head. "If you would have come to me, Embry, I would have gone along with your plan," she informed him. "All of this wouldn't have been necessary."

"I couldn't risk you not believing me," Embry informed her. "The price of failure was too high. This way, Colton and I would still be in your good graces if anything went wrong. We could still protect you from the inside."

"That's something else we'll need to talk about later," Kasey informed him, then straightened and drew a deep breath. "But, for now, is there anything we can do to help?"

"If you'd like to help," Embry announced. "The two of you can cover our backs by watching the monitors and tell us their positions."

Embry handed both women ear transmitters. Kasey stood while accepting the transmitter and then looked Embry in the eyes.

"Be careful, okay?" Kasey said softly.

Embry smiled and gently pulled Kasey into his arms. As Kasey hugged him affectionately, he appeared pleased and clung to her a moment longer, not wanting to release her. Kasey kissed his cheek and pulled away.

"When you get back," Kasey announced, then turned stern. "I want you to tell me the truth about *everything.*"

"Fair enough," Embry replied, maintaining his smile as he gently caressed her arms. "Just promise me something, darling."

"What's that?"

"If I die," Embry announced, then glared at Hunter by the doorway and frowned. "Don't sleep with him."

Hunter tensed while hovering near the open doorway.

"So, as long as you don't die, it's allowed?" Kasey asked while offering a mocking grin.

Embry's eyes widened in something resembling horror. "Oh, God. I'm already too late, aren't I?" he asked, then groaned while shaking his head. "I can't say I'm surprised. He's been like a love-sick puppy around you for the last eleven months."

Kasey managed a tiny chuckle. "I've only known him for two months."

Hunter quietly slipped out of the room with an embarrassed look while Jamie pretended she wasn't listening.

"Yes, but he and Diesel have been keeping an eye on you since Vincent made me suspicious after Natalie's death," Embry informed her matter-of-factly. "Originally, I wanted to put him in Colton's place, befriending you, but Colton looked younger and blended better with the nightclub scene. Honestly, I didn't want Colton too close to you." His look turned stern. "He's a little too *friendly.*"

"No kidding," Jamie muttered and managed a tiny laugh.

When Embry eyed Jamie, she turned away while attempting an innocent look. Something Embry had said then caught Jamie's attention, and she looked back at him.

"Wait," Jamie remarked. "What do you mean Colton *looked* younger?"

"He could pass for a twenty-five-year-old man," Embry remarked.

"He *is* twenty-five," Jamie corrected.

Embry smiled and chuckled. "No, he's actually thirty-one," he replied. "Same age as Hunter and Diesel."

Jamie gasped with surprise at Colton's actual age. Embry then looked back at Kasey.

"If you really like Hunter," Embry announced almost delicately and nodded, "I won't stand in your way."

Having heard the comment, Hunter quickly reappeared in the doorway and stared at them with an enthusiastic look.

"He's actually not bad with relationships and commitments," Embry announced, then cringed. "He's certainly not Diesel. Besides, you'd probably be good for him too."

"I appreciate your approval," Kasey remarked. "And, actually, he has respected your wishes. Nothing happened."

"I'm glad to hear," Embry replied while flashing a menacing grin. "I really didn't want to beat him impotent."

Kasey gave him a stern, disapproving glare, then managed a smile. Embry flashed a grin, but it was uncertain whether he was joking. He kissed her on the cheek and then turned to leave when he saw Hunter standing in the doorway. He paused by Hunter and glared at him.

"Knock up my little girl, and there won't be enough of you left for your mother to identify," Embry scoffed, then left the room.

Jamie read the looks between Hunter and Kasey, then quickly jumped off the bed. "I'm just going to see Colton off."

Jamie hurried from the room as well, giving Kasey and Hunter some privacy. Hunter couldn't contain his smile as he approached Kasey and pulled her into his arms.

"You certainly know how to smooth talk him," Hunter announced while holding her. "Admit it; you love me."

Kasey couldn't help but smile at him. "I've thought a lot about what you said, and you're right," she announced. "There's no rush, and I am happy you're willing to wait."

"Oh, no, you don't," Hunter announced as his expression dropped and his eyes widened. "You can't change your mind now. I just got the official green light here."

"I'll tell you what," Kasey announced while attempting to hide her humored smile. "Don't get yourself killed out there, and we'll leave it open for discussion."

"I guess I'll just have to turn up the charm," he announced.

Hunter kissed her warmly and with a sense of urgency. Kasey eagerly returned the kiss without hesitation.

"Let's go!" Embry was heard shouting from the corridor.

Hunter broke off the kiss and groaned softly while hiding his slightly nervous smile. "Do me a favor," he announced. "Warn me if he sneaks up behind me while we're out there."

Kasey smiled, kissed him quickly, and then moved away. "I will."

Hunter returned the smile and left the room.

Chapter Forty-three

Kasey and Jamie closely watched the monitors, hoping to cover the guys' asses via the security cameras. Both women were anxious, knowing the men could easily be shot and killed. The stakes were high, and they were outnumbered. Any edge Kasey and Jamie could give them would help their chances of survival.

"Is everyone in position?" Embry asked over their ear transmitters. "Master bedroom passageway."

"Game room passageway," Diesel replied.

"Library passageway," Colton announced.

"Kitchen passageway," Hunter replied.

"Eagle one, what's the enemy's position?" Embry asked. There was a long pause without a response. "Kasey, you're Eagle One."

"Oh, uh, two men are outside," Kasey replied while scanning the security cameras. "Between the main entrance and the helicopter."

"I have one in the kitchen and one in the second floor hallway," Jamie responded as well. "The one in the second floor hallway is heading toward your location in the master bedroom from the main stairs."

Both watched the monitors and swiftly switched between rooms, keeping eyes on the enemy as they moved.

"Oh, wait," Kasey announced, spotting more movement. "Dillon and Davy are between the stairs and the front door."

"One just outside the kitchen as well," Jamie added.

"I think there's one more, but I'm not seeing him," Kasey announced, becoming flustered. "Be on the lookout for him."

"He might be in a bedroom, bathroom, or a dead zone," Embry informed her over the ear transmitter before reporting to his men. "Move out on my mark." There was a pause. "Mark."

All four men appeared from their respective secret passageways with their assault rifles aimed and ready. Kasey and Jamie each took two men and scanned their surrounding locations, keeping an eye on the enemy.

§

Embry hurried across the master bedroom from the secret passageway and positioned himself alongside the open doorway.

"Embry," Kasey announced urgently. "The man in the second floor hallway is nearly upon you. Coming from the main stairway."

Embry waited just inside the master bedroom alongside the doorway and saw the armed man walk past with his weapon prepared to fire. When the man passed the master bedroom doorway, Embry silently stepped into the hallway just behind him. Alerted to his presence, the man quickly turned. Embry spun into a series of roundhouse kicks and punches, knocking the rifle from his hand first and then striking him multiple times in the face, taking him down almost effortlessly.

§

Dillon and Davy stood within the grand hallway listening to reports from their men roaming the hallways and searching the estate. They heard something loud coming from the second floor, not far from the stairs. As they looked up the staircase, the man Embry had been fighting suddenly tumbled down the steps. When he struck the bottom, it appeared as if he'd sustained a broken neck, although it was unclear if it had happened from the fall or from the altercation. Davy eyed his dead man at the base of the steps.

"All units, we have one on second," Davy announced into his own ear transmitter, alerting their men.

Dillon positioned himself safely near the front door and appeared partly concerned and partly annoyed at his man.

"What the hell is going on?" Dillon demanded while attempting to sound tough, despite his apparent cowardice. "Your men can't handle one bodyguard and a middle-aged butler?"

Davy glared at Dillon. "They're not alone," he snarled in response, turning angry. "Was there something you failed to mention about this bodyguard?"

"Of course not! I saw his resume," Dillon snapped back. "He was a mall security guard and a weekend warrior."

"Well, he obviously lied," Davy scoffed in response. "Mall security guards don't typically break a man's neck. Wait here!"

Davy charged up the stairs to confront the enemy while another guard rushed down the hallway from the back of the house, heading for the grand stairs as well. Dillon heard something nearby and glanced toward the front sitting room, taking his eyes off the approaching man for only a moment. Diesel suddenly appeared from the game room doorway and swiftly plucked the man from the hallway. When Dillon looked back, the approaching man was gone. He looked around a moment, slightly puzzled, then glanced back up the staircase, waiting for Davy.

§

Hunter darted behind the island counter in the kitchen to avoid being seen by the man just near the back stairs. Dillon's hired man heard Davy on his earpiece and hurried across the kitchen to the interior door to assist the others. Hunter suddenly catapulted over the counter and struck the man in the chest with both feet. The man was thrown backward without alerting the guard just outside the back door. The man on the kitchen floor slowly moved to his feet, saw Hunter, and lunged for him. Hunter spun into a backward kick and swiftly dropped the man. He then pulled the man behind the island counter while keeping an eye on the guard just outside the door. The guard outside remained blissfully clueless.

"Hmm, nice moves, Hunter," Kasey announced over his ear transmitter.

Hunter looked at the camera in the corner of the kitchen and winked while grinning.

"Two down," Kasey announced over Hunter's ear transmitter. "Be on the lookout, Embry. Davy is heading up the grand stairs."

"We have one down in the game room," Jamie remarked over their ear transmitters. "Very *crudely* done."

§

Diesel walked across the game room for the secret passage entrance, leaving a man bleeding from his neck on the floor after having his throat crudely torn out.

"That's how I operate, princess," Diesel scoffed while glaring at the security camera as he passed and gave her the middle finger, which was covered in blood.

"Cut the chatter," Embry was heard over their ear transmitters.

§

Hunter crept toward the outer kitchen door, where the armed guard remained clueless about what was happening inside. They avoided using their weapons to keep the men unaware of their attack for as long as possible, but there was no way to avoid that now. Hunter kept low and positioned himself to the side of the door, then lightly knocked on it. The door was suddenly thrown open by the guard holding his assault rifle. Hunter turned, fired two shots into the man, and dropped him. Hunter casually straightened and shut the door, hiding his mess.

"The shots alerted the two on the beach," Kasey announced over their transmitters. "They're heading for the front door."

"Davy is going back down the stairs as well," Jamie informed them over their transmitters. "You'll see him soon."

"All four are about to meet in the grand hallway," Kasey added.

"Sounds like a party. I'm heading for a little aerial recon," Embry announced from his communication device.

"I'm taking a sneak-around approach," Hunter informed them while approaching the nearby back door.

Hunter opened the back door, unslung his assault rifle, and jumped over the dead man on the ground, heading around the mansion.

Chapter Forty-four

Dillon remained near the front door in the hallway while listening to what was happening through his own ear transmitter. His hired men weren't talking much, which was starting to concern him. Davy rushed down the stairs, catching Dillon's attention. As Davy reached the bottom of the stairs, the two men from the beach hurried through the front door, joining them.

"The shots came from the kitchen," Dillon informed them while pointing.

The two men and Davy ran down the hall to the kitchen.

"We have three heading toward the kitchen," Kasey announced over her guys' ear transmitters. "Dillon is still by the front door, Hunter."

Colton and Diesel appeared simultaneously from the game room and library and opened fire on the three men, effectively mowing down the first two. Davy pulled back, narrowly avoiding their rapid-fire, and ran for the front door, where Dillon waited.

"Where are you going?" Dillon demanded as Davy hurried past him and to the front door.

"It's over, Dillon," Davy snarled in response as he approached the open doorway. "No one is reporting. I don't know how they did it, but they're all gone. It's time to go."

Davy didn't wait for permission and ran from the house. Dillon considered it only a moment before hurrying to the dead man at the bottom of the stairs and grabbing his rifle.

"Wait for me!" Dillon cried out while turning toward the front door.

Embry slid down the banister, caught onto the railing near Dillon, and catapulted into a kick, striking Dillon in the chest. Dillon was thrown several feet across the hall, striking and sliding down the wall. He appeared to be unconscious. Davy was the last man standing, and he wasn't getting far. Embry casually sat on the second to last bottom step, removed a cigar, and lit it. He puffed on the cigar without care and seemed to be waiting for something.

§

Davy hurried toward the beach and the first of the two older helicopters, not waiting to see what happened to Dillon. Hunter casually sat within the open side door of the first helicopter and spotted the man before he reached the sand. When he saw Davy step onto the beach, Hunter leaned out and fired several rounds into the sand at Davy's feet. Davy cried out and returned fire while running away from the beach, heading back for the mansion. Hunter grinned and chuckled, moderately amused, before tapping his ear transmitter.

"One coming back at you, Finn," he announced. "Not very menacing for a mercenary. It's possible he pissed himself." Hunter chuckled, amused. "I'm going to need confirmation on the pissing part."

§

Embry sat on the stairs, still puffing on his cigar without a care in the world. Davy ran into the house, saw Embry, stopped, and aimed his rifle at him. Embry casually put his hands in the air with his cigar between his front teeth.

"Easy, you've got me," Embry announced with a slightly twisted smile.

"You're my ticket out of here, old man," Davy remarked.

"Old man?" Embry asked, somewhat offended with the cigar still between his teeth. "I really hate being called that."

"Get up!"

As Davy approached Embry, where he still remained comfortably seated near the bottom of the stairs, Colton suddenly appeared from the front room. He kicked the rifle from Davy's hand, knocking it to the floor with a clatter. Davy turned toward Colton and took a karate stance, intriguing Embry. As Davy lunged for Colton, both men went into a series of kicks, punches, and blocks. Hunter entered only a moment later with his rifle aimed. When he saw the two men fighting, he lowered his weapon and leaned in the doorway.

"Colton can fight?" Jamie was heard over their ear transmitters.

Embry continued casually puffing on his cigar without moving and made a so-so motion with his hand. "Eh," he replied to Jamie's question. "He's slightly better than average."

Diesel approached the stairs by the railing, saw the men fighting, and lit his own cigar. All three watched Colton and Davy continue to fight, kick for kick and punch for punch. Surprisingly, Davy got in a good shot, striking Colton in the mouth.

"Come on, Colton," Embry groaned while leaning back on the steps. "Stop playing with him and finish it already."

"Let him play," Diesel remarked with a soft chuckle as he puffed on his cigar. "We get so little entertainment these days."

Davy got in another shot, knocking Colton back several steps.

"He enjoys getting his ass kicked," Embry insisted while gesturing with his cigar. "There's something off in that boy's head."

"It's like watching a cat play with a mouse before killing it," Diesel replied while chuckling. "Sometimes, you feel bad and just want to root for the mouse."

When Davy attempted to punch Colton in the groin, Colton deflected the shot and immediately became annoyed. Davy turned arrogant and again took his karate stance, possibly preparing to finish Colton.

"Okay, now you're just pissing me off," Colton announced while sneering.

As Davy made another attempt to attack Colton, Colton spun into a high, roundhouse kick, caught Davy around the neck, and flipped him through the air to the ground. Colton rolled and gracefully sprang back up to his feet, leaving the man motionless on the floor.

Diesel cheered and slow-clapped. "Nicely done," he announced. "I think he may even be alive."

Chapter Forty-five

The Coast Guard removed the remaining five men from the basement cell and took them into custody. At the same time, a swarm of law enforcement officers buzzed around the house, collecting evidence and statements before removing the bodies. Embry took several officers into the kitchen, where Dillon and Davy had been handcuffed together and locked in the pantry for safekeeping. Embry eyed the officers as they approached the pantry at the far end of the kitchen.

"After seeing the video footage of the two men executing Kasey's uncle," he announced, then indicated the pantry door. "We feared putting them in the holding cell with the five other men, who may not have been involved in double-crossing Vincent." Embry flashed a tense smile. "We didn't want to endanger any more lives until it could be straightened out. So handcuffing them together in the pantry seemed the smart decision."

The officers nodded as they paused before the pantry door. The outside bolt, although heavy, was busted.

Embry's eyes widened at the sight, and he lunged for the door. "No, that's impossible!"

As Embry yanked the pantry door open, two officers aimed their weapons. The pantry was empty. Both men had escaped!

"We'll send a search party out for them," the first officer announced. "Since both helicopters are still on the beach, they're probably still on the island unless there's another way off that we don't know about. A boat, perhaps?"

"No, there isn't a boat," Embry replied, then sank into his own thoughts. He then hesitated and looked at the officers. "Well, there's the life raft we used after the incident on the cruise ship. It's on the beach about a mile from here."

"We'll check it out," the first officer informed him.

"My friends and I would like to help search for them," Embry insisted.

"It could be dangerous," the officer replied. "We couldn't--"

"Look around, Officer," Embry remarked while indicating the covered bodies on the kitchen floor. "I think we'll be fine."

§

Dillon slowly woke to the sound of gently lapping water. He groaned softly and looked around. Still handcuffed to an unconscious Davy, Dillon saw they were in the life raft from the cruise ship and just far enough from the island that they could see it in the distance. One boat ore and a small backpack were in the middle of the raft. Dillon angrily thrust the palm of his hand into Davy's shoulder several times.

"Wake up, you idiot!"

Davy woke and looked around with disorientation. "What the hell--?"

"Is this your idea of an escape?" Dillon demanded. "A raft with one ore? We're not going to get very far. The mainland is too far away."

Davy looked around, genuinely surprised, then looked back at Dillon. "My idea?" he demanded. "This wasn't my idea."

"If it wasn't you," Dillon announced, still enraged, "then how did we get out here?"

Davy scratched his head, then eyed the handcuffs they shared and frowned. "It had to be the men that went missing earlier," he insisted. "They must have joined forces with the girl and her friends. Their plan must have been to get rid of us so they wouldn't have to explain anything to the authorities."

"Great," Dillon scoffed. "Just great!" He looked back at the island in the near distance. "We have to paddle back to the island and steal one of the helicopters."

"We need to be quiet about it," Davy insisted. "We can't let them see us coming. We don't have any weapons to fight them."

"Maybe there's something useful in the backpack," Dillon announced, then opened the bag. There were a few bottles of water and a revolver. He checked the cylinder and frowned. "We've got four bullets and four bottles of water."

"Not much help," Davy muttered. "We'll have to figure out a way out of these handcuffs once we reach the island."

"It's pretty simple. We'll use the gun and shoot the links," Dillon insisted. "But we should do it here, where the shots won't be heard."

Davy glared at Dillon. "You've watched too many movies," he remarked. "You're not shooting through that chain with a .38 special, and even if it would work, look where we are. We're in a raft. One hole, and we sink."

Dillon glanced at the raft and frowned. "Yeah, I guess you're right," he replied. "We need something we can shoot into."

"Save the bullets," Davy insisted. "We'll find another way out of the handcuffs when we reach the beach."

Dillon studied the revolver a moment and seemed to consider their options. He raised his brows as an idea struck him.

"I've got it," Dillon announced with renewed enthusiasm. "I have a plan."

Davy eyed Dillon, somewhat skeptical. "What's your plan?"

Dillon turned the gun on Davy and pulled the trigger without hesitation, striking him in the chest. Davy gasped with surprise before falling against the raft, almost instantly dying. Dillon casually shrugged and offered a sly grin.

"We can use your body to cushion the blow and protect the raft," Dillon replied.

Dillon positioned their cuffed hands over Davy's lifeless body and placed the gun's muzzle against the handcuff links. He took a few deep breaths and then pulled the trigger. With a loud bang from the gun, the handcuff jolted against his wrist. Dillon looked at the handcuff that remained intact, although now covered in blood.

"Son-of-a-bitch," Dillon scoffed and repositioned their hands for another attempt.

Before he could squeeze the trigger, the raft began sagging. It only took Dillon a moment to realize the raft was losing air. Alarm swept over him as he swiftly pulled Davy away from the side of the raft. There was blood and a hole in the side. The bullet went directly through Davy and into the raft!

"Oh, shit!"

As the raft quickly lost air, Dillon and his lifeless accomplice began sinking into the water. Dillon attempted to stay afloat, but Davy's lifeless body sank with the raft, pulling on Dillon's cuffed wrist like an anchor.

"Fuck!"

Dillon floundered for a few minutes, attempting to stay afloat before finally being pulled under with the dead man attached to his wrist.

§

Kasey and Jamie were concerned when they learned Davy and Dillon had escaped. Obviously, Davy and Dillon were a little craftier than any of the guys had imagined. After all they'd been through, Kasey would have expected Embry to be a little smarter than that. Embry, Diesel, and Hunter helped the Coast Guard search the mansion and parts of the island for the two men, while Colton remained behind to ensure Kasey and Jamie were protected until the two men were found. When they heard shouting from the beach, all three ran from the mansion and headed onto the sand. Colton stopped his two friends just short of the action happening not far from the helicopters.

Two officers pulled Dillon and Davy from the surf and onto the sand. The deflated raft floated further away on the small waves.

"Looks like they attempted to escape in the raft," the first officer announced while examining the bodies. "One's been shot twice, and the other appears to have drowned."

"Probably got into a deadly argument," the second officer reported. "The first man shot the second twice in the chest at close range."

"Which obviously punctured the raft," the first officer remarked, then shook his head. "Takes a real genius to shoot someone in a raft. No wonder the bastard drowned."

"Well, saves time on a trial," the second officer muttered as they heaved the bodies further onto the sand.

Jamie and Kasey gently rubbed their chilled arms while watching the events unfold.

"I can't say I'm sorry," Kasey muttered to her friend. "Dillon got what he deserved."

"Your cousin wasn't too bright," Colton informed Kasey. "A little teamwork, and they probably could have gotten away."

"You'd think the idiots would have taken something to cut through the cuffs or pick the locks before escaping in the raft," Jamie remarked.

"Colton's right," Kasey scoffed. "Dillon wasn't very bright."

Chapter Forty-six

Avoiding most of the action, Kasey and Embry sat on the terrace, sipping tea, while the bodies were removed and others gave their statements to the authorities. It had been a long day; never-ending seemed appropriate. Kasey had been through a wide range of emotions, from learning Embry was her father to her cousin Dillon ordering the hit on Nat and then killing her uncle. The mansion looked like a war zone, and Kasey just wanted a moment of peace away from dead bodies and spilled blood. Sitting on the terrace with Embry, sipping tea, was familiar, and it helped her relax.

They sat silently for the longest time before addressing the elephant in the room.

"So, what happened with you and my mother?" Kasey finally asked, now looking at Embry. "Why did she tell me you were dead?"

"Your mother and I met while I was on a two-week shore leave," Embry informed her while smiling warmly. "We had the most amazing two weeks of my life. When I shipped out, we wrote to each other every week. Two months out, she told me she was pregnant. I asked her to marry me, and she said yes." His smile then faded as he sank into despair. "A few days later, I was on a mission that went south, and I was declared MIA. I'd been severely injured and was smuggled to safety by a nice family who risked their lives to help me."

"No one knew you were alive?"

"No." Embry hesitated, then continued his story. "I recovered in a small hospital for months before the military even discovered I was alive. Ten months had passed by the time I got back to U.S. soil. You'd already been born, and your mother was married to the man you knew as your father." Embry sighed softly while off in his own thoughts. "She believed I was dead, and for your sake, she moved on. The guy she met and fell in love with was a good man from a wealthy family, and I knew you'd be taken care of, so I never told her I was alive."

"So why show up nine years ago?"

"Eight years," he corrected her, then offered a warm smile. "Just because I stayed away, that never meant I didn't think of you. When your mother died, I went to work for your aunt and uncle. I wanted to make sure you'd be cared for and get to know my little girl."

"Why didn't you tell me?"

"Would you have believed me?" he asked while raising a brow. "We had a good relationship the way things were. In many ways, it was already a father-daughter relationship. I wasn't about to ruin that, but I was afraid you'd be in danger after your aunt was killed. That's when I devised my own plan to keep you safe."

"But I was friends with Colton several months before my aunt was murdered," Kasey remarked. "If you didn't get involved until after--?"

"I knew the sort of men your uncle associated with long before your aunt was killed," Embry informed her. "I wanted to ensure you were safe when I couldn't be there. Colton was sent to the nightclubs to operate as a casual acquaintance. I didn't count on the actual friendship that ensued. That was real."

"Well, I'm glad to hear that," Kasey remarked. "I'd hate to think that was all a lie. Jamie and I really like Colton." She then glanced around and considered everything else that had happened. "This island and the mansion. Who really owns it?"

"Oh, it's mine," he replied, hiding his smile. "I sort of won it in a poker game."

"A poker game?"

"Some prince with a lot of money," Embry replied and chuckled. "Lousy card player."

Kasey laughed softly and then eyed him, turning serious. "So what now?"

"Whatever you want, Kasey," he announced while offering a warm smile. "The mansion back home belongs to you. It was your grandparents' wish that the house would be passed down to their grandchildren. Your uncle knew that but chose not to share that information with you. When you turned twenty-one, you would take control of the house and receive your trust fund. Somehow, your cousin must have learned about that, which is probably why he made his move before you found out."

Kasey tensed slightly while eyeing him. "You're not leaving, are you?"

"As long as you want me around, I'm not going anywhere."

"Well, I want you around," she replied. "Even if you weren't my biological father, I'd still want that. You've always been like a father to me."

"I'm glad to hear that," he remarked, then chuckled. "Although, I doubt you could have gotten rid of me even if you had wanted to."

There was a long pause before Kasey finally spoke. "About Hunter--?" she questioned and raised her brow. "You're not going to make things awkward, are you?"

Embry drew a deep breath while in thought. "No," he replied. "Honestly, I've made my peace with it." He then sighed. "I'm actually surprised he was able to keep up that emotionless bodyguard act as long as he had. That lovesick little puppy. I had to read him the riot act in our stateroom before dinner that first night of the cruise." Embry appeared baffled and shook his head. "For some reason, he was unusually agitated about you and your friends going to the club that evening, but he wouldn't say why."

Kasey's expression dropped at his words, and she immediately shifted. "Is it possible Colton shared some of our personal conversations with him?" she asked.

"Colton and Hunter are actually pretty good friends," Embry replied. "It's quite possible." He then turned suspicious. "Why do you ask?"

She remained tense. "Well, it's possible Colton may have told him about my birthday plans."

"Your birthday plans?"

"That's as much as you need to know," she informed him.

Embry stared at her a moment, stiffened, and then turned uncomfortable. "Yes, that's as much as I need to know," he muttered, then eyed her suspiciously. "Did those plans include Hunter?"

"No," she responded a little too quickly.

Embry eyed her and seemed to read her thoughts. "You don't have to lie," he remarked. "You're not good at it."

She fidgeted at his response. "Well, not initially."

"That may have explained his edginess," Embry replied. "Knowing how he felt about you."

Kasey slipped back into her own fantasies of that night before everything went to hell. A tiny smile crossed her face.

"That actually explains a lot," she remarked mostly to herself.

"Oh?"

She managed a tiny laugh and shook her head. "That night in the club," Kasey replied. "He smiled at me differently, and I saw something I hadn't before. I thought it was just the alcohol."

Embry frowned at the comment. "The moment I saw you in that dress, I knew he was going to lose his focus," he remarked, shaking his head before meeting her gaze. "Well, I suppose it all worked out in the end. All bets are off." A sly smile crossed his face. "If he wants to date you, he can no longer object to me asking his mother out."

"His mother?" Kasey asked, now curious.

"Hunter's mother is insanely hot," Embry informed her. "Pisses him off when the boys and I casually point out that little fact."

Kasey raised an arrogant brow. "Casually point out?" she asked. "You mean torment relentlessly."

"It's a guy thing," he informed her. "A soldier with a hot mother opens himself up to relentless ribbing, but we draw the line at making moves on them. It's sort of an unspoken code." Embry then shrugged. "He wants to date my daughter; then I'm allowed to date his mother."

"So you're going to go out with his mother just to piss him off?"

"Not *just* to piss him off," Embry insisted while cleverly raising a brow as he gazed into her eyes. "Did you miss the part about his mother being insanely hot?"

Kasey groaned, minded her business, and sipped her tea. She hoped Hunter knew what he was getting himself into. Embry was already working on his passive-aggressive plan to torment him. On the bright side, she was happy Embry was considering dating.

§

A few hours later, after the investigation had concluded and the authorities had left, the helicopter that had initially towed them to the island landed on the beach with Diesel at the controls. Jamie and Colton were eager to leave and climbed inside. As Embry approached them, Kasey and Hunter stood nearby while in each other's arms.

"Are you sure you want to stay?" Embry asked, directing the question more to Kasey than Hunter.

"The clean-up crew will be here tomorrow," Hunter informed him, then shrugged. "Someone should be here to keep an eye on things."

Embry eyed them, frowned, and shook his head. "I'd say behave," he remarked, "but I don't see that happening."

Kasey and Hunter just grinned without offering any comment.

"I'll see you back at home in a few days," Embry replied and hugged Kasey. He then glanced at Hunter and flashed a devious smile. "I'll tell your mother you said hi."

Hunter's expression suddenly dropped. Before he could comment, Embry approached the helicopter and jumped inside. Hunter and Kasey moved closer to the house to avoid the blowing sand, then waved as the helicopter took off and flew away. Without warning, Hunter grabbed Kasey and tackled her to the sand. She let out a surprised scream and then laughed.

The End

Other books by Holly Copella!
Reviews left on Amazon are appreciated!

"The Battle for Andrea Maria"

A cruise ship attack turns six survivors into overnight celebrities after they take credit for the heroic act of a stowaway who died saving them.

The cruise is just what Jess needed--a bit of harmless fun far from her daily grind. But what begins as a relaxing vacation turns into a desperate fight for her life when terrorists take over the ship and start piling up bodies. Teaming up with a mysterious stowaway, Jess attempts to send out a distress call but knows they cannot wait for help to come. If she or the few remaining passengers have any hope for survival, Jess must act now. The papers dub it "The Battle for *Andrea Maria*," but to Jess it is the moment she fought side-by-side with her enigmatic Romeo, saving the ship--and losing him. She thinks the story ends there, but really, the nightmare is just beginning...

"Insanely Deadly"

When the dead return to life, it's up to an admiral's daughter and a mildly insane, former war hero to save their small town.

Jetta Cross, a Navy Admiral's daughter, is tasked with keeping her father's comrade, a former war hero turned town crazy, grounded in the real world. Capt. John Hunter is still fighting the war in his head, where imaginary dead people are part of his world. When a viral outbreak brings about a zombie uprising, Hunter is left to his own devices. He must resume his role as a one-man commando unit in order to destroy the ravenous undead. With Hunter still fighting his own inner demons as well as the undead, the townspeople fear their zombie neighbors may not be the only threat. Stranded at the island's luxurious resort with a handful of workers, Jetta is forced to live up to her father's reputation and take charge of the deteriorating situation at the hotel. She must wage her own war against the infected before the government declares her hometown a total loss.

"Deadly Institution"

A town recluse suspected of killing his wife teams up with a young woman in order to stop a killer.

After being accused of murdering his wife, Konrad Churchill turns his back on the town that once adored him. Ten years later, he still holds his grudge and the title of the most feared man in town. With the reopening of the burned mental institution, where his wife had died, former employees are now murdered one-by-one, throwing suspicion back on Churchill. A young local reporter, Jacey, is forced to reveal her long-time friendship with the infamous recluse in order to clear his name not only in the recent murders but to exonerate him in the death of his wife as well. Will Jacey's relationship with Churchill invite the killer closer to her? Or is the killer already in her life?

"Death Displacement"

A grief-stricken man travels back in time to seek revenge on the woman who murdered his girlfriend but inadvertently falls in love with her.

Kane is about to marry the woman he loves. His life is perfect. A few weeks before the wedding, a vindictive woman from his girlfriend's past mysteriously arrives and kills her. He learns of a traumatic accident that happened five years earlier, which triggers Riley's hatred for his girlfriend. Distraught over his girlfriend's death, Kane uses an antique time machine to travel into the past in order to find and destroy the woman responsible. When he runs into Riley's younger self, he realizes she's not the monster she later becomes, and he can't bring himself to destroy her. With a little help from his oddball friend from the past, they formulate a plan to prevent the accident that sends Riley down her destructive path. Kane's plan backfires when he falls for the younger Riley. His new tortured existence is further complicated when future Riley, his girlfriend's killer, shows up with her own devious agenda that doesn't include him. Will he be able to stop the time ripple, which ultimately ends with his girlfriend's death? Or will future Riley take him out of the timeline forever--

"Dead Village"

After strange happenings isolate a small resort town from the rest of the world, nearly one hundred residents seek refuge at the closed hotel. Only eight survive the night. And that's just the beginning...

One day after the entire population of Fox Ridge Village disappears, a car wreck forces several unsuspecting crash victims to seek help at the closed summer hotel. Within the hotel, they discover the grisly aftermath of a brutal slaughter. Crash victims Vander and Devon, a reluctant clairvoyant, team up to solve the riddle of the "haunted hotel" and the mass hysteria plaguing the remaining survivors. By the time they discover the hotel's secret, they're already drawn into the hysteria. As the body count continues to climb, it's a race to isolate the source and bring everyone back to reality before they kill one another. Will Devon be able to communicate with the traumatized spirits before their fate becomes her own?

"Town Darling"

After surviving a brutal attack that claims the lives of those she loves, a young woman seeks revenge on a corrupt town.

Going back home is never easy, but for Casey, it means returning to her corrupt hometown where she barely survived a brutal attack. Accompanied by two family friends, she seeks justice for the night that destroyed her life. Her physical scars are nothing compared to her emotional ones, forcing the local sheriff to believe that the town darling is back for revenge. As the conspiracy for her revenge appears to be leading up to the coveted town fair, the sheriff is determined to stop her from fulfilling her vengeful scheme...but guilt over his role on that fateful night continues to haunt him. Will his desperate need for Casey's forgiveness be his undoing? Or will Casey's desire for revenge destroy them both?

"Basement Dwellers"

A viral outbreak at a hospital leaves a mortician, sheriff, and coroner fighting for their lives against a horde of undead and the CDC.

After a massive car wreck leaves several survivors in critical condition at the local hospital, a surgeon uses experimental drugs on his critical patients and accidentally causes a zombie outbreak. When local mortician, Lexx, receives an infected corpse as her client, she becomes stranded in the hospital basement during CDC quarantine along with the local sheriff and the coroner. The infamous surgeon struggles to find a cure for his infectious blunder by using the other survivors as test subjects. Meanwhile, Lexx and the sheriff attempt to locate his missing sister, who's stranded somewhere in the battle zone that once was the emergency room. It's a race against time and the ravenous undead. Can they survive the undead before CDC sanitizes the hospital of all infection?

"Misfits, Inc."

A seemingly ordinary, young woman meets four misfits who claim she has given them supernatural powers.

While on a business trip to a remote island paradise, a bored secretary, Hailey, has her world turned upside down when her path collides with a psychic freak, Skyler. He attempts to convince her that they had met in his dreams, and she had chosen him as one of her four mystic warriors. After Skyler foresees a woman's death, they discover an unidentified creature has killed one of the guests. They are joined by a lounge pianist and a rich playboy, who also claim they had met her in their dreams. If Skyler's prophecies are genuine, the evil entity controlling the ravenous creatures needs to destroy Hailey to ensure its survival. Reluctantly accepting her fate, Hailey has to locate the last and most powerful of her chosen warriors, The Guardian. Their fate is in doubt when The Guardian turns out to be a self-absorbed, former cat burglar with a bad attitude. Can Hailey turn her company of misfits into an elite team of mystic warriors? Or will The Guardian's secret agenda destroy them all?

"Deadly Institution 2"

When blackmail turns into murder, a young woman finds herself caught in the killer's crosshairs.

The small town of Stony Ridge is no stranger to scandal and persecution of the innocent. When a brutal killing shakes the town's prestigious country club, Jacey McMurray seeks help from a self-proclaimed vigilante, Konrad Churchill. As her professional and personal worlds collide, Jacey fears the stress of the country club killings have finally taken their toll on Churchill. Can a stressed out vigilante stop the killer before he strikes again?

"Witness Protection"
Also available in audiobook!

After witnessing an execution, a resourceful young woman attempts to disappear while being pursued by a hitman and a handsome federal agent.

A helicopter pilot, Jackie Remus, reluctantly agrees to go on a date with one of her clients, but her date is unexpectedly cut short when she witnesses a man being murdered. After narrowly escaping with her life, she is placed into protective custody. When the safe house is breached, Jackie makes a daring escape from both the hired killers and the handsome FBI agent, who wants to return her to protective custody. With a little help from her sly and crafty friend, Monroe, Jackie is convinced she can disappear until the trial. While on her journey to meet with her friend, she solicits help from a few shady but lovable characters along the way. Although she manages to stay one-step ahead of the hired killers, the federal agent remains in hot pursuit. Will Jackie reach Monroe before she's captured by the FBI and returned to protective custody? Or will the hired killers silence her first?

"Unconditional"

A young woman puts her life on hold to care for an unstable, highly skilled combat soldier, who believes someone is trying to kill him.

A botched military coup leaves a team of elite fighters injured with one clinging to life in a coma. When Harlan wakes from his coma, he's left with no memory of his past life. His commander's daughter, Indy, takes it upon herself to care for the fallen war hero. She's challenged with more than just his physical care as she combats with not only his memory loss but also his newly found desire for her. His infatuation with her becomes the least of her worries when he sinks back into his role of a combat soldier. Believing his life is in danger, his fighting skills surface, turning him into an unpredictable and dangerous man. Will his memory return to him before Indy is forced to commit him? Or will he finally find his nemesis, "the coyote", and possibly claim the life of an innocent person?

"The Pen Pal"

In order to save her friend, she must enter the mind of a serial killer.

When her best friend is abducted, no one believes Jolynn saw it in a psychic vision. With nowhere to turn, Jolynn reluctantly joins Agent Harris Slade and his team on their hunt for a sadistic serial killer known only as "The Pen Pal". Finally confronted with the killer, Jolynn realizes she must enter the mind of the psychopath in order to stop the brutal killings. But when her vision reveals a particularly disturbing death, can Jolynn sacrifice her lover for her friend?

"Witness Protection 2"
The Return of Whiskey Tango Foxtrot

Believing she holds the clue to millions in missing laundered money, a young woman is placed into the protective care of a former Navy SEAL team.

Feeling sorry for her recently separated co-worker, Leeann invites Wiley to join her and her friends on their night out. Little does she know that finding her co-worker murdered is just the beginning of her nightmare. Leeann unknowingly holds the key to fifty million dollars in potentially laundered mob money. With hired killers pursuing her, the FBI places her into a different kind of protective custody. Former Navy SEAL team Whiskey Tango Foxtrot reunites to keep Leeann alive at their secret hideaway. What should be an easy assignment takes an unscheduled turn when secrets, lies, and betrayal threaten to derail their mission. Is the team prepared for a war on their own doorstep? Will Leeann's misguided trust endanger the lives of those sent to protect her?

"Witness Protection 3"
Alpha Mike Foxtrot

A helicopter pilot risks her life to help a team of retired Navy SEALs rescue two girls from a killer.

When former Navy SEAL team Whiskey Tango Foxtrot asks for a simple favor, Jackie reluctantly offers her air-taxi services. What could go wrong? What begins as a search and rescue for two girls turns into a fight for survival against a heavily armed drug cartel. Wanted by the law with the cartel in hot pursuit and their home base breached, the team is forced to call in a favor from a questionable ally. Unfortunately, their new safe house isn't what it seems. Without knowing who the real enemy is, can Jackie and the team save their young witnesses from the hands of a killer?

"Already Dead"
Supernatural Collection

From the already dead to the undead. Three supernatural tales of "things that go bump in the night".

"Bloodletting" - A vampire themed resort allows guests to *participate* in their Bloodletting Ritual to celebrate the island's legendary vampires.

"Reaper of Souls" - A young woman must outwit an evil sorcerer in order to save her brother or become one of his minions forever.

"Already Dead" - When Flight 220 crashes, ten passengers make it to an isolated island, but only one man lives to tell the lie.

"Witness Protection 4"
O-Dark-Hundred

A simple assignment turns deadly when a retired Navy SEAL team uncovers a plot to kill a notorious mob boss.

When Whiskey Tango Foxtrot embarks on a simple stalking case, they're not prepared for a trip to a private island paradise owned by an infamous mobster. With one of their own suffering from traumatic head injuries, the team is left scrambling to decide what is real or imagined. The situation escalates even further when they uncover an assassination plot where everyone is a suspect. Now targets themselves, can the team survive their trip to paradise?

"Witness Protection 5"
Outside the Wire

After suffering several casualties on their last assignment, a retired Navy SEAL team discovers their misery is just beginning.

When Whiskey Tango Foxtrot returns home after suffering a devastating loss, they're hit with even more bad news regarding the rest of their team. Their grief is cut short when they discover their names are all on the same hit list. Hunted by relentless assassins, the scattered team must decide whether to remain safely hidden or find the man who put the price on their heads. Against the wishes of her teammates, Jackie strikes out on her own in order to save a friend who wants her dead. In a kill or be killed situation, will Jackie's emotions finally betray her?

"The Murder of Emily Fisher"

After finding their favorite teacher murdered, the lives of two teenage girls are forever changed.

Everyone loved Emily Fisher. While walking home one afternoon, two teenage girls, Sidney and Trisha, stumble upon a gruesome murder scene. The brutal murder of Emily Fisher, a young, attractive schoolteacher, shocks the small town of **Marilina**. After graduation, Sidney moves far away from the memories of the small town while Trisha retreats deeper into denial. Eight years after the murder, Sidney receives a desperate call from her childhood friend, forcing her to return home. Trisha believes Emily's killer was falsely accused, and she manages to turn the entire town against her while attempting to prove it. When Trisha receives a death threat, Sidney realizes there may be some credibility to her friend's wild accusations. Is Trisha's mental breakdown a result of childhood trauma? Or is the real killer actually attempting to silence her? In order to save her friend, Sidney must answer the eight-year-old question. Who murdered Emily Fisher?

"Once Upon a Disaster"

A young homicide detective finds herself at the mercy of a hitman in the aftermath of an earthquake

While investigating the murder of a hitman, Detective Jade Wesson pursues a lead connecting the dead man to a break-in at a computer programming company. She's drawn into the world of nightclub owner and front man for the mob, Cody Riley. Her investigation keeps pointing to Cody's right-hand man and possible hitman, Vahn Lott. Despite her efforts to keep her investigation on track, Vahn has plans of his own for the attractive detective. When an unprecedented earthquake rocks their east coast town, Jade must put her life in Vahn's hands if she wants to survive. Can she trust a man who might be the killer she's hunting?

"Awaken the Dead"

A grieving innkeeper struggles to keep her haunted hotel out of foreclosure.

After losing her parents in a suspicious boating accident, Harley Brandon is determined to keep the family hotel out of foreclosure. Unfortunately, the hotel ghosts have other plans. Built with tainted money, the century old Horizon Hotel thrives on a tradition of murder, scandal, and suicide. As the paranormal activity increases to alarming levels, Harley discovers the truth about the hotel and its residents. Can Harley save her friends from the hotel's frightening hidden secrets?

"Castle Bloodshed"
Murder Collection

From a deadly island paradise to haunted castles. Three novella length tales of murder, mystery, and malicious intent.

"Castle Bloodshed" – A tour of Wesley Castle turns into a fight for survival as six stranded tourists discover the haunting secrets within the castle walls. A mystery writer teams up with an uptight butler in order stop a killer who may already be dead. Novella length paranormal murder mystery.

"Fleshies" – Is Uncle Rutger crazy? Five years ago, four business partners died within their newly purchased, fixer-upper castle. Their bodies were never found. The surviving partner, Rutger, claims a demon keeps him as its slave. Rutger's nephew schemes to save his uncle by sacrificing the lives of a group of stranded motorists and a high-profile novelist. Novella length supernatural murder mystery.

"Demon Island" – A group of strangers are invited to a remote island for the reading of a will. The guests soon discover they were brought to the island to be executed one-by-one. It's up to a private detective and a tenacious young woman to solve the murders and find a way to escape paradise. Novella length murder mystery.

"Brighton Island"

When a psychic visits a haunted island mansion, he inadvertently awakens the ghosts' tortured souls.

Something's not right with Simon. When Jacklyn brings her eccentric friend to her uncle's island mansion, she didn't expect him to slip into psychic overload. As Simon attempts to solve a decade-old, double homicide, Jacklyn is confronted with the possibility that she could be next to join the mansion ghosts. When they find themselves stranded on the secluded island, her Uncle Hyland wages his own war to save them from a flesh and blood killer. Will her uncle's "shock and awe" military tactics save them or get them killed? Can Simon bring peace to the tortured souls or unexpectedly join them?

"A.L.F. Resort"

A fantasy vacation turns into a nightmare when the resort's artificial life forms are compromised.

Welcome to A.L.F. Resort where you can live out your fantasies with safe, state-of-the-art artificial life form robots! When a young journalist and a photographer are sent to A.L.F. Resort to do a story for their magazine, Shay and Becka believe they've hit the jackpot of all work-cations. The engineers pull out all the stops to make their fantasies memorable. Unfortunately, the newly designed A.L.F., the Gen X, is smarter than his programming and creates havoc within Shay's fantasy. A computer malfunction removes their safety inhibitors and the A.L.F.s play out their own hostile fantasies. Zombies, bikers, and mobsters run amuck, turning fantasies into nightmares. Shay gets more of a story than she anticipates, but will she survive long enough to write it?

"Jungle Princess"

While stranded on a prison island, a young woman discovers a creature of "unknown" origin.

After their cruise ship sinks, Alex and two of her shipmates are stranded on a deserted, tropical island. Unfortunately, the castaways soon realize they're not alone. They discover an abandoned prison with over two dozen inmates living on the island's south side. While avoiding the prison on the far side of the island, Alex discovers a strange but loveable creature of unknown origin. When one of her fellow castaways is in trouble, Alex reluctantly seeks help from the prisoners. After the brutal murder of several inmates, their questions surrounding the abandoned prison are about to be answered. What really killed over one hundred prisoners? And is it still out there?

"Murder in Wax"

A series of brutal murders plague a quiet farming community when beautiful women audition for the same acting job.

While all the young women in town are fighting over a once-in-a-lifetime acting opportunity, Devon Vincent is excited about her new job at the local wax museum. Although supportive of her friend's acting aspirations, Devon has a hard time understanding the rivalry among the women in town. When the aspiring actresses are brutally murdered one-by-one, Devon fears her friend may be the next victim. Devon finds herself in the middle of a murderous revenge plot that leads back to the wax museum's doorstep and possibly implicates her boss as the killer. Will Devon's newly found feelings for her boss bring a killer closer to her? Or is the killer already in her circle?

"Witness Protection 6"
Alpha Dogs

An easy rescue turns into a wild ride for retired Navy SEAL team Whiskey Tango Foxtrot when everyone wants to kill their client.

It was a simple task. Rescue a young woman from her mob boss father-in-law. Little did Jackie and company realize that rescuing the young woman was the easy part. Keeping her alive would be a massive undertaking, especially when everyone wants a piece of the mafia heiress. The team fights for survival against their toughest adversaries yet. How many innocent people must die in order to save one woman? Can the team survive the ultimate battle between mercenaries and assassins?

"Midnight Requisition"

A series of brutal murders leaves a traumatized young woman on a hunt to find a killer.

When they were just babies, Scorpio and her twin brother, Kane, tragically lost their parents under mysterious circumstances. Refusing to accept his father was dead, Kane set off on a mission to find a man he'd never met. A home invasion gone wrong leaves Scorpio grieving the loss of those she loves. Out of the tragedy of her loss, two fallen heroes are thrust upon her. Scorpio soon realizes someone wants her dead and the killer may already be in her circle. As her entire life unravels in a web of betrayal and lies, can Scorpio trust her new, slightly questionable friends?

"Until Death"

Liars, cheaters, blackmail and murder. It would be a wedding no one would forget.

Despite knowing he's making the biggest mistake of his life, Raina Steele reluctantly attends her father's third wedding. What should have been a boring reception turns into a web of lies, betrayal, and murder. With no one above suspicion, Raina must put aside her feud with the arrogant yet insanely handsome butler in order to catch the killer before he finds his next victim. With a murderer waiting to strike and lives hanging in the balance, the real question remains...the bride is wearing white? Seriously?

"Tainted"

What happens at the Dark Forest Hotel, stays at the Dark Forest Hotel...for all eternity.

What secrets surround Dark Forest Hotel? After her parents die under mysterious circumstances, sixteen-year-old Jeri escapes foster care and seeks refuge at a "closed for the season" hotel. Over the next six years, Jeri graduates from teenage runaway to the hotel's assistant general manager. When she learns a convention is secretly held every year in her absence, she demands answers from her boss, friends, and co-workers. After getting conflicting stories, Jeri sets out to discover the truth. She's suddenly thrown into a horrifying new world where vampires and vicious creatures are craving her virgin blood. After six years of everyone lying to her, is there anyone she can trust?

"Witness Protection 7"
Bravo Foxtrot

An Army deserter on the run brings mayhem to a retired Navy SEAL team when his teenage daughter is caught in a mercenary's cross-hairs.

A weekend of fun turns into a race for survival as Monique and Colleen's surrogate big brother, Bogart, rescues the girls from mercenaries hunting Colleen's Army deserter father. With the girls safely stashed at their Colorado hideaway, trouble brews when the team discovers Colleen's father was framed by his former commander over a stolen, high-tech weapon. In order to clear Colleen's father and bring him home, the team must fight one of their toughest advisories yet...a high-ranking military officer with countless mercenaries and the U.S. military behind him.

"Midnight Requisition 2"
Amateur Night

A brother and sister duo team up to catch a potential kidnapper.

After finally reuniting with her not-so-dead brother, Scorpio and her friends are taunted into helping him with his new case. A wealthy cattle rancher believes someone wants to abduct his daughter, but the team suspects her ex-boyfriend is pulling off an elaborate scheme to win her back. What appears to be a slice of paradise in the Colorado Mountains turns out to be a venomous snake pit filled with lies, lust, betrayal, and murder. Surviving the depraved family becomes the least of the team's worries when a botched kidnapping turns into murder.

"Cemetery Stalkers" Horror Collection

Four tales of horror from flesh eating alien monsters to blood-sucking vampires.

"Night Creatures" – When a rescue party becomes stranded on an abandoned cruise ship, they discover the terrifying secret unleashed from the cargo hold. What starts out as a rescue mission rapidly deteriorates into survival as the small group is hunted by a frightening creature with a taste for human flesh. Novella length horror book.

"Ravenous" – After escaping a carjacking in the back woods, a young woman seeks refuge in a mysterious mansion with a terrifying secret. Despite promises of a ride to town in the morning, she's convinced she's being held prisoner by a cult leader. Short paranormal story.

"The Feast" – Five years ago, a killer went on a murderous rampage at the church picnic. Despite eyewitness accounts of a non-human killer, the local law refused to believe the town's citizens. When a group of teenagers stumble upon the contained remains of the killer, they unwittingly set him free to continue his terror upon the small town. Novella length paranormal book.

"Cemetery Stalkers" – When 'The Reaper' stalks a cemetery, death follows. Following a series of bizarre incidents within the cemetery, a young woman fears for the safety of her friend, who lives in the middle of spook central. Short horror story.

"Jumpers"

When a cruise ship is exposed to a deadly virus, the fate of the world rests in the hands of a lounge dancer and a conman.

An infectious outbreak threatens the passengers and crew of the "Queen Anita" and the entire world if the virus makes it back to civilization. Lounge dancer, Maxine, must find a way to prevent the destruction of the world, but in order to do that, she needs to trust a conman with unique insight into the virus.

"Witness Protection 8"
Midnight Requisition

A brother and sister duo finds themselves on an explosive collision course with a team of retired Navy SEALs.

Obsessed with the belief that his father is still alive, Kane Wayland embarks on a foolhardy mission to confront the elusive, former Navy SEAL, Zack Kinsley. Despite heavy protests, Kane's sister, Scorpio, joins him on his quest. The disastrous "reunion" comes with a steep price that none are prepared to pay. With the haunting reality of the botched mission, Midnight Requisition, still looming over each of them, can the two teams pull together in time to prevent another tragedy?

"Midnight Requisition 3"
Circular Run

A brother and sister reopen a hotel with a tainted history only to discover its past refuses to stay dead and buried.

Scorpio and Kane Wayland finally realize their dream of reopening their grandfather's old, cliffside hotel in Maine. With the hotel's checkered past behind it, the relaunch is a dream come true. Unfortunately, history has a habit of repeating itself. When guests mysteriously vanish, the hotel's somewhat seedy clientele are all now suspects. In order to save their hotel, Scorpio and Kane must stop a killer. When your guests are mercenaries, bounty hunters, and mobsters, who can you trust?

"Raven Force"

An inn keeper becomes involved in a game of espionage after picking up a mysterious hitchhiker.

After surviving a nightmare of a date, Maxine Croft didn't think her evening could get any worse...until she nearly hits a stranger on a dark back road. This unprecedented meeting would turn Max's world upside down as she's thrust into a world of murder, corruption, and deception within her own backyard. As she gets in deeper with an elite, special task force, Max inadvertently puts her sisters' lives in danger. Will Max and her sisters become just more "collateral damage" to facilitate the team's mission?

"Midnight Requisition 4"
Charlie Foxtrot

A mob convention at a remote cliffside hotel has murderous consequences.

Hotel owner, Scorpio Wayland, reluctantly books a "mob" convention at her quiet, cliffside resort. What could go wrong? When former mob boss, Salvatore Romano invites friends for a "family" reunion, disaster swiftly follows.

"Witness Protection 9"
S.N.A.F.U.

A notorious mob boss turns to a retired Navy SEAL team to keep his son alive.

They were made an offer they couldn't refuse. When his son is accused of murdering known mobsters throughout Colorado, Giovanni turns to the retired Navy SEAL team of Whiskey Tango Foxtrot to keep his boy alive and prevent a war between the "families". With the mobster's son in the crosshairs of every hitman and bounty hunter on the West Coast, Jackie and the boys need to find Marco and go completely off-grid. But is the team risking their lives to protect a serial killer?

"Witness Protection 10"
Bravo Zulu

It's all hands on deck when the mob declares war on the team and those they love.

Whiskey Tango Foxtrot reunites with Midnight Requisition when war is declared by a notorious mobster and his army of highly trained soldiers. After several deadly attacks shake both teams, their skills, loyalties, and limitations are tested in an explosive and bloody rampage that will scar and change their lives forever.

"Pretty Little Dead Things"

Romance, scandal, and an unsolved murder. Welcome to snob central!

After a disastrous evening at the exclusive country club gala, Marley Temple doesn't think her life can get any worse. When someone close to her is murdered, Marley is left devastated. Although everyone else seems to move on after the unsolved homicide, Marley can't let it go. She's suddenly thrust into the inner circle of a wealthy playwright recluse, whose stage actress wife was brutally butchered just two years earlier. Although Marley fears falling for the infamous Devlin Ryker, forming a strange alliance with him brings her closer to solving the perplexing murder. But as she gets closer to learning the truth, the killer gets closer to her. Will Marley discover the killer's identity before she becomes his next victim?

"Dead Again"

After barely surviving a murderous attack, a young woman believes a cold-hearted cattle rancher holds clues to that night.

After the murder of her mother in an attack that nearly claimed her life as well, Sage Remington believes moving to the country with her sister will heal her emotional scars. Sage's near death experience leaves her with memory loss surrounding that fateful night. A bizarre encounter with an infamous cattle rancher, Jackson Morgan, brings back fragments of Sage's lost memory. If she wants to piece together what happened to her mother, Sage needs to get closer to Jackson, who somehow holds the clues. Unfortunately, discovering Jackson's secrets opens the door to a whole other world where nothing is what it seems.

"Dead Again"

After barely surviving a murderous attack, a young woman believes a cold-hearted cattle rancher holds clues to that night.

After the murder of her mother in an attack that nearly claimed her life as well, Sage Remington believes moving to the country with her sister will heal her emotional scars. Sage's near death experience leaves her with memory loss surrounding that fateful night. A bizarre encounter with an infamous cattle rancher, Jackson Morgan, brings back fragments of Sage's lost memory. If she wants to piece together what happened to her mother, Sage needs to get closer to Jackson, who somehow holds the clues. Unfortunately, discovering Jackson's secrets opens the door to a whole other world where nothing is what it seems.

"Dead Woods"

Two magazine reporters get more of a story than they want while investigating strange happenings in a cursed forest.

While interviewing a small-town hero, two adventure-seeking magazine reporters, Kara and Lenox, hike into the infamous Dead Woods in search of a story. Their simple outing takes a chilling turn, and they soon find themselves involved in the town's haunted history filled with curses, witch burnings, and zombified minions. Narrowly escaping with her life, Kara runs into local legend Daemon Archer, a distant relative to a man accused of witchcraft and burned in Town Square in the 1800s. In order to survive a panic-stricken village prophesizing 'evil will take a mate', Kara has to trust the town's most feared citizen.

"Cinderella of Yardley Manor"

Never believing in love at first sight, a young woman finally thinks she's met the man of her dreams, only to discover he's the wrong man.

After graduating college, Ramsey O'Connell reluctantly agrees to travel with her uncle on his business trip to England. However, when she discovers her uncle's true intention, fixing her up with his wealthy colleague, William Yardley, she has some reservations. Falling in love was the last thing she expected, but falling in love with an emotionally unavailable man turns her fairytale into a nightmare.

ABOUT THE AUTHOR

Holly Copella has been writing since the age of twelve when her frustration at a book's poor plot drove her to author her own story. Over the last decade, she's written a number of screenplays, some of which she's now adapting into novels. Her fascination with zombies and other darker material lends an edge to her writing, which tends to lean toward horror. As a fan of Agatha Christie, she appreciates the craft of a good plot and the importance of creating significant characters.

Hailing from Pennsylvania, Copella lives in the Endless Mountains on a farm with her new horse, Maverick, and other animals. In addition to writing and reading fiction, she enjoys riding horses and traveling to Las Vegas.

www.ingramcontent.com/pod-product-compliance
Lightning Source LLC
Chambersburg PA
CBHW060531180626
46817CB00002B/524